TERRAFORMING
MARS™

T0061707

SHORES OF A
NEW HORIZON

M Darusha Wehm

ACONYTE

First published by Aconyte Books in 2024

ISBN 978 1 83908 275 7

Ebook ISBN 978 1 83908 276 4

Cover art by René Aigner

Distributed in North America by Simon & Schuster Inc, New York, USA

Printed in the United States of America

9 8 7 6 5 4 3 2 1

ACONYTE BOOKS

An imprint of Asmodee Entertainment Ltd

Mercury House, Shipstones Business Centre

North Gate, Nottingham NG7 7FN, UK

aconytebooks.com // twitter.com/aconytebooks

TERRAFORMING MARS

Mankind is on the brink of achieving a second planet to live on: Mars.

Vast corporations spend fortunes to compete to transform the Red Planet into an environment where humanity can thrive. The potential rewards are enormous, the risks colossal.

As the biosphere becomes habitable, immigration from Earth increases, and social and political pressures stress the already fierce corporate rivalry. While scientific advances are daily miracles, not everyone is working toward the same future.

In a savage place like Mars, the smallest error can be lethal.

More Terraforming Mars from Aconyte

In the Shadow of Deimos by Jane Killick
Edge of Catastrophe by Jane Killick

For Steven, Ange, Stephen, Jo, and John

CHAPTER ONE

Zambrotta Kaspar stared out the viewport at the familiar rocky red landscape, a few dots of green speckling the ground as the newly planted cactus began to take root. It was not a window, and if it had been, there would be nothing to see but the side of the neighboring Zero Gravity Engineering building. The port was a screen set in the wall of Zammi's office and it could have shown anything – a live view of the Oort cloud, scenes from Earth, the latest Lovzansky film – but Zammi preferred a closer approximation to real life. It was the view out someone's window, at least.

The brief flash of a visual notification warned Zammi moments before there was a loud knock at his door.

"Yeah," he said, and the door slid open.

"Congratulations, professor!" Beryl Fernandez strode into the small room and pinched the fingers of her left hand together, then flung them apart, releasing a holodisplay which hovered over her open palm. The garish logo of Mars University sat in the space before Zammi's eyes, the year's tenure list in a dull sans serif font below. He spotted his own name near the middle of the page.

"Thanks, Fern," Zammi said, not sure how to feel. "I really didn't expect it this year."

"Because you're under thirty? Come on, it would have been ageism pure and simple if they'd made you wait," she said, folding her large frame into the single free chair in the office. She was one of the few people Zammi had ever met who he didn't tower over. "You've been doing great work."

"The department is full of great teachers and researchers," Zammi demurred, but his colleague made a rude noise.

"Whatever. There are, what, three full profs in Earth Studies?"

Zammi nodded, even though Fernandez knew the number perfectly well – as the department chair of Engineering, she was on the university's Chairs' Committee and there was little that went on without Fern noticing. "We need a full professor who focuses on the Exopopulation Period," she continued, "and there's no one else for that job."

Zammi shrugged, knowing she was right. Still, it felt vaguely unreal. He wasn't sure if he was the university's youngest ever tenured professor, but it was probably close.

"Come on," Fernandez said, launching herself out of the chair. "There's a party in the faculty café. Let's go before the cake is all gone."

"Ugh," Zammi said, making no move to leave the office. "Cheap wine and departmental heads bloviating on about their own ascensions to the vaulted halls of higher learning? No, thank you."

Fernandez shook her head, dark curls bouncing into a froth

around her brown face. "It wasn't an invitation, Dr Kaspar. With great power comes great responsibility. Up you get." She grabbed him by the arms and lifted Zammi bodily out of his chair.

"*Spider-man*? Really?" Zammi said, eyebrows meeting in mock derision.

"You aren't the only one who took an Old Earth Media elective," she said, grinning. "Come on, let's go."

Zammi held up a forefinger. "One glass of wine, then I'm out."

Fernandez shrugged gleefully and said, "We'll see," then she pulled Professor Kaspar into the hall.

There was plenty of cake still sitting on the serving counter, with a stack of plates waiting to be filled. Fernandez lifted two off the top and artlessly dumped a chunk of the heavily iced pink sponge on each. Zammi lifted a hand, palm out, as she thrust a plate toward him.

"Suit yourself," she said, and dropped one of the forks back into its tray, before scraping a slice of cake onto the other plate. She dug her fork in and took a bite. After swallowing, she said, "You better get something. It looks weird otherwise."

Zammi nodded and selected a chilled clear pouch of pale beer. "They really pulled out all the stops." He smirked at Fernandez. "Beer *and* wine."

She chuckled and polished off the first slice of cake. "Told you it would be fun."

Zammi shook his head and scanned the room. He recognized about half the people, mostly other members of the History Department or chairs of other departments. Marius Munro, the History Department chair, caught

Zammi's eye and waved him over. Zammi didn't recognize the two people Marius was talking to, but the three were of a similar vintage and looked like they shopped at the same tailor's.

"Department heads," Zammi whispered derisively, while forcing a smile in Marius's direction.

"You get on with Munro just fine," Fernandez said.

"Yeah, I do. But he's the exception that proves the rule."

"That's not a thing," Fernandez said, and shoved Zammi firmly toward the knot of people. "Go get congratulated."

Zammi acquiesced, and Marius slung an arm around his shoulders when he approached. It was awkward in more ways than one – he was a head shorter than Zammi.

"Here's to our newest rising star," he announced to anyone within earshot. "Finally a voice for Exopop, eh, kid?"

Zammi tried to smile gamely and sipped from the pouch of beer. The liquid went down wrong, and he coughed, sputtering. Marius slapped his back, and he managed to get his diaphragm under control. What a nightmare.

"I remember my first beer," a stranger in a tweed, floor-length tunic said, not entirely unkindly, as the others chuckled. "It will be good to get some fresh blood in the place." Zammi glanced around for an identification panel and saw the translucent holo floating just over the person's left shoulder.

Dr Lora Evistar

Linguistics, chair

"Thank you, Dr Evistar," Zammi said, after clearing his throat one more time. "I hope to be useful to the department."

"I'm sure you will be, Dr Kaspar," she said, then took a deep pull on her drink. "I remember when I got tenure, back – oh, it must have been nearly twenty years ago, wasn't it, Marius? – we were still such a new institution in those days..."

Zammi tried to keep his face neutral as he tuned out the droning reminiscence. It wasn't a conscious choice. He just naturally stopped being able to process boring, self-referential exposition. At least, that was what he told himself. He nodded at random intervals, then made a show of catching a glimpse of something in the distance.

"Please excuse me," he said when Dr Evistar paused to take a breath, then Zammi strode purposefully over to the corner of the nibbles table where Beryl Fernandez was parked.

"I hate this," Zammi said.

"Hummus?" Fernandez held up a flatbread smeared with a paste so strongly flavored that Zammi could smell it from a meter away.

He shook his head, with a wry smile at Fern's gambit. "No, you know I don't hate hummus." He dipped his own chip and popped it into his mouth. Creamy, garlicky, peppery. He took another one. Across the room, someone laughed a little loudly and Zammi flinched.

"Whoa," Fern said, dropping a hand lightly on Zammi's arm. "You *are* jumpy."

"I'm fine." He shrugged and turned away.

It had been over two decades, surely he should be over it by now. But no, every party was always the same, every ostensible celebration internally morose. A reminder of that night.

He'd been just a kid and so excited to be at a grown-up party with his big sister and all three parents. And when Mom and Papi had left early, it had been even more exciting to be allowed to stay behind with Val and Dad.

The music was loud and people were laughing and dancing. There was a buffet of food on one table, glasses and drinks on another. Dad got them each a plate and filled it with little pastries, mini quiches, and veggies with dip, then told the kids to go have fun before he went off to talk to a group of adults Zammi didn't recognize. He turned to his sister, worried she would abandon him for the small knot of other teens awkwardly milling around near where people were dancing, but she grabbed Zammi's hand.

"Come on, kiddo," she said, grinning, "you heard Dad."

They wove through the crowd and, when she thought no one was looking, Val grabbed a half-finished glass of beer and led Zammi over to where some of her friends were sitting on the floor near the speakers. She held a finger to her lips, then sipped from the glass. She made a sour face but took another drink anyway.

Zammi sat cross-legged and nibbled on his food as he watched the older kids dance. The music was loud but in a fun way. Val was laughing and maybe even a little tipsy from the purloined beer. She'd become so much more grown-up lately, never wanting to play puzzles or hide and seek with Zammi anymore. But now she grabbed his hand again and pulled him to his feet. She was gripping Zammi's hand so tightly he just went along with it. Zammi didn't dance very often – he was shy, and more than a little awkward in social situations – but he tried to follow along. He wanted to be part of the group, part of Val's new life. She twirled, pulling Zammi along. The other kids were all laughing and smiling as they danced together. Zammi felt like he belonged, like he was on the cusp of something new.

They were laughing so hard that when they heard the sound of a plate breaking, it took them both a while to realize something was wrong. But then he saw Dad's face from across the room, and it was like the whole planet stopped. The party went completely silent. All the kids were staring at them, as Val's face morphed from the cool teenager back to a little kid, running over to their father.

The implant in Zammi's left hand vibrated and for a moment he wasn't sure if it was real or part of the memory. But, of course, he hadn't had a communicator back then, and it had been Dad who'd received the notification. Dad who'd dropped his plate of cake on the ground before sinking to the floor next to it, his face a mask of disbelief.

Zammi shook his head as if clearing the image away. He gestured a holo open with his fingers and saw a message from the UNMI. The United Nations Mars Initiative had begun as an arm of Earth's world government, but over the hundreds of years since its inception it had become more inherently Martian. Now, in addition to carrying out terraforming projects of its own, the UNMI took on many administrative roles on Mars, including supporting the relatively new independent and impartial Citizens' Oversight Committee.

The message was from the Committee asking for someone to take point on investigating a new incident. Some shipping crash on an unnamed asteroid – maybe an accident, maybe something more sinister. The memory of that night came back to him again, and the terrified heart-stuttering feeling returned too. His vision blurred around the edges and if he didn't do something about it, the panic would take over.

"I have to go," he said to Fern, handing her his unfinished beer.

"Anyone else would have planned this," she said, a smile on her wide face. "You should think about that for next time."

"I don't know what you mean," Zammi said, genuinely confused and still reeling from seeing the words "fatal crash."

"I know," Fern said, patting his arm. "Off you go, then."

Zammi nodded earnestly and made for the door.

Once he'd gotten away from the hubbub of the party, Zammi's heart slowed and his breathing evened out. Twenty-two years had compressed to a singularity in that crowded cafeteria, but now he was able to put some space between himself and the memory. The two parent-shaped holes in Zammi's life were always present, but the edges lost their sharpness as Zammi walked toward his office. By the time he was seated at the desk, he was almost able to read the details of this new crash without feeling like a bewildered and bereaved seven year-old.

Lupa Capitolina was a private vessel, larger than a personal shuttle but smaller than a yacht. It was an unusual design, but wealthy prospectors and corporate officers could afford to commission unique ships and often did. When humanity had first taken to the stars it was almost all under the auspices of corporate ownership, the search for profit at least as strong a draw as the search for adventure. Years of conflict and progress had reshaped the governance of the human exopopulation, but the asteroid belt was still a wild mix of private enterprise, corporate exploitation, freehold settlements, and general lawlessness. If anything shady was going on, it probably had something to do with The Rocks.

The ship had been en route from Mars to one of the asteroids when it suddenly veered off course and crashed into a small ice asteroid. There were no survivors.

The cause of the crash was still unknown, and some unusual aspects had been flagged. First, it appeared that the ship's transponder had been disabled, making it difficult to track. Secondly, the debris indicated that the ship was carrying a large amount of specialized mining equipment which was highly unusual for a private vessel.

The asteroid belt was a well-known danger zone, and most private vessels were equipped with state-of-the-art navigation and safety systems. But this ship was old and had apparently been flying without any of those things. Honestly, it was a miracle it hadn't crashed sooner. Zammi couldn't help but wonder if somebody had deliberately sabotaged the vessel from the jump.

But who would do such a thing? And why? There were so many questions, and Zammi knew that getting to the bottom of this crash was going to be a long and difficult process. But he also knew what he'd signed up for when he joined the Oversight Committee.

Spaceflight was inherently dangerous, and just because it was commonplace, that didn't change the reality. You simply got used to the risk. The void of space was incompatible with life, and there was only so much technology could do to insulate people from that fact. Still, the few times he'd done it, Zammi never worried about traversing space per se. So long as your ship kept the air inside and the vacuum outside, it would be fine. It was interaction with matter where things went wrong – takeoffs, landings, running into rocks.

It had been a small, pebble-sized meteor that got Mom and Papi. Something that would easily be dealt with by modern safety features, but in those days private crafts weren't as protected as they should have been.

Progress, Zammi thought, forcing himself to focus on the positive. Learning what had happened wouldn't bring back the people who died, but it might lead to changes so that the same thing didn't happen to anyone else.

You can't change the past, but you can learn from it to make the future better. It was what drew Zammi to history, what made him volunteer for the COC. The desperate hope that one day he would truly believe that something good could come from tragedy.

CHAPTER TWO

"I don't know what I expected, but it wasn't this."

It was the day after the party, and Zammi was sprawled on the couch in Marius's office, his tall frame taking up both seats as he leaned against the armrest. The space between Zammi and Dr Munro was filled with a large holo, showing dozens of documents, images, videos, and three-dimensional reconstructions.

"The days when the Committee had to fight for access to data are mostly long past," Marius said. "I'd like to think it's because people have begun to realize the utility of having a third party involved, but I suspect it's nothing so noble."

"We're supposed to sort through the data dump for them?" Zammi suggested, idly flicking through the mountain of material on the holo which had been sent from Utopia Invest, the owner of the mining rights to the asteroid where the wreckage of *Lupa Capitolina* had been found. "They're trying to use us as free data management."

Marius snorted, the corner of his mouth barely twitching

in his version of a wry smile. "They're trying to drown us in crap," he said. "They've forgotten that manure makes a great fertilizer."

Marius was a dapper, brown-skinned man somewhere in his fifties or sixties. The slate gray handlebar moustache he wore was really the only indicator of his age, other than his stories from the old days and his early years at Mars University. Of course, he wasn't a professor then, rather one of the students in the relatively new history department. He'd never left, going on to graduate work, then tenure, then department head. He was personable, passionate, and his students generally loved him. Of course, Marius roped his favorite student – now colleague – into his pet project as soon as he possibly could, convincing Zammi to sign on with the COC.

"They've obviously been busy," Marius said, indicating the dossier with his finger. "The first thing to keep in mind is that this is just a preliminary report. It's a compilation of everything that's known about the crash to date, but it's not complete – it never is. And, in case it wasn't abundantly obvious, there probably won't be another report. Anything else we find, we'll have to get on our own."

"On our own?"

Marius shrugged. "It's a free system. Even more free in the Rocks. There isn't a single authority out there – anyone can ask questions."

"You mean on the ground investigating?" Zammi's voice rose in pitch. "Like actually go out there and sift through debris?" The thought of trawling through a crash site made his stomach tighten.

"If you like, sure, though that's not quite what I was thinking.

What we really need is a proper scan. It won't take long before the site is contaminated or, worse, 'cleaned up.' We need to get someone there before that happens. If you were inclined to ask a few questions… well, that would be fine, too."

Zammi nodded. That was more like what was in his wheelhouse. "I guess I was assuming that everything would be in the data dump."

"Even in the best circumstances things get missed, and this is anything but the best circumstances. You never know what gets overlooked in the rush to make a buck out here. You want to start with the report?"

Zammi leaned forward, pulling his long dark hair up into a knot, an unconscious habit before he set to work. The holo showed a standard virtual desktop, with the deep green logo of the company that owned the mine floating in the top left corner. The data was divided into several categories. The first, a so-called executive summary which was distinctly lacking in detail.

The rest of the report contained a description of the ship as well as a list of the wreckage found at the crash site. There were images of the ship, several renderings of the debris field, schematics of the vessel's components, timelines of the flight. It was all pretty standard stuff and at a cursory glance told Zammi nothing.

He glanced over at Marius, whose gracefully curved eyebrows were knitted as he peered at some part of the report, deep in thought. Ever since he'd taken his first class with Dr Munro as an undergrad, Zammi had thought of the teacher as a vaguely parental figure. He'd had two fathers of his own, one of whom was still alive and well – at least as far as Zammi knew. But while Dad had never stood in the way of Zammi's scholastic endeavors, he'd never understood them – or him. The only history that had mattered to Ivan Michelson then was his personal history, and maybe that of Helion, where he'd worked his whole life. Who knew what mattered to him now?

Zammi remembered when they'd been a happy family of five: Ivan and his wife, Hadley; their husband, Julián, and their two kids. The Kaspar-Vallejo-Michelsons on official forms, though the adults all stuck to their original surnames and Zammi and Val were Kaspars, their mother's name. When she and Julián died and Dad had disappeared into himself, there hadn't been much to connect Zammi or his sister Val to Ivan Michelson beyond the home they shared and the rudimentary conversations they had in the evenings over awkward dinners. Until even those became rarer, then Val left, and then…

Zammi shook his head. This was typical – getting lost in the connections between thoughts, falling down the gravity well of cause and effect, the weight of history as massive as a star. He needed to use that ability to find connections to help figure out this crash, not to zone out thinking about his childhood.

"I'm thinking," Zammi tapped the holo with a finger, dragging the report back into focus, "that there's nothing terribly strange here."

"That's because you're looking at the forest, not the trees," Marius replied. Zammi understood the reference, even though there was nothing even remotely like a forest anywhere other than Earth, and there were precious few of those left where people tended to live. The temperature and atmosphere on Mars was getting to the point where it might have been possible, but there was nowhere near enough water yet. Maybe in Zammi's lifetime, though. Mars was still a work-in-progress, but that progress was visible and active. Change was the only constant on the planet.

Marius pointed at the holo. "Take a look at reference SR073-27. That's where the weird stuff starts."

He entered the reference and a section title "Causal Factor" popped up on the holo. The preliminary report blamed the accident on navigation error. The ship's approach was awkward, attempting to land the craft on the asteroid's surface after a too shallow approach. Unable to compensate, the ship plummeted to the ground, breaking apart upon impact.

"The debris field covers an area of about six square kilometers," Zammi said, gesturing toward the holo in a circular motion, trying not to think about other crash sites. Other people lost. "That's a lot of wreckage."

"Indeed," Marius replied. "We shouldn't rule out an explosion prior to impact."

"Could there have been something onboard that caused the navigation system to fail?"

"Sabotage?" Marius asked.

Zammi shrugged. "Maybe. Or something fried the control system…" He squinted at a table of data. "Look here – the nav system was offline at the time of the crash. And had been off for nearly an hour."

"So they'd been running manually long before whatever happened to cause the crash," Marius said. "So much for nav system error as the causal factor, eh?"

Zammi pursed his lips. No one wanted to pin the blame on a person when a computer could shoulder the load, but why would they have turned off the navigation system in the first place? Hand-steering was a nightmare combination of being both tedious and difficult. No one would have chosen to do it for a second longer than absolutely necessary.

"You think there was some kind of failure on board that took out navigation?" Zammi conjectured, flipping back to the report's index to try to find an explanation. The error logs showing nothing untoward at the time navigation was turned off… except that it was *turned* off. Not a failure, not a system crash. It was manually, deliberately, terminated.

"It's a possibility," Marius said, but he sounded dubious. "But there's something else that's bothering me."

"What's that?"

"Look at the ship's layout. It's not big. It's made for cargo, not passengers. And look at the crew manifest – you've only got a captain, flight engineer and technical specialist listed here."

"Three people is a reasonable crew for a machine like this."

"Sure." Marius flipped through screens rapidly. "But who else was on board?" He pointed at a line in a table. *Personnel Loss – based on debris data: 5 – 7.*

"Who were those extra people?" Marius asked. "This was listed as a private run."

Zammi nodded, but all he could think about was how those five, six or seven lives had been reduced to a line in a database. The math that had to have been employed to guess at the number of people on board. *People*, who doubtless had families, friends, colleagues. Others who cared about them, but now they were not even statistics.

Zammi swallowed and shook his head, trying to dislodge the morbid thought. "So maybe they were all crew," he said, trying to focus on the problem at hand. "Could be they were short-handed and took on a few extra bod– er, people."

"Possible," Marius said, seemingly oblivious to Zammi's discomfort. He flipped back to the executive summary, pulling it into focus and tapping it with his finger. "But we've got no names here. Just stats. According to the story, the flight had no fixed destination, but I must assume they collected a privately negotiated cargo from the Utopia Invest outpost. There's nothing else in the vicinity and the UI operation is the only one on that asteroid. They must have smelled an opportunity for a quick payday – short term speculation is their bailiwick. There are no details about that here, of course. No registered flight plan, no cargo manifests. All because of *industrial confidentiality*, no doubt." Marius blew a stream of air from his nose, forcefully enough to cause his otherwise solid moustache to tremble. "What a load of insufferable, ludicrous nonsense. They redact almost as much data as they send us in these things, all legally, in the name of protecting their competitive advantage. These investment brokers… they're nothing more than parasites."

Zammi was familiar with Marius's many strong opinions about the power and authority that Martian corporations enjoyed, and he didn't bother to argue.

The human exopopulation – everyone, everywhere throughout history who had lived and died somewhere other than planet Earth – owed its existence to a series of corporations taking a gamble on space really being the final frontier. It wasn't only business, of course. There had been political agencies, private cooperatives, pretty much every kind of human organization involved, but the business of expansion was lucrative and compelling. It was a complicated legacy, for some people a shameful one. Some human settlements had gone through their individual struggles to wrest control away from corporations and form self-governments, but on Mars, in the asteroid belt, and in the race to reach other planets and moons there was still plenty of money to be made from the resources space offered. And that meant that there were plenty of areas that were barely controlled, businesses large and small exploiting resources mineral and human, their employees citizens of nowhere. These were the domains of gamblers, grifters, and the desperate.

At least, that was the common view in places like Mars University, where most people never approached within an astronomical unit of the asteroid belt. The closest most Martians came to a rock-jock was as a stock character in serial entertainments – or a dire warning of what could befall young students who ignore their studies and fall in with a bad crowd.

The reality was that the people who worked the Rocks were as diverse as any other group of humans anywhere. Some were there because they loved the challenge and adventure of the frontier, some were paying off a terrible debt and mining was the best way to make fast money, some were even born into it – the family business. It was a hard life, though, especially when compared to the relative ease of living in a domed city. Being misunderstood and stereotyped was the least of their concerns.

The relationship between the individuals who worked the

Rocks and the companies who benefited from their labor was strained. In the years since the first permanent settlement in the Rocks was established some organization had taken hold, and the Martian-based Mining Guild had made some good footholds in the Rocks, but plenty of independents operated easily in the gaps, playing the unions and corporations against each other. The asteroid belt belonged to no one, so oversight was relegated to operations like the PSCOC, but when wrongdoing was found, consequences were thin. Getting all the authorities to agree was hard enough, and even when that did happen, there was a lot of space in space. Even groups that were banned from trading "everywhere" could manage to operate in the margins if they tried.

But Zammi believed that poor oversight was better than none, and even if for every one exploitative operation they exposed there were dozens more under way, they had still improved the lives of the people they helped in the moment. He had to believe that the individual successes mattered, or else nothing mattered.

"So they're hiding the important data," Zammi said to Marius's still disgusted face. "How do we find it?"

Wrinkles appeared at the edges of Dr Munro's eyes. "That's the fun part, kid."

CHAPTER THREE

The next day, Zammi met Marius in his office first thing. Which, for Marius, was after Zammi had already been to the gym, cleaned up, read several chapters of a colleague's thesis, set a pot of beans simmering on the cooktop, and finally recorded a message to Val.

His sister hadn't picked up any of his calls, but that wasn't out of the ordinary. However, Zammi hated leaving messages. It was time to get it over with, though, so he took a deep breath, faced the camera on his desk, and tapped record.

"Hey, Val. I hope things are going well with you. I just wanted to let you know that I did it: I got tenure! So, you know, I'm stuck here, I guess." Zammi made a noise that was intended to sound like a laugh, but he was pretty sure it didn't come out that way. "Anyway, I wanted to share the good news. Let me know when you're back in Tharsis…" He cut the recording and scrubbed back a few seconds. For all he knew, she was in Tharsis now and was just too busy to talk to him. He cued up the recording to deliver an edited ending. "Anyway, I just wanted to share my good news. Talk to you soon."

He ended the recording and sent it, not even bothering to review the final product. His filial duty was now done, and he could get back to work. Val probably won't even care; she'd always thought that the university life was dull as dust. Still, a part of him wanted her to be happy for him.

He got into the History Department just before eleven and expected silence to answer his knock on the department head's door. Marius Munro was a known night owl and not an early riser, so it surprised Zammi when the door flung open and Marius waved him in, pointing Zammi at a holostation.

"I feel like we've gotten everything useful we're going to get out of this report," Zammi said, after several minutes flipping through holo pages. "But all we have is speculation. And not even enough of that to develop a hypothesis. Where do we go from here?"

"People like to talk," Marius said. "Especially when they don't get to talk much."

"What do you mean?" Zammi asked.

Marius leaned forward and put his hands flat on his desk. "We're not likely to be the only ones looking into the crash," he said.

"You mean like the corporate interests of the owners of the vessel?" Zammi asked.

"That's one," Munro said, nodding, then glanced away as if unsure. "There are also the families."

Zammi took a steadying breath. "But that's part of the problem. We don't know the identities of the crew."

"Someone must," Marius said. "There might be someone looking for them even if they don't know what happened."

"Missing persons reports."

"Yeah."

Zammi considered that for a moment. "The crash only happened a few days ago. Would someone have reported them missing already?"

Marius frowned, and for a moment he looked old. "Depends on your definition of missing. When my sister Cassie was a pilot, she called home every thirty hours or there was hell to pay. I don't think my folks were all that strange."

Zammi thought about how Dad changed after his parents' accident, how he retreated into himself almost as if both Zammi and Val were gone, too. Val's friends all assumed that he'd become overprotective, never letting his remaining family out of his sight, but the truth was that if Zammi had hotwired a rover and gone for a desert joyride, Dad wouldn't have noticed. Not that it was the kind of thing Zammi would ever have done. Val got away with that and more plenty of times, though.

He released the thought and turned back to Marius. "What about the ship? There must be records somewhere."

"Agreed," Marius said, then arched an eyebrow. "Why don't you follow up on the owner of the ship and I'll look into the … other stuff?"

Marius could have a gruff demeanor at times and most people who didn't know him well assumed he was blunt to the point of cruelty, but the truth was that he was as sensitive to others' feelings as anyone Zammi knew. It made him an excellent teacher and, now, mentor.

"It's a plan," Zammi said, standing and waving his hands to close the holo. "I'll let you know when I find something."

"Same here."

Zammi set to work at his terminal tracing the ownership of the ship and, by the next day, had a name: Jocasta Rew.

He discovered that Jocasta Rew was the owner of a small pilot-for-hire outfit called Starry Vistas. A quick check of the financial records showed that the business was doing nowhere near well enough that it would be able to afford its own ship – even an old, barely functioning bucket of bolts like the *Lupa Capitolina*. And, indeed, the company hadn't purchased the ship – the *Lupa Cap* was registered to Rew personally, not Starry Vistas. It was very odd.

He did a little more digging in case Rew happened to be independently wealthy and merely ran the business for fun, but there was no indication that such was the case. Not surprising since Starry Vistas appeared to be barely scraping by, taking on risky jobs for a quick pay transfer, their financial office regularly robbing Peter to pay Paul when payroll came around. There was no accounting for some folks' idea of entertainment, but running a struggling business was an unlikely idle pastime.

He sent a message to Rew's public comms address asking her to contact him, then waved the holo away and leaned back, gazing at the viewport in the office. This time it offered a live view from one of the cameras on the Tharsis City dome. It was objectively spectacular – the glint of sunlight on distant domes, majestic ranges on the horizon, a sky beginning on take on the blue tint that came with an atmosphere – but to Zammi it was just "outside."

He breathed in, the air inside the dome a mixture of recycled, filtered, and newly processed gasses, but he couldn't smell anything he hadn't smelled a thousand times before. He wondered what it would be like to live somewhere where you could stand in the open under the stars for more than a few very uncomfortable minutes. He'd never been to Earth. Zammi's entire existence had been lived inside one containment or another – a dome, a suit, a rover. Even though it was one of the goals they all worked toward, the idea of being exposed to space, even under the protection of an atmosphere, was inherently terrifying.

A blip on the desk caught Zammi's attention and he brought up the messenger screen again. It wasn't from Rew, instead it was a reminder of the faculty meeting next week. It would be Zammi's first as a full professor, his entrée into the world of departmental politics. He scheduled the message to resurface the day before the meeting; that would give him enough time to prepare. The message blinked out of sight, and Zammi scanned his inbox and frowned. There was nothing remotely personal in here, no sign that he had any life outside of the university. It was probably an accurate assessment. It had been months since he'd seen Val, and as for Dad… well, that man had made the decision to be alone years ago.

It was a little odd that his sister hadn't responded when Zammi let her know about getting tenure, but Val's life was as chaotic as Zammi's was orderly. For all he knew she was hitching a ride on a cargo steamer out somewhere beyond the reach of a comms beacon and hadn't even seen his video message. Val never stayed anywhere very long. She'd left home as soon as she was old enough to make her own way and since then she'd never held down a steady job as far as Zammi knew. She always seemed to be doing fine, though. She messaged just often enough that Zammi felt like he had some semblance of a family and they managed to meet up once a year or so. The notion of the two of them together in one place for good seemed ludicrous now. It was hard to believe they'd spent over a decade sharing a room.

Zammi went back to the holo, this time looking deeper into Starry Vistas' pilots. It was a small-time, independent operation that made its way freelancing for whichever corporation or organization needed extra help, and their job logs made it clear that they were barely making ends meet. There were no shortage of folks working a similar grind – people or groups who did what needed doing for whoever was paying. It wasn't easy, but there was a freedom to be had in taking jobs on one's own schedule. Not to mention that corporate contracts tended to be long-term, with punitive non-competes, so quitting a job meant no one else was going to hire you. How had their owner ended up with a new – well, new to her – ship? There had to be another source of the funds to buy the ship, but what? And why didn't whoever it was just put their name on it?

"Hey, you."

Beryl Fernandez poked her head into Zammi's office, then knocked twice on the doorjamb. The reverse order of her actions was typical and Zammi closed the holo.

"I'm going to take the waters. You should come with."

Zammi had met Fernandez in the faculty chandlery, on his first trip for supplies as a brand new lecturer. He was struggling with the automated payment system when he felt a hand on his shoulder.

"Come with me," she'd said, as if they were old friends. "You need to get set up with credit." She steered him to the small hatch where a human staffer helped Zammi open a new account with the store and access his stipend balance. Thanks to his mysterious savior, he'd only had to say his name. Ever since then, Fern had been a constant in Zammi's days on campus, whether he'd wanted the companionship or not.

Now, annoyed at the interruption, Zammi bit back the childish response, *I don't wanna have my bath,* then nodded. Honestly, a steam would probably do him good, and he needed a break one way or another.

There were public baths of wildly variable quality in all the large settlements on Mars, but the university facility was both decent and affordable. Water regulation meant that few individuals could afford private shower facilities – daily ablutions were dry chemical rubs. It was sufficient for good hygiene but most people enjoyed a soak or a steam every once in a while, and long ago a bathhouse had become a symbol for civilization among the exopopulation. Zammi could have lectured extemporaneously for at least an hour on the topic, but Fern knew the history just as well.

For no obvious reason the bathhouse was in the Philosophy Department's building, next to the combination spa and gym, artlessly named *The Platonic Ideal.* Zammi groaned every time he saw the sign and the obviously doctored before-and-after images of satisfied customers. He opened his mouth to make a sharp remark, but Fern cut him off.

"Yeah, yeah, it's tasteless and worse yet, it's not even funny. Let's skip the commentary and get to the tubs already."

They checked into the baths, individual towels dispensed

by the automated kiosk when they swiped their staff credentials, then opened the first door to the airlock. Once it was securely shut behind them, the door to the baths swished open, misting them in scented steam. When it had closed, the vapor that had escaped into the airlock would be reclaimed and recycled. Not a drop of precious Martian water was to be wasted.

Zammi stashed his clothes in a locker and padded into a single steamer for a minute's blast. The warm droplets coated his body and saturated his long hair, the uncanny sensation of additional weight on his head always oddly comforting. He ran his hands through his hair, now a mass of dripping curls, as the steam shut off, and wrapped the large fluffy towel around himself. He pulled his thick tendrils up into a fat, black knot on the top of his head then walked to the shared pools, the non-slip texture of the flooring like pebbles underfoot.

Fern was already lounging in a four-person tub, the water up to her chin, the steam in the room nearly obscuring her from sight. Zammi folded his towel carefully and set it in a cubby near the tub, then slipped in across from Fern. A sigh escaped his lips as the warm water surrounded him.

"I know what's good for you," she said, her eyes still closed and mouth only barely above the lapping water.

"Yeah, yeah," he said, dismissively, but sank deeper into the warmth.

They sat in silence for a while, letting the steamy air saturate their lungs, and the tension flowed out of them both.

Fern let him relax for a few minutes before asking, "So, do you wanna talk about it?"

"Talk about what?" Zammi replied, legitimately confused.

"You know." Fern opened her eyes and looked at Zammi, her gaze expectant. "You've been moping around here for days, since the tenure news. Have you even stepped foot anywhere besides your office and your room? I mean, I know you're normally a head-down keener, but this is a lot – even for you." She cocked her head, then said uncharacteristically softly, "Did something happen?"

"I…" Zammi started, then sighed. "I've just been feeling a bit… abandoned lately. It's nothing new, just family. Or, you know, lack of family. But I guess I'm noticing it more right now is all."

"You have a sibling, right?"

"Yeah, Val. We get along OK, I guess, but she's not around much. Hasn't been for a long time." He stared off into the steam. "It's fine, really. Besides, Marius has me on a case for the committee, so there's plenty to keep me busy until the term starts."

"You don't say." Fern sloshed around in the tub, making tiny waves lap on the surface. "What's it about?"

"A ship crash on one of the asteroids," Zammi said without inflection.

Fern stared at him, conspicuously keeping her face neutral. "Oh," she said, eventually.

"Yeah," Zammi admitted, avoiding her gaze. "Like I said, it's fine."

"Sure," Fern said. "You know–"

"Look," Zammi said, surprisingly heated. "If you're going to tell me that you're always here for me to talk about my feelings, you can forget it. I don't want your pity. And if I wanted a counselor, I'd go see a professional."

A beat later Fern barked out a laugh. "Zambrotta Kaspar, the last thing I want to do ever is listen to people talk about their feelings. I was going to say, you know that's what you get for joining up with Marius and his pack of do-gooders. Trouble… and having to think about things."

Zammi's anger broke and he chuckled. "That's true enough. I knew what I was getting into."

"Yes, you did," Fern said. "Now quit your bellyaching and enjoy this tub, or leave me to it."

"I hear and obey," Zammi said, leaning back into the water and closing his eyes.

CHAPTER FOUR

"I'm not sure I'm ready for this," Zammi said.

Marius put a hand on his shoulder. "You'll be fine. We've gone over everything a thousand times. You know what to do."

"But what if something goes wrong?"

"There's always a risk, but we've minimized it as much as possible. We'll be in near instant communication, and if something unexpected happens, I'll be there to talk you through it."

"I know, but…" Zammi paused, not sure how to explain. It wasn't that he was heading off to some desolate asteroid. It wasn't that he was looking into a crash that no one involved seemed to want investigated. It wasn't even that the very thought of seeing wreckage made his stomach turn. It was all of it and more.

"Look, they have to let us view the site. It's part of the agreement – independent observers aren't only allowed in a case like this, it's mandatory. No one is going to try to stop you."

Zammi nodded. Maybe that was the problem. He wanted someone to step in and give him an out, a reason to stay on Mars where he had his books and lectures, where he could spend his days contemplating people whose descendants were long dead. The distance was a kind of emotional security.

"I'm sorry," Zammi said. "I'll get over myself."

Marius shook his head. "It's fine. I'm sorry I didn't give you more time to get your head on straight. It's just… we have a window, and I wanted to seize it."

"I know," Zammi said.

"I would go if I could, but they don't let department heads skip off on side trips like this willy-nilly."

"Of course. I just didn't think it would be so soon."

"It has to be this shuttle run, or we'll be waiting a month, and by then the scene will be contaminated beyond belief. I'll be with you the entire time, I promise," Marius said. "You'll be fine."

Zammi nodded. "Yeah, I know."

"Now go on," Marius said, nudging him toward the shuttle. "You don't want to miss your flight."

Zammi would have been perfectly happy missing his flight, but he reminded himself of why he was going: Ethelbert Tipton, Pia van Niekerk, and Jocasta Rew. Marius had managed to identify three of the downed crewmembers and Zammi repeated their names to himself as he packed. Apparently Starry Vistas was a family crew, the three of them a package deal – pilot, navigator and mechanic. Zammi guessed that they'd been hired to run the *Lupa Capitolina* for the true owner as part of whatever deal Rew had made. There was no indication who the other people aboard might have been – the actual owners, passengers, stowaways, incidental crew hired on by Starry Vistas. There was no record of them anywhere.

The data files weren't going to be of any more use, Marius had made it clear that he was sure of that. So it had to be the personal touch, and with Marius's duties as department chair, he couldn't disappear off to an unnamed asteroid for however long it took. There was no time to ease Zammi into it – his debut was going to be the real thing.

The stress of the day had taken a lot out of him. The commuter flight from Mars was smooth and boring, as was docking at the transfer station, then another, similar flight to the landing pad on the asteroid.

Apparently, only a few ships came in to offload cargo and pick up the chunks of ice being mined here for delivery to Mars and select other colonies for use as their main sources of fresh water. Most of the daily business was done remotely or through automated systems, which meant for a couple of days every month the dock would be busy, filled with maintenance workers, pilots, and dockhands, but the rest of the time the place was a ghost town.

Zammi was the only person to disembark through the airlock, and he was struggling with the low gravity when he was met by a tall figure in a heavy uniform with security tags, who kept uncomfortably close to him as they skip-walked down a series of corridors. Maybe it was a good thing Marius wasn't here – he had a clear and obvious distrust of authority.

"Anyone else with the investigation team?" the security officer asked.

"No, it's only me."

The officer nodded once then said, "They've got you a temporary spot in berthage. This is all we have for quarters, sorry."

Zammi shrugged. "It will be fine."

"You're here to look at the wreckage, right?"

"Right," Zammi said, "and take some scans. I'd love to speak with anyone with any information."

"It happened pretty far out from the active mine. I don't think anyone saw it."

"I have to try," Zammi said, hating how unconfident he sounded.

They walked in silence for a few minutes, then the officer spoke again in an oddly confidential tone. "You know, I'm not sure you fully realize what happened here."

"I know it was a bad crash, and a lot of people died," Zammi said. "I know it's hard to go on after something like that."

"No, that's not what I mean," his escort said. "I mean they weren't supposed to be here. That ship… it just came out of nowhere and slammed into the asteroid."

That's how it always happens, Zammi thought as they arrived at a large, unmarked metal door. His escort pounded on the door and the sound of several locks being worked on the other side came through. The metal squeaked as the door was pushed open from the inside and a large, unshaven head poked through.

"This is the Citizens' Oversight person," the officer said to a grunt from the one on the inside, then turned back to Zammi. "Karl will show you to your bunk."

"Welcome aboard," the man said, opening the door and

gesturing him inside. "Sorry about the accommodations, they actually get worse the farther out you go."

The place appeared to be nothing but a series of small, unadorned rooms with quad bunks, but Zammi was surprised to find himself steered toward an even smaller cubby, made up with a single cot with fresh blankets and a pillow. The walls were bare metal and the room was lit by a single overhead lamp.

"This all for me?" Zammi asked.

Karl shrugged. "I thought you might want something a bit more comfortable than the workers' quarters." He paused. "We don't spend much time in here, pretty much just to sleep. Figured you'd need privacy to do whatever it is you're here to do."

Zammi frowned. "You heard about the crash?"

Karl nodded. "Don't know nothing about what you folks do, though. I hope it'll keep you busy."

"Oh?"

"It's pretty boring out here." Karl jerked his head toward the wall, indicating the entire asteroid, Zammi guessed. "We don't got any holos or interactives. You want some reading material?"

"That would be great," Zammi said.

"No problem," Karl said. "One of the other workers brought in a batch of books, if you don't mind a random selection."

Zammi smiled weakly. "That's fine."

"I'll drop them off later," Karl said. "I need to get back to work. Chow'll be in the mess in a few hours. There's a bell, you can't miss it."

Karl left him alone and Zammi stared at the empty cot and

tried to think of what to do next. Part of him wanted to curl up and sleep for a week, but the sooner he got what he needed the sooner he could get back to Mars. He did lie down, just for a moment, and the cot was surprisingly comfortable.

The next thing he knew, he woke up, mouth gummy and eyes bleary. He gestured open a screen to check the time – he'd only napped for a couple of hours. He paged over to the comms setting and searched for the local network, but nothing came up. His university comms could reach a nearby satellite, so he still had the promised connection to Marius, but there were no signs of public communications, or even a local net. That seemed odd, so he stood up and looked around the small room for a hardwired screen or other device.

It didn't take long to be certain there was none. The room's four walls were completely unadorned and the only furniture was the cot. Maybe there would be a common room with a shared holo, or something. Karl had mentioned a mess hall – maybe there?

As if on cue, a loud bell sounded like a gong, heavily amplified. A fuzzy piped-in voice came over a speaker somewhere outside the room, and said in several languages, "Food time." Zammi wondered if it was a weird translation or if whoever had programed the voice was unusually literal. Whichever, he understood what was going on, and joined the stream of people outside the door headed down the corridor. No one said anything to him, but Zammi could tell by the way everyone kept their eyes elsewhere that new arrivals were uncommon here.

The mess hall was as utilitarian as the rest of the facility, a cavernous room with a series of long tables with hard benches on either side. A serving station was set up along one wall, and an orderly queue formed on the way. Zammi slotted into line, which moved briskly. When he got to the front, he could see why. The choices were minimal – a runny looking gray stew, bread rolls, some lumps of obviously inexpensive vat-grown protein. Zammi avoided the latter but accepted a double scoop of the stew. Even this unappetizing meal was making his stomach growl.

He found a free seat and tucked into the stew. It tasted a lot better than it looked, even though it was mostly broth. He tore off a hunk of bread to dip in the sauce when a shadow fell over him. He looked up to see a hard-faced woman slip into the seat across from him.

"You must be Doctor Kaspar," she said, making the word "doctor" sound vaguely insulting. "I'm Vera Baughman."

"Of course," Zammi said, wiping his hands on a napkin and sticking an arm across the table. Vera shook his hand briskly, then dropped her hands back into her lap. "You're the foreperson here, right?"

She nodded once and said, "I'm aware that your presence here is required, but I have to admit that this crash has been extremely inconvenient." She pursed her lips, as if it were Zammi's fault personally.

"I understand, but surely you want to know what happened? Your people…" he trailed off, as Vera's face softened for the first time since she'd sat down.

"You don't know," she said and Zammi made a "what don't I know" face. "That ship wasn't one of ours," she explained. "We had nothing on the schedule and we'd never seen it before. Either it was in the wrong place at the wrong time, or…" She gazed over his shoulder at nothing in particular, then looked back at Zammi. "Or it was trying to land here undetected."

"Why would anyone do that?" Zammi asked and a twitch appeared on Vera's face, only for an instant, then it was gone.

"I couldn't say," she replied, then stood. "Whatever it was has nothing to do with me or my team, which is all I'm concerned with. I will do what I must to help you, and you are welcome to the amenities of our facility." She chuckled. "I hope you get what you need quickly, and with a minimum of fuss. Enjoy your meal, doctor." She turned on her heel and walked away.

There was obvious subtext to her words, but Zammi couldn't figure out what it was. He focused on his dinner and nearly didn't notice that someone was standing just behind and to his left.

"Hey, Big'un," a gravelly voice said, and Zammi turned to look up into a face that had seen better days. It wasn't just the wrinkles, but a brace of scars including at least one vacuum burn. The eyes had a distinct lack of friendliness to them.

"Uh, hi," Zammi said, sticking out a hand out which was ignored. He awkwardly withdrew it as the other person stared him down.

"Didn't think we were getting any new inmates," the person said with narrowed eyes. "It just you or are there more?"

"I'm not – uh, *new*," Zammi said. "I'm here because of the crash. Part of the independent investigation team."

"Oh. Oh!" The interloper's tone changed and he helped himself to the seat that Vera Baughman had vacated. "My name's Rufus. You need any help while you're here, you know, a bit of information here and there, a little local knowledge to ease your time, I'm your man." He glanced toward Vera Baughman then dropped his voice, genuine concern in his tone. "Boss give you a hard time?"

"She's not my boss," Zammi said. "I'm from the Citizens' Oversight Committee."

"Sure thing. Independent, you said. So are you, ah…" Rufus glanced around the mess as if someone might be trying to eavesdrop. "You're getting a ride out of here when your investigation is complete?"

Zammi shrugged. "Yeah. Probably in a few days. I don't expect to be here long."

"Cool. Cool, cool, cool," Rufus said, obviously reining in excitement. "Well, like I said, anything you need, and I mean *anything*, you just call on old Rufus here, OK?"

"Sure thing," Zammi said, not meaning it at all, when a ruckus on the other side of the hall drew both their attention.

"Stars on fire, Billie, I am not trying to take your job away from you, just… whoa!" The clatter of food trays broke the yelling, and a wiry person with long black hair tied up in a complicated braid leapt across one of the tables in a high arc, which, due to the gravity difference, would have been impossible on Mars, pulling someone on the other side down in the process. The yeller, certainly.

Surely it couldn't be…

Zammi's stomach clenched and he stood briskly, taking only a few strides of his long legs to cross the hall and join the knot of people now surrounding what was clearly in the process of becoming a fistfight. The person with the hair – Billie – was taking a swing at the other party, who'd spryly rolled out of the way and was now picking herself up.

Her hair was nearly shaved to the scalp and she was at the more muscular end of her natural body shape, but Zammi knew that voice anywhere. The voice, the delighted grin as she ducked another of Billie's haymakers and drove a fist into her opponent's midsection. The gleam in her eyes as Billie stayed down, groaning.

"Val?" Zammi said aloud, but he was inaudible among the din of the other workers hoping for more entertainment. "What the hell are you doing here?"

CHAPTER FIVE

The fight ended as quickly as it had begun, as a pair of security officers charged into the mess hall and the combatants disengaged. Val caught Zammi's eye, and her face cycled through confusion, surprise, panic and amusement, then settled on a false contrition that Zammi knew well from their childhood. She spoke earnestly and quickly to the officers, and even clapped Billie once on the shoulder. Whatever line she'd spun obviously worked and she was given a talking-to, but ultimately let go. She made her way to where Zammi was standing and jerked her head for him to follow.

"What are *you* doing here?" Val whispered angrily, wiping her face with a grubby napkin. "And before you say anything, call me Tina, OK?"

They sat at the end of a table in the nearly empty mess, once Billie had limped off in ignominy and everyone else wandered away, bored now.

"Is that a permanent change or just for here?" Zammi asked.

"Just for here," Val replied, without further elaboration. "Don't screw this up, OK?"

"I'll try," he said, frowning. "I don't know what *this* is, though."

Val glanced over her sibling's shoulder, although there was no one within earshot. She ignored the implied question and reiterated her own. "You are the last person in the solar system I thought I'd see here, Zambo. You were up for some kind of nerd promotion the last I heard, weren't you? Something go wrong at the university?"

So she hadn't even seen his message. That was better than being ignored. "It's called tenure," Zammi said, simply, not commenting on her use of the hated childhood nickname. "And I got it. I'm here because of that crash."

He watched Val's face for any reaction but there was none. She had always been good at stuffing down any hint of feelings and pretending to be made of stone.

"But why?" she asked.

Zammi explained about the Citizens' Oversight Committee, how he was working with his department head to try to make sense of what happened. Val's eyes began glazing over and Zammi knew better than to bother explaining further. If it didn't interest her, or affect her directly, Val didn't give a damn. About anything.

"So, what about you?" Zammi asked, trying to get her attention. "You need to make some quick cash or something?"

Val's face twitched, then she laughed, briefly but with real feeling. She was gorgeous when she laughed, always had been, but it was a rare moment when she allowed the hard set of her jaw to relax enough.

"Or something," she said, then glanced behind Zammi again. He fought the urge to turn to see what, if anything, she was looking at.

"You don't know what this place is, do you?" she asked, her voice low.

"I'm getting the distinct impression that I do not," Zammi replied. "Wildcat ice mining operation?"

Val shook her head with a "try again" expression on her face. "I mean, it is that, technically," she allowed, "but me and my compatriots aren't exactly making quick cash."

Zammi frowned, then thought, then his eyes widened. "Surely not BeSADs?"

Val nodded, her face warning Zammi not to make a big deal of it. Bonded Service Against Debt was legal everywhere off Earth, though it had been outlawed there centuries previously. Zammi knew that in the early days of settlement most of the people who created livable communities on Mars had been indentured – the cost of passage into the stars far more than the life savings of anyone willing to do the work. The early system was set up so most people paid off their debt within a few years, then were able to start building savings of their own. It worked reasonably well to start, but over the years became more and more exploitative – but also much less common. Now most people regarded bonded service as the terrible legacy of a less civilized time.

Of course, never in human history has civilization been equally distributed, and it was certainly not now. Not to mention that one person's just and free society was another's repressive regime. Philosophically, it was a complex issue. Practically, though, Zammi knew that nowadays most sites that used BeSADS were effectively prisons. It explained rather a lot about the last few hours.

"I had no idea things were so bad for you," Zammi said, the realization of his sister's situation finally sinking in. "Why didn't you tell me? I'm sure we could have found a way to manage your debt, something other than this."

Before Val could say anything, one of the station's staffers – perhaps *guard* was the more accurate term – walked into the mess.

"Lights out in ten, you two," she said to them gruffly from just inside the door. "Better get a move on."

Val stood and gave Zammi a "follow my lead" look. "We're on our way." She turned to Zammi and whispered angrily, "I don't need a handout from you. Or anyone. Just leave it, OK?"

It wasn't a request, and she didn't look back as she walked briskly out of the mess hall.

Zammi perched on the cot in his tiny room and reflected on what Val had told him. The bare walls, the lack of communications, and the regimented life he'd observed here now took on a more sinister tone. It was one thing to suffer austerity by choice – even if that choice was limited by the constraints of capitalism – and it was quite another to think that the people he'd met were trapped here. That Val was trapped here.

She'd seemed remarkably comfortable with her lot, though. Val had never been one to just go along to get along, and Zammi struggled to imagine how she was managing here. Given the fistfight in the mess, maybe she wasn't. She absolutely was one to put up a brave face even when she was in terrible pain. Seeing Zammi was probably the last thing Val wanted. She'd be mortified to think that anyone, especially her own brother, felt sorry for her.

A dull buzzer sounded, and the yellow overhead light winked off. A dim blue illumination came from strips along the edges of the floor, presumably so it wasn't pitch black in the windowless space, but it was dark enough that sleep seemed the obvious choice. Zammi pulled the rough blanket up to his neck and between his earlier nap and the many things he now had to fret about, he wondered if he'd ever get to sleep.

The next thing he knew, the overheads snapped back on to full brightness and a klaxon sounded. For a moment he was disoriented, reaching for the screen by his bed back at home at the university to dim the lights and silence the alarm. But then his mission and the reason he was on the ice asteroid came back to him, and he swung his legs off the cot and went to find the ablution block.

It felt a very particular kind of indescribable way to put on the borrowed vac suit and drive off across the asteroid's surface while the rest of the workers were literally trapped in either the mine or the desolate habitat. The buggy was driven by a member of Vera Baughman's staff; the nametag on his tatty suit read *Milton, A.* It was a good distance out to the crash site, and they passed groups of suited workers manipulating the large boring machines used to extract ice from below the rocky surface of the asteroid. Rickety-looking prefabricated huts dotted the landscape, acting as staging grounds for what Milton explained were test shafts. There was ice on this asteroid, but it was only found in a few underground pockets, so they were using the old trial-and-error method. It would never have been close to cost-effective if the staffing costs were competitive. Once they'd passed the last abandoned test site, Zammi's curiosity got the better of him.

"Can I ask a possibly rude question?"

The face inside the helmet grinned. "Go for it."

"Are you a BeSAD?"

Milton chuckled. "I'm disappointed. That's not even close to a rude question. Everyone here is bonded, except Baughman probably. Maybe even she is, I dunno. It's how UI operates."

Utopia Invest. Zammi didn't know much about the investment consortium.

"All their staff are bonded?"

Milton's helmet bobbed up and down in the affirmative as he jerked the joystick to avoid a large crater, the buggy bounding off the surface for a disconcerting moment. "On the mines, they are. It's a great investment opportunity – they buy up debt all over the system then pick up cheap deeds on marginal rocks. There's usually not enough ice on these little rocks to make a proper operation pay off, but cheap labor goes a long way. And once in a while these little rocks really pay off."

Zammi knew what he meant. Scans could only give a hint of what exactly lay below the surface, and occasionally a large vein could be discovered in an unlikely location.

"What happens when it does?"

"The investors get the lion's share, of course," Milton said without rancor. "But the contract is for a day rate plus a small sale bonus. If we struck a frozen ocean, pretty much everyone here would pay off their debt on the first shipment."

"So coming out here is one of those high-risk high-reward choices?"

"Yeah, but it's also not exactly a choice. If UI or some other outfit like it buys your debt, they own you. If you can't pay, you have to work. Choice doesn't really enter into it."

Zammi didn't know what to say to that, but he was spared having to come up with a response as debris began to spot the landscape.

"We're here," Milton said as the buggy slowed. "We've got enough air for a couple of hours, so take your time. You know, up to a point," he chuckled again, then pulled a lever which reclined the seat. "Wake me up when it's time to go back," he said, then the faceplate of his helmet darkened.

Zammi hopped out of the buggy, startled by what felt like falling in slow motion. Then, when his feet were safely on the ground, he checked the gauge mounted on the left forearm of the suit. Oxygen was at eighty-three percent and he watched as that ticked down to eighty-two. Right, he needed to slow his breathing. He'd only been out in the open a few times in his life, and it was mildly terrifying. He'd be fine. Just get the data and get back – he didn't need to do any analysis out here.

He pulled a handheld scanner from the leg pocket of the suit, checking that its tether was secure before fumbling it on with gloved fingers. He realized now that what he'd thought were loose asteroidal rocks were actually metal and carbon fragments. There was debris everywhere, tiny pieces of what once had been a feat of human engineering. There was a lot more of it a couple of meters away. He walked toward it, identifying it as obviously the main crash site, waving the scanning beam over anything he noticed. He tried not to think about anything beyond individual movements. Step forward, scan left and right, take another step, scan again. Don't think about what part of the ship this twisted, scorched piece of metal might be. Don't contemplate that organic-looking stain. Just step forward, scan, and step again.

Time lost all meaning, but he let the oxygen meter keep the pace, and he'd scanned everything visible and was shaking Milton awake at forty-two percent.

"You got everything you need?" Milton asked, jerking the lever and returning the seat to its upright and locked position.

"I think so." Zammi's voice was hoarse. "Let's just get back."

"You got it, boss," Milton said in his incongruously jovial manner. How anyone in his position could be cheerful, Zammi would never understand.

The ride back to base went by without incident, Milton carrying the conversational weight while Zammi stared ahead blankly. He managed to thank him for the ride after fumbling his way out of the suit and walked back to the small room. He flopped down on the cot, his mind beyond processing. It was as if his brain was filled with static.

This had happened to him a few times before, mostly in the years following Mom's and Papi's deaths. The counselors had said it was normal, a coping mechanism, so long as it didn't negatively impact Zammi's life for long periods. Still, whenever he used to shut down it had been disturbing to everyone around him. Val used to try to shake him back to life, though that never did anything except agitate her more. At least this time, he was alone. There was no one to be bothered by his staring eyes and unmoving body.

Not that Zammi was having those thoughts now. He was having no thoughts now. And even when his personal comms chimed with notifications, he didn't notice. It wasn't until there was a banging on the door to his room that he came back to himself and shook his head with a start.

"Yeah?" He opened the door to see Karl, an ancient looking tablet in his hand.

"There are a bunch of novels on here," he said, thrusting the reader toward Zammi. "I hope there's something you like in there."

"Sure," Zammi said, the fog slowly dissipating from his mind. "Thanks, I appreciate it. Uh, what should I do with it? When I'm ..." He didn't want to say *leaving*. "When I'm done."

"Just leave it in the room," Karl said. "I'll pick it up once you're gone."

"OK," Zammi said, feeling foolish for not just talking like a normal person. Apparently, he was the only person here who felt uncomfortable about the fact that he was free to leave. "Thanks again."

"No problem. You find anything out at the site?"

Zammi was momentarily confused about what he was talking about, then shook his head. "I haven't looked through the data, and it wouldn't mean anything to me if I did. It will take someone with more specialized knowledge than me to make sense of it. Really, I'm just here to be a set of arms and legs."

Karl nodded sagely. "I hear that. You'd think with all of this..." He twirled a finger as if to encompass the base, the mine, maybe even the entire exoplanet infrastructure. "You'd think we'd have gotten past needing people to do the dirty work, but here we all are." He made a "what can you do" face and turned. "Enjoy the books."

Zammi closed the door and looked at the tablet in his hand. He'd only ever seen anything like that in a museum, and it took him a moment to figure out how to turn on the screen. All it showed were the cover images of the titles which had been most recently opened. From what Zammi could tell there were a couple of romances, a mystery or thriller, and something with a horse on the cover. He tossed the tablet onto the cod, inadvertently opening a western as he did.

The text didn't look like it was from a novel. It was formatted in bullet points and seemed to have a section for notes, and Zammi could see at a glance that it was the kind of thing a person would get in trouble for in a place like this. He recognized literature describing how to organize a union when he saw it. He tapped the file closed. He was pretty sure that Karl wasn't trying to recruit him. If the tablet with the uploaded books were passed around as much as he said, he'd probably forgotten it was even in there.

Well, good for them.

Zammi pulled out the scanner and connected it to his personal comm, uploading the data to a file that would automatically be sent to Marius on the university's system net. Zammi knew he was just a tool here; a more complex version of the scanner. It was just like Karl had said, sometimes it still took people to do the dirty work.

He picked up the reader Karl had left and selected the book with the dark cover. He wouldn't be leaving until tomorrow and there really wasn't much else to do around here. It would kill some time before the mess opened.

It was a by-the-numbers action thriller, with a larger-than-life hero who wound up in prison after a series of improbable mishaps. She had a whirlwind romance with one of the guards, broke up an extortion racket, then masterminded a daring and utterly implausible escape. It was not exactly Zammi's usual choice for reading entertainment, but he found himself reading chapter after chapter. When the chow bell finally sounded, he was reluctant to put the book down. After all, Cherry Lazereyes had just busted down the door to the executive office of the corporation that owned the prison. But Zammi's stomach growled, so he carefully laid the tablet down on the cot, open to where he left off so he wouldn't lose his place.

He joined the throng headed toward the mess and was struck by how similar this facility was to the prison in the book. He stopped dead in his tracks, causing the person behind him to knock into his side.

"Watch yourself, buddy!"

Zammi rejoined the group, but the thought that had struck him was now making its presence insistent. What was the downed ship doing there? Why was its ownership being masked? Could it have been trying to get someone out of here?

Had the crash been a failed prison break?

CHAPTER SIX

The mess hall was filling up when Zammi got there, and he couldn't see "Tina" anywhere. He picked up a tray and got in line for the food. It moved quickly and soon Zammi was peering at the possibilities on offer.

Someone behind him tapped on his shoulder. "Not planning on budging, are you?"

Zammi turned. She was about Zammi's age, and was almost the same height, but her build was much more at the wiry end compared to Zammi's more muscular frame. She wore a crewcut and was dressed in a neatly pressed jumpsuit.

"Oh, uh…" Zammi had no idea what to say.

"I'm not trying to be a jerk, but you're blocking the whole line, you know?"

"Sorry," Zammi said, "I just—"

"Look, this one's meat and this one isn't." Crewcut pointed at the two basins of brown, apparently unwilling to let Zammi's awkwardness play out any further. "There's not much else to pick between them, yeah?"

"Right, thanks," Zammi stammered and took a hefty helping of not-meat then moved on to an empty spot. To his surprise, Crewcut followed and swung a thin leg over the opposite bench seat then sat.

"Anjali."

"I'm Zambrotta."

"Good to know you," Anjali said after a bite of stew. "So, I saw you talking to Turner yesterday."

"Turner?"

"After the fight."

Oh no, you didn't, Val. Tina *Turner*? Really? Clearly, no one else here had been forced to listen to ancient American music as a kid, but still. Surely, she could have come up with something else.

"Yeah, what about it?"

Anjali smiled, though it seemed more menacing than friendly now. "I don't know what she is to you and I don't want to know. But I do know that she doesn't belong here. You get me?"

Zammi felt his body warm and took a couple of deep breaths. This was just like when they'd been younger. He'd been small for his age as a kid, but by the time he was a teen Zammi had been bigger than Val, bigger than pretty much everyone else, and every once in a while, when his sister had gotten into a scrape, some other kid would think that Zammi was the one to sort it out. He'd learned to talk himself out of a fight early on.

"I'm only here to collect data about that crash," Zammi said as casually as he could manage. "I don't have anything to do with anything else around here."

Anjali nodded, though she didn't look entirely convinced. "Good. Great. You should probably keep it that way."

"You bet," Zammi said, gesturing with his fork. "Thanks for the tip." Anjali cocked her head. "About the food," Zammi added, digging into the stew. "I'm a vegetarian."

"Sure thing," Anjali said, standing and picking up her still full tray. "Good luck with the crash." She walked away and Zammi shoved a forkful of stew into his mouth. It was spicy, but he didn't taste it. What fine kettle of fish had Val gotten herself into now?

When he got back to the room there was a message from Marius. A university shuttle was stopping off in the morning to pick him up. This time tomorrow he'd be on his way back home. He picked up the book reader and tried to focus. He'd just gotten to the part where Cherry was framed for the murder of her lover when there was a loud bang at the door.

He opened it up and found Vera Baughman standing there.

"I understand you'll be leaving us tomorrow," she said, her hands clasped behind her back. "You get everything you need?"

"As far as I know," Zammi said.

"Good. We've had enough distraction from this incident." Zammi searched the woman's face for clues to whether or not she knew anything more about the crash. Was it some breakout mission gone wrong or really just another casualty of the very real dangers of space travel? She didn't give anything away, and Zammi reconciled himself to the fact that he might never know.

"Please do inform the powers that be that we've been

entirely cooperative with the investigation," she went on. "I trust you've had everything you need provided for you?" She glanced into the room, and for some reason Zammi turned his body so she couldn't see the book reader that Karl had lent him.

"Everyone has been extremely helpful," Zammi assured her. "I'll do my best to expedite the process, but it might be some time before anyone comes to clear the scene." He shrugged. "There's nothing much we can do about that."

Baughman waved a hand dismissively. "The wreckage doesn't bother me, it's not in an active work zone. It's all this administration that's so disruptive." She gave Zammi a look that made it clear that he was one of the things that fell into the category of *administration*.

Zammi bit back a retort about how he'd do his best to make sure that this site was designated a "no crash zone" from now on, and instead forced a thin smile.

"We appreciate all the help you've provided."

Baughman pursed her lips then nodded once. "Your shuttle is scheduled to arrive at 09:30. I recommend you are ready and waiting with plenty of time. No one wants you to miss your ride."

"Of course."

Vera Baughman turned abruptly and walked up the hall. Zammi closed the door and went back to the cot, picking up the tablet. He hadn't even flipped it on when there was another bang on the door.

"What can she want now?" Zammi muttered to himself and pressed the unlock button. The door flew open, and Val threw herself into the room, flinging the door closed behind her. Zammi fully expected to shortly hear a pounding on the door by whoever was chasing her, but nothing of the sort came.

Val stood there, unflustered, and looked around the room, whistling low. "Nice digs. I didn't know there even were singles in here." She sat on the cot and bounced a couple of times as if testing the springs.

"What's going on, Val?"

"Were you really going to leave without saying goodbye?"

"I got the distinct impression the last time that you didn't want me talking to you. And I'm pretty sure you've been avoiding me."

Val made a face and picked up the tablet, turning it on and skimming the text. "This is a good one," she said. "Especially the love interest." She waggled her eyebrows, looking more clownish than suggestive.

Zammi waited a beat. "What's love got to do with it?"

Val grinned widely, dimples forming in her cheeks. She smacked Zammi lightly on the arm with the back of her hand. "Ah, you got the reference! Though, to be honest, it's more like the Thunderdome around here." The grin evaporated and a furrow appeared between Val's eyebrows.

Zammi sat down next to her and looked at his sister. "What's going on here? Are you in trouble?"

"What makes you say that?"

"Oh, nothing. I only happened to get warned off by a hardcase at dinner, just for talking to you. The name Anjali mean anything to you?"

Val scowled but didn't say anything. She riffled through the pages of the book, then set it down on the blanket. "Yeah,

OK, look. Maybe things are getting a little hot around here. It's probably time for me to bail. So, it's a good thing your ride's just about here, am I right?"

"Oh, no," Zammi said, jumping up to his feet, then pacing as much as the small footprint of the room would allow. "I'm not getting caught up in your shenanigans. What is it, a failed romance? You make a move on the wrong person's partner? Again?"

"No!" Val was indignant. "I'm not looking for that kind of trouble anymore. Mostly. Anyway, no, that's not it. Far from it."

"Whatever," Zammi said. "It doesn't matter what you did to piss off whoever you pissed off. You said you didn't want a handout, so I'm not giving you one." He turned and gestured to the door.

Val didn't get up from the cot. She looked at Zammi and the usual sparkle was gone from her eyes. She looked like she wasn't even trying to come up with a funny zinger.

"Zambrotta." Her voice was low. "I need your help. If it hadn't been you, I'd still be in here asking whoever was getting on that shuttle tomorrow for a break. I have to get off this rock, and that's the only game in town. Please."

Zammi sighed. This wouldn't be the first time he'd bailed Val out of a jam. It wouldn't even be the strangest. He wondered idly what would happen to him if they got caught, and then wondered why he was even entertaining Val's request at all. Why was it that Val could get him to do just about anything, anytime?

"You know they are only expecting one person on that shuttle, right?"

Val's smile split her face. "You leave all that to me. Just follow my lead tomorrow and I'll see you at the landing dock." She picked up the book reader, then placed it back on the bed carefully. A strange look passed over her face. Zammi thought it was pride, but that didn't make any sense.

"Thanks, Zambo," Val said, getting up and going to the door. "It's worth it this time, I promise."

Before Zammi could ask what she was talking about, she'd slipped out the door and was gone.

Zammi never found out what happened to Cherry Lazereyes, but he wasn't about to abscond with the only entertainment the people here had. He left the tablet on the cot, along with the bedding bundled into a neat pile, and headed to the mess for breakfast bright and early.

There was no sign of Anjali or Val in the morning queue, but a familiar voice interrupted him as he dithered over oatmeal or toast.

"Morning, Big'un." Zammi turned to see Rufus standing rather close, his empty breakfast tray loose in his grip.

"Oh, hi, Rufus."

"How's your investigation going? Anything I can help with?"

Zammi thought back to their odd initial conversation. Now that he knew what kind of facility this really was, it was obvious. There wasn't anything he could do for him, though. He didn't even know how Val was going to sneak aboard the shuttle, and there was no chance he could get this guy on board, too. The desperation in his face broke Zammi's heart though, and he didn't know what to say.

"Hey, put up or shut up, you." A uniformed staffer smacked Rufus's tray with a gloved hand, and he visibly shrank back.

"Yeah, of course, sorry," he stammered, grabbing a couple of slices of toast, then scurrying off to a table. He furtively tried to catch Zammi's eye, but he took a ladleful of oatmeal and briskly walked in the opposite direction. It felt awful, ignoring him like that, but what could he do? This wasn't some pulp adventure story, and he wasn't a hero.

Val would probably have tried to rescue him, Zammi thought bitterly. And she'd probably get them both arrested for her trouble. Which made Zammi wonder what was going to happen when he got to the shuttle. Val was remarkably good at landing on her feet, but she'd also had her share of trouble. Zammi even had to bail her out of a private detention facility once. He had less than zero interest in winding up in one himself.

He scraped the last of the oatmeal and returned the tray to the kitchen slot, slinging his light duffel over his shoulder. There was nothing for it but to head back to the dock and deal with whatever awaited him there.

The pale sunlight illuminated the dull ground of the asteroid visible through the small shockglass window next to the door to the bridge, which he could see was already deployed, ready to be attached to an arriving ship. Zammi was the only person at the lock, and as he waited for the university shuttle, no one else appeared. Val, conspicuously, was nowhere to be seen. He watched the shuttle approach and land, ground crew in vac suits tethering the other end of the bridge to the shuttle's lock.

Zammi's heart sank as he realized what must have happened – Val had been caught. Well, there was nothing he could do about it now. A green light next to the door illuminated and a buzzer sounded. Zammi pressed the button and the door to the bridge opened. A blast of cold hit him, but he trudged forward toward the shuttle's open airlock.

A figure in a vac suit stood just on the inside of the shuttle and lifted a hand in greeting. Zammi felt a brief surge of adrenaline squirt through his body. Should he have been wearing a suit, too? How secure was this bridge? He found himself hurrying to get into the shuttle, and once inside looked around frantically for the ship's emergency suits. On a bulkhead adjacent to the airlock was a locker with the universal bubble-headed human-shaped pictograph indicating that it contained the required items. Zammi took a deep breath as he heard the shuttle's lock being cycled and the clamps disengaging the bridge. He turned toward the suited figure and gasped in realization.

The face inside the helmet grinned mischievously.

"How did you get in here?" Zammi hissed.

"I told you this was my exit strategy all along." Val's tinny voice came from the suit's speaker. "I've been planning this for a while. Come on." She undid the clasps around her neck and lifted the helmet off, tossing it toward Zammi's fumbling hands, then shimmying out of the suit. She stuffed the suit and helmet into the emergency locker then walked toward the passenger compartment.

"Come on," she repeated, not looking back. "Ship can't fly until we're belted in."

Zammi followed, speechless. There was no one else in

the small seating area, and Zammi settled into the couch across from Val after stowing his bag in the luggage locker. He secured his harness and depressed the large button on the seat arm labeled "Ready." Val was already belted in, and a cheery *bing-bong* chime sounded before a synthesized voice informed them that take-off was imminent. Zammi knew that until they were ballistic and the rockets turned off, there was going to be no conversation, and that didn't bother him at all. He had no idea what he was going to say, anyway.

Another chime sounded, then the sound of ignition filled the compartment. Zammi felt like he was mashed against the foam of the couch as the shuttle shot away from the asteroid and into space.

CHAPTER SEVEN

"It's an automated pilot," Val explained once he could hear again. "We're the only ones on board. All I had to do was add the extra mass to the manifest and Bob's your uncle." On another day the smug look on her face would have annoyed Zammi, but right now he was legitimately impressed.

"I am full of questions," he said, finally. "But for now, I'm just glad we aren't in some tiny windowless room awaiting a visit from some corporate authority."

"Pfft." Val waved a hand dismissively. "For all that that place likes to pretend that it's a prison, their 'guards' are not exactly the most loyal of staffers."

Zammi stretched as much as the couch would allow and looked at Val. He tried to remember how long it had been since they'd been face to face in the same physical space. Months, certainly. Maybe a year? With the day-to-day busy work of teaching, and the added pressure of tenure review, time had gotten away from him. What had Val been doing all that time?

She looked well, at least. A lot fitter than the last time

Zammi had seen her. She'd certainly held her own in that mess hall fistfight, and the definition in her arms was visible in the snug long-sleeve top she was wearing. It suited her. Zammi wondered exactly why she'd become so strong – hopefully it was manual labor, rather than fighting.

He didn't know how to broach the subject, and now they had three day's worth of traveling as they headed back to Mars. Ever since they were kids, Zammi and Val had been two objects flung into different trajectories, ellipticals that crossed only rarely. Val's life was her own and she'd made it abundantly clear that she was fine doing it her way. Not that Zammi had any skills that would be useful to… what? Whatever it was that Val had become.

"You've got that look," Val said, interrupting his thoughts.

"What look?"

"The one where you're trying to figure out what's going on but, for some reason known only to the depths of your own weird little subconscious, are utterly incapable of asking."

"Well, then why don't you just tell me things?" Zammi barked, angry. "I'm not the one who goes radio silent for weeks at a time. I'm not the one who doesn't answer messages. My comms work just fine, which apparently is more than I can say for you. If you actually talked to me, I wouldn't have to wonder."

Val snorted. "Oh, sure. Then I'd have to put up with Judgey McJudgerson over here? No thanks." She crossed her arms in front of her chest and stared at a bulkhead.

Why was she like this? Really, why were they *both* like this? Zammi loved his sister, but every time they got together it was as if they were trying to set the system-wide speed record for the fastest time between "hello" and "get lost."

"Val," Zammi said, forcing himself to be calm. Well, to act calm, anyway. "How much trouble are you in?"

He expected another defensive blowout, but Val didn't move. Without facing Zammi she said, "I saw the boo readers in your room. You take a look at the western?"

"No, I read the thriller…" Zammi paused, things starting to slot into place. "The information for the workers' organization meeting, I did see that file. You have something to do with that?"

Now Val looked at Zammi, achievement evident in her face. "You could say that. The whole reason I was there was to help them get organized. I was there to start a union."

"Wait, what? You weren't there working off some debt like everyone else?"

Val shook her head. "I mean, I was. There is a debt, there had to be, or I wouldn't have been targeted by their 'recruiters.'" She made air quotes with her fingers. "But it's not real. I mean, I can pay it off anytime I want. There's some complicated financial thing I don't really understand with shell accounts and some kind of doing-business-as thing I had to sign, but really, I'm doing fine."

Zammi gaped at her.

"Oh, I'm not going to be commissioning a yacht or anything anytime soon," Val explained, "but I'm solvent. It was all a set-up to get me onsite so I could help the grassroots organization that was already going on. They had the interest and there are people doing the work, they just needed some practical guidance." She jerked her two thumbs toward her chest. "And that's me!"

Zammi's mouth had fallen open of its own accord during this speech and he consciously closed it. He'd once thought there was nothing Val could do to surprise him, but he was wrong. He was full of questions, but the pleasant *bing-bong* sounded and the shuttle played the automated warning that they were about to execute a course correction, so the carrier would not be held liable for any injury sustained by a passenger not properly tethered into a couch. Both Val and Zammi had stayed strapped in, and shortly the roar of the rockets filled the small space. By the time it was quiet again, Val was asleep and Zammi's questions would have to wait.

The rest of the trip went by in an oddly solitary manner. Val was consumed with some kind of task – brushing him off by saying she had to do paperwork. Conversation was difficult and not easy to come by. When Zammi came upon Val taking another nap he wasn't sure if he should be annoyed or grateful.

Val didn't wake until the deceleration burn had begun, and soon the shuttle was arcing toward Picinae Locks, Mars's north docking station. There would be no more conversation until they landed, and Zammi wondered what was going to happen when double the number of passengers disembarked. Probably nothing – these shuttles were as automated as possible, so there likely wouldn't be anyone besides the ground crew at the dock. They wouldn't care about the manifest, either. Their only job was to keep vacuum on the outside of the places where humans were.

Once they'd landed, the rocket noise evaporated and that chime – now rather more annoying than cheerful – sounded again. Zammi unclamped his harness and grabbed his bag from the locker, keeping between Val and the airlock.

"Are you going to be around for a while?" he asked, shy all of a sudden, as if she were a stranger.

Val looked up at him. "A few days at least. You want to hang out a bit?"

"Yeah, I do." Zammi didn't move.

"Cool," Val said. "Look, I'm sorry about the messages. Between my cover story and the general lack of facilities on that asteroid, I didn't have access to comms. I wasn't ignoring you, I promise."

"Yeah," Zammi said. "So I'll hear from you soon? Maybe dinner?"

"Definitely dinner," Val said, and Zammi finally started moving out of the airlock. "Does the university pub still do those burgers? With the fried onion rings?"

Zammi's stomach clenched at the thought, but he just said, "Yeah, of course. How about tomorrow?"

"It's a date," Val said, passing Zammi on the bridge toward the interior of the spacedock. "See you there at six!" She jogged ahead without waiting for an answer.

Zammi arrived at Biblio's Bar shortly before six, but he expected to be waiting. Punctuality was never Val's strong suit. The place was quiet and he was early enough to secure a table and have a quiet drink with a bowl of nuts, pretty much the only thing the pub served that he would be willing to eat. The so-called salad was a watery lump of yellowish "lettuce" covered in chunks of cold vat meat, and that was the only thing on the menu that wasn't fried. Sometimes they served a creamy, salty soup whose principal ingredient Zammi couldn't identify. He was pretty sure that it was meant to be a dairy product, but it certainly hadn't come from any type of animal he'd ever heard of. It was oddly satisfying, though, but it wasn't on the specials board today.

When Val arrived Zammi was hunched over his beer, staring at the pattern of foam that had settled on the side of the glass. He sat up in his seat when Val entered the room, a broad smile on her face, and she wove her way through the tables towards Zammi. She was wearing a plain T-shirt with well-worn jeans and an undone button-up shirt as a jacket. She hadn't brought anything back with her from the Rocks – where had she gotten these clothes? Did she still have a bolthole near the university somewhere?

Val dropped into a chair opposite Zammi and grabbed a handful of nuts. She took a deep breath then tossed one into her mouth.

She was still chewing when she said, "Smells great in here."

The place was filled with the pungent, rich scent of fresh-cooked beef. Neither the meat nor anyone else in the bar would have ever come within several astronomical units of an actual cow, but the meat was beef, right down to the DNA. Zammi's stomach growled even though he hadn't eaten meat of any kind in years and the thought made him vaguely queasy. He tapped the tableside menu to ask for another bowl of nuts.

"Good idea," Val said and poked at the menu herself. Shortly, a human staffer approached with a large beer and the snack.

"Double beef burger, fries, side of rings?" the waiter confirmed and Val nodded. "OK." The waiter shrugged. "It's your gut."

The waiter left the nuts, sloshing the top of Val's beer onto the table as it was set down, then ambled back to the bar. While the bar didn't need to employ human staff – most restaurants used a combination of automatic servers and human chefs – students worked the front of house to make a little extra money. The service would probably improve if they let the students go, but it was part of the campus charm. At least that's what people kept saying. Zammi wasn't sure as he mopped up beer with a wadded napkin.

Val took a large swig, leaving a foam moustache which she did nothing about. "It's been a while," she said, leaning back in the chair.

"You mean me, or–" Zammi waved a hand to indicate the bar.

"I was thinking about burgers," Val admitted, "but yeah. A lot's gone down since we talked last. Tenure! It sounds like a trap to me, but I know it's what you wanted. Congrats, bro."

"Thanks," Zammi said. "Honestly, it kind of feels like it came out of nowhere. I mean, I knew I was up for consideration and there were so many meetings and forms and submissions, but still. Somehow, it was a surprise."

"You're happy, though, right?" Val asked, sincere.

Zammi thought before answering. "Yeah, I think so. It will be good to be able to direct my own research and I'm looking forward to advising students. I love the work. There is so much history out here, and we're making more every day. It's a wild time to be alive and I can't imagine going through my life without really sitting with all of that, you know?"

Val's face went blank.

"Oh crap," Zammi said, "that's not what I meant. I'm not trying to judge anything you're doing, I just meant for *me*, you know, that I want to be more intentional…" He stopped talking, knowing he was getting close to babbling. "So, what have you been doing, anyway?"

Just then the server reappeared with an enormous platter,

filled with a burger the size of Val's head next to a mound of French-fried potatoes and a heap of onion rings.

"Marry me?" Val said, whether to the waiter or the burger, no one knew. The waiter made a face then walked away without another word. "Oh, yeah," Val breathed as she picked up the burger and seemingly dislocated her jaw to get it in her mouth. She made no effort to conceal the obscene noises she made as she chewed.

"Ew. How long has it been since you ate?" Zammi asked, conspicuously looking elsewhere.

"Mmpf," Val grunted, then swallowed. "Ship rations and the food on the Rock doesn't count. It's either disgusting or primarily–" she made a face "–the kind of stuff you eat."

"Vegetables, you mean."

"Unf," Val moaned, another massive bite of burger in her mouth.

"You're a barbarian," Zammi said, but he was smiling.

Val demolished the burger in an astoundingly short time, then began methodically working on the onion rings. After she'd polished off several, she held one out to Zammi.

"Live a little. Onions are vegetables, after all."

Zammi sighed, but took the ring, biting into its crisp, golden shell. It did taste good, though he couldn't imagine eating half a dozen of them. Let alone everything else that had been on the plate.

"Where do you put it all?"

Val shrugged. "Gotta have fuel for the machine," she said, cramming several fries into her mouth at once. Zammi and Val had grown up on a potato-rich diet, the staple of Martian cuisine for years until successive lines of the tuber began to lose their nutritional enrichment, and became the stock varieties again. Regardless, Zammi was well over potatoes. Val, it seemed, still couldn't get enough. "That reminds me, after we're done here, I gotta show you something at the public dock."

"Sure," Zammi said. He finished the last of his beer, then gestured with the empty glass to Val. "You want another?"

Val nodded and Zammi entered the order. Val was down to the last fry and was licking her fingers when the waiter appeared with the beers.

"Whoa. Nice job."

Val patted her stomach. "My compliments to the chef."

"Sure thing, boss." The waiter took Val's empty plate and walked away, head shaking in disbelief.

"What's up with that?" Val asked. "Does no one eat here or something?"

Zammi opened his mouth to explain but decided it wasn't worth it. It wasn't as if Val ate like that *every* day.

Surely.

Val drained a third of her glass, then set it down in front of her. "The Citizens' Oversight Committee, eh? Your boss got you into that, right?"

"You mean the department chair?"

"Yeah. You mentioned that he was into that kind of thing once."

Zammi was surprised that she remembered. "He's not my boss, not really. But yeah, it was his suggestion. I'd seen his involvement in it through the years and I figured I'd take it on even before he brought it up. They do good work. It's a way of giving back."

Val nodded, no hint of irony in her expression. "Yeah, I

can see that." She lifted her glass and tilted it toward Zammi. "Here's to giving back. Helping people help themselves."

Zammi felt something strange in his chest, a mix of nostalgia, warmth, and a little pinch of anger. It was a phrase his parents had often said about their work, work which had taken them away when they'd been needed most. Well, when Zammi had needed them, anyway. Val always did her best to be self-sufficient, even as a kid. She wore her independence like a fancy suit.

"I suppose so," Zammi said, and lifted his own glass then drained it. The beer sloshed in his stomach, and he wished he'd eaten more than some nuts and a greasy onion ring. "I should probably go," he said, pushing the empty glass toward the middle of the table.

"Nah, you've got to come with me to the docks," Val said, finishing her own drink and standing. "It won't take long, I promise. Then you can get back to reading ancient cargo manifests or whatever it is that professors of the history of the human exopopulation do."

Zammi grinned despite himself. She'd said it sarcastically, but Val had gotten his title exactly right.

"OK," he acquiesced. "But you have to let me stop at the Beanery on the way. I need to eat a real vegetable."

Val sighed deeply, then said, "Fine, I'll allow it." As she pushed open the door to the pub she said, "They still do those fruit cobbler things? I could go for one of those."

CHAPTER EIGHT

After leaving the campus, they stopped at a food stall, Zammi choosing a burrito with microgreens, seitan, and a large dollop of The Beanery's famous sauce that they called "so much vegetable goodness." Val somehow managed to find room for an apple tart, which she devoured in three bites. They ate in silence at a nearby bench, and when Zammi was done Val said, "OK, let's go." As they made their way along the crowded streets of the residential section, Zammi sensed a tension appear in Val that hadn't been there before.

Zammi followed Val down a winding alleyway, the press of people and buildings slowly dying away until they reached the edge of the city. The hangar came into view, massive structures stretching out past the dome. Dozens of rovers were parked at ground level, with off-world ships on the rooftop landing pads, their hulls reflecting the multicolored light from the docking bays.

Val led Zammi to the airlock leading to the rover hangar, a safety protocol since the corridor on the other side was protected from the elements and had its own life support. The habitats on Mars had been built with many redundancies like this. One failure would not lead to complete collapse. The hangar side of the lock was much quieter than the city side and the silence was nearly tangible. Zammi found himself whispering when he asked Val what they were doing there.

"You'll see," Val said, her voice a tone higher than usual. Was she nervous? Why?

They walked a long way, out to the less expensive berths, and finally stopped at a toughened touchscreen panel next to a locked gate. The panel would allow access to the shared bridgeway, the charging pads this far out not having their own dedicated connection to the main hangar.

"There it is," Val said, her voice small now, as she pointed toward one of the rovers. Zammi crowded next to her at the porthole, squinting to see what she was indicating. "The Oryx."

As if he were looking at one of those images that appears to be random shapes and colors until one's perspective changes just enough for it to resolve into a clear picture, Zammi suddenly saw what Val was pointing at. It was as if the life support had failed. Zammi's lungs seemed to cease their natural bellowing, his stomach clenching into a hard stone.

It was a small, personal rover, not much more than a four-seater with a small cargo hold. The hull was a sleek black that would reflect starlight when it was out in the desert, and its engine would be powerful enough to make a cross-planum run faster than a transport. It was an older model, not the kind of thing anyone would choose nowadays, but stylish in its own way. And terribly, painfully familiar.

"That's…" He wheezed, his mouth dry. "Mom and Papi's car."

Val nodded, swallowing visibly. "I found it at a chop yard, got it dirt cheap. I've spent years fixing it up. Upgraded engine, all new armor-glass, a couple other bells and whistles. It runs like a dream now, almost as efficient as a brand new Sublight Zipper."

Zammi wrenched himself away from the window, leaning against the cold bulkhead, the only thing between himself and the void. He fought his body, forcing himself to breathe, willing his heart rate to slow.

"I don't believe this. You found an old Oryx, the exact same model of rover our dead parents had, and you thought to yourself, 'I know what I should do. I should buy it!'?"

"No," Val said, her voice shaking but her face stony. "Not the same model. It's the same car. It's Mom's actual car."

Zammi didn't know what to say, so he did what he always did when Val said something outrageous. He laughed.

"I guess it is kind of morbid," Val admitted. Zammi's maniacal laughter had faded, and they both sank down to sit on the floor of the hangar. "But I had so many memories of it, with Mom and Papi – and you and Dad," she added. "It was in really good condition, considering…"

"Considering that it's two decades old?" Zammi said, without heat. The fight had gone out of him. He was numb.

"Yeah, that." Val stared intently at the bulkhead on the other side of the corridor. "Dad sold it right after… I'd always wished we'd kept it, though."

Zammi nodded, dazed. The rover had been more than

a way to get from point A to point B. His mom had loved that car, and her job as a skills development officer for the Mining Guild had meant that she spent a lot of time going from place to place, sometimes with all or part of the family in tow. She and Papi had been a team, working with people to improve their expertise to keep up with the changing demands on Mars. Helping people help themselves. Dad's job at Helion was the stable income that kept them going, but it had always been demanding on his time. So, at various times those aft seats had been a home for Zammi and Val, a safe place, a retreat to listen to music, to watch holos, to eat meals together. To do homework and play computer games and share secrets.

"If I had a chance to be with Mom and Papi again, even for five minutes…" Val's voice trailed off. "Five minutes, Zambo. I'd trade it all for five minutes."

Zammi didn't think Val had ever said anything like this about their parents, not in all the years since the accident. Her obvious hurt shook Zammi to the core, and his throat constricted just as his sinuses felt like he'd inhaled a fistful of Martian dust. His vision blurred and he gave in, blinking once and letting the tears fall down his cheeks.

"Same," Zammi said, surprised to see that Val's eyes were wet, too. She was trying her best not to cry. Zammi recognized the stiffness in her body as Val forced herself to keep control. Zammi reached out and Val hesitated for a moment, then sank into his arms, a single tear escaping her will and making a track in the dust on her face. The two of them held each other silently, sharing in each other's warmth. Zammi cried until his eyes were puffy, Val holding him tightly.

Eventually Zammi was all cried out and pulled away. Val got up to leave, but Zammi didn't follow. Something had been mended here, but something else had been broken. Val mumbled a goodbye, then walked out of the docks, back toward the habitation dome, her shoulders hunched, and hands balled into the pockets of her jacket.

Alone, Zammi looked at the rover, its familiar shiny smooth body giving no indication of its history. Sure, it looks great, he thought, but you can't just buff out the dings and upgrade some parts and make everything OK. What happened to their parents – to their family – would never be OK.

What had Val been thinking?

Zammi walked back through the commercial district, toward the campus and back to his room. The workday was long over but it wasn't late, certainly there was no chance that he'd fall asleep. But Zammi knew he wouldn't be able to concentrate on a book or game.

He hit the wall button to configure his room, the combination dining table desk sliding into a depression in the floor and his bed dropping down from the wall. He flopped onto the mattress, its soft foam contouring to his body, and brought up a large screen. He scrolled through the entertainment options, nothing grabbing his interest, then waved his hand to switch the input, and pulled up the data from the Citizens' Oversight Committee.

Once he'd received it, Marius had submitted the information Zammi had gathered to the COC's analytics team, but it had just been a day, so there was only the automated analysis so far. It hadn't really added much to the data: there were now six confirmed individual casualties, but otherwise it was nothing he didn't already know. Zammi flipped through the information he'd already read, then something caught his eye.

The flight plan submitted to the Astronautical Safety Commission claimed that the ship had been on a scouting run with no fixed destination and Vera Baughman had been very clear that, as far as she was concerned, the ship had nothing to do with her facility. But the trajectory had been making directly for this asteroid.

Was Baughman lying, trying to cover something up? Or was the flight plan inaccurate? Did no one check whether Utopia Invest was expecting them? Zammi wondered how many ships were operating on a given day – there couldn't have been that many of them. Perhaps the *Lupa Cap* was there to pick up some off-the-books cargo – or were they actually on the asteroid for some*one*?

His hand implant vibrated, and he waved the large holoscreens away. It was late enough that the only messages that would pass his *do not disturb* filter would be coded "emergency," and his heart rate ticked up as he flicked up a small screen to see the line of text there.

"What do you want, Val?" Zammi spoke aloud. "It's the middle of the night."

"You're awake, aren't you?"

Of course. Zammi's filter was smart, his implant sensing the difference between waking and sleeping. Middle of the night plus awake meant that family got through, too, emergency or not. That exact situation had never come up before, so he'd forgotten.

"Can't this wait until morning?" Zammi asked. "I am awake, but wasn't planning to be for long."

"Sure, I just..." There was a pause. "I wanted to make sure we were OK."

Zammi sighed. She was trying. Really trying. "We're OK. But we'll be a lot more OK once I've had some sleep. Is that OK enough for you?"

"Yeah. Maybe see you tomorrow?"

"Maybe," Zammi said, then knowing that the speech-to-text synthesizer wouldn't pick up his inflection, added, "Yeah, let's. I'll ping you after I get into the office."

"Great. Sleep well."

The conversation ended and the screen closed itself. Zammi padded to the washroom and got ready for bed. He had to admit that Val being difficult was still better than Val being absent, and he fell into bed looking forward to seeing her again. It was always nice when he got to pretend that he was part of a family.

When Zammi got into the office the next day, Marius was waiting for him.

"Is there a problem?" Zammi asked, tossing his bag onto the desk.

"I mean, when isn't there?" Marius replied, an easy smile on his face. "But that's not why I'm here." He frowned, then sank into the guest chair across from Zammi's desk. "Well, I guess it is, but that makes it sound more dire..."

"Why don't you just tell me what's going on?"

"So, you've looked at the data about the crash," Marius asked and Zammi nodded. "I don't know about you, but to me there are a whole lot of questions still unanswered."

"Agreed."

"The Oversight Committee has the authority to poke into a lot of places, but we're a voluntary organization. What we are allowed to do and what we have the capacity to do don't always align. I'm swamped with these interminable budget meetings, for example."

Marius was taking his time getting to the point, but in Zammi's experience there was no way to short-circuit his meanderings. He just waited for Marius to get there, knowing he would eventually.

"Classes don't start for a few weeks," Marius said, and Zammi nodded again, trusting the process even if he didn't understand the non-sequitur. "How's your preparation going?"

"Fine. Better than fine, really. I'm building on the courses I taught last semester, so the main difference will be the individual study I'll have with my students. Until they start, there's nothing much to do."

"Good, good." Marius ran a finger along his moustache, his gaze on the viewport and its familiar landscape. "So, if you were to take a little trip out to, oh, let's say the shipwrights at the Arcadian Communities, and have a chat with anyone who knows anything about Starry Vistas and the *Lupa Capitolina*, I would agree as your supervisor that it wouldn't negatively impact your work here at all."

"I see." This was, of course, the first Zammi had thought about such a thing, but he was just as bothered by the holes in the official record as Marius seemed to be. And whatever it was that they'd been doing, those poor people onboard the *Lupa Capitolina* deserved better.

"Hey, did I hear something about the Arcadian Communities?" The voice from the hallway outside Zammi's office reached his ears easily – just as easily as his conversation with Marius had obviously been heard out there.

"Val?"

She poked her head into the doorway, and when she spotted Marius, she walked all the way in and stuck out her hand.

"Well, if it isn't Marius Munro! Nice to see you again." She leaned back to give him the once-over. "You're looking fine."

"Likewise, Valentina," Marius said, shaking her hand.

"You two know each other?" Zammi asked, only a little surprised. Val had always been one of those people who seemed to know everyone.

Val and Marius glanced at each other sidelong, and Zammi thought he saw a slight flush appear on the professor's face.

"Yeah, but how do you…" Val stared at Marius and her mouth made an O. "*You're* the boss!"

Marius scowled, but it was very obviously performative. His moustache still twitched from his smile. "I'm the chair of the History Department, yes."

Val shook her head. "What do you know, Mars really is a small place. Anyway, Zambo, don't you worry about our thing." She wiggled a finger to indicate herself and Marius. "It's been years. So what's this about the Arcadian Communities? I've been meaning to get out there. There's a dealer who specializes in parts for classic rovers and there's something just not right in the Oryx's starboard intake manifold…"

Marius's eyebrows nearly climbed up into his hair. "You have an Oryx? A functional one?"

Val grinned. "I should've known a motorhead like you would appreciate it. Yeah, I do. And the car could definitely use a shakedown cruise." She turned to look at Zammi. "Why not a little jaunt to the Arcadian Communities? So, what do you say, Zambo? Road trip?"

CHAPTER NINE

Zammi didn't know which was worse, that Marius and Val had apparently had a past together or, as he soon learned against his will, that they'd met at a classic ship show, ogling souped-up old flyers, rovers and shuttles. Regardless, he didn't want to know anything further about either, so he'd agreed to go with Val to the Arcadian Communities and shooed Marius out of his office.

Once they were alone, Val said, "I know you're kind of weird about the car, so if this is a bad idea, I get it."

Zammi was taken aback. Seconds ago, Val had been verbally shoving him into the passenger seat but now she had cold feet? Oddly, her newfound reticence made Zammi feel less uncomfortable about taking a trip on the vehicle which embodied his lost childhood.

"No, it's fine." He frowned. "Unless *you* don't want to–"

"No, I do," Val replied quickly. "I just didn't want to railroad you into anything. I kind of forgot myself for a second there."

Zammi laughed. "*Marius*, though?" He couldn't think

of him as anything other than a mentor. He'd never really considered that Professor Munro had a life outside the university, and he didn't especially want to think about it now.

"Oh yeah, Marius," Val said, all trace of shyness suddenly gone. "Have you seen him? How you haven't been hot for teacher this whole time is a mystery for the ages."

"Gross," Zammi said, "and totally inappropriate."

"Whatever, sexy is sexy," Val said, dismissively. "So, when do you want to get underway?"

Zammi thought. "I can leave any time, I guess. Do you need to do anything to get the rover ready?"

Val nodded. "It won't take long. We could take off this afternoon."

"Sounds like a plan." Zammi wasn't great at spontaneity, but he couldn't think up a legitimate reason to stall. "I guess I'd better pack."

Now that he knew to expect it, the sight of the Oryx didn't immediately make Zammi's stomach lurch. Actually, he didn't even see it as the same vehicle he'd spent so much time in as a kid – it had never been this lovingly detailed back then. It had been a tool, rather than an heirloom. Even so, Zammi still expected to see a carpet of old food boxes, school tablets, mismatched mittens, and random toys when he pulled open the aft doors. But the interior of the rover was spotless, shining, and even smelled like a showroom. It had never smelled like that before.

Zammi popped the rear hatch and threw his duffel inside. The storage compartment wasn't as devoid of personality as the rest of the vehicle, Val's own battered backpack already lying next to a bound mechanic's manual and an ancient portable hardware screen displaying a mechanic's manual.

"You ready?" Val's voice reached him from the front of the rover.

"Ready as I'll ever be."

Zammi settled into the co-pilot's chair, the rover adjusting automatically for his height and weight, the seat shifting beneath him. Val began the startup protocol – it was a more involved process than Zammi had realized. He'd never paid any attention to his mom when she'd fired it up. Zammi was surprised to learn that the rover was fitted with a full automation module, which Val powered up then verbally entered their destination. Zammi watched the external camera feed cycling through images fore, aft, and on all four quarters.

"So... does it drive itself?" Zammi asked, after a few minutes.

"Yeah, but I really only like to use it in mesh mode," Val said.

"What is mesh mode?" Zammi's stomach tightened.

Val grinned. "I told you I gave it some upgrades." She pointed to the ground with a finger. "It's got these amazing expanding wheels made of mesh and bands. It's great. You're up so high, it's almost like flying."

"So, do you even have to do anything?"

Val made a face. "Of course. I mean, there is an autodock feature, but I don't like to use it."

"Control freak," Zammi said, teasing.

"That's not the only kind," Val replied and actually winked, then pulled the harness straps down across her chest and clicked the tabs into place.

"Ready?"

Zammi tugged on his own harness, proving to both of them that he was safely strapped in. Not that any kind of seat belt would help if…

No. He wasn't going there.

Val pulled up a hard console and it illuminated with simple controls. She reached up to hit the start button when Zammi interrupted her.

"What, no countdown?"

"Not necessary. Plus, it's just the two of us, so… you know."

"Aw, come on. Give me something."

Val sighed. "Fine. *Engaging thrusters.*" She gave her voice the resonance of a pulp holo actor then tapped a large square on the console.

The rover rolled smoothly on the ground, then the massive hangar door opened automatically, and they coasted toward it. The process was nearly silent.

They cleared the area near the dome, then Val said, "You can't use mesh mode on paved roads or in a dome because it'll chew up the surface. But once we get off road, it's the ticket." She turned the nose of the vehicle off the track and the car bounced as it encountered the bare Martian surface. Val pressed a button on the console. There was a whir and then Zammi lurched as the car began to rise as the wheels expanded.

"What is happening?" Zammi asked.

"Mesh mode!" Val grinned. "Hang on to your butt."

Then he was slammed back into the faux-leather of the seat as the rover's drive engaged and they shot across the Martian desert.

•••

The acceleration didn't last long and when the cruising drive clicked in, the noise of the engine softened and Zammi heard Val laughing.

"Whoo! She's got a heck of a pickup."

"I definitely don't remember it being like that," Zammi said, his breath returning as he felt himself settle back into the seat, the three-point harness slackening.

"Upgrades, I told you."

The Martian surface flashed past them, but it felt as if they were hovering above the ground. "Could we drive right over a crater?" Zammi asked.

Val made an exaggerated thinking face, then Zammi said, "I'm kidding! Please, no, let's stay safely on flat ground."

"Aw, you're no fun," Val said, mock disappointed, but she tapped on the console lightly to engage the automation, and the ride continued, easy and smooth. "Besides, they say you want to slow down before you drive over anything larger than a meter. Though I bet it would be fine." Zammi rolled his eyes while Val unclipped her harness and deftly turned around, angled so that she could slip into the aft passenger compartment. A moment later a lumpy paper sack appeared next to Zammi's head. He grabbed it and peeked inside, holding it carefully lest its contents fall out.

"Potato doughnuts?"

"Is there any better road trip food?" Val's voice replied from the rear before she wrangled herself back to the pilot's seat.

Zammi reached into the bag and pulled out a chocolate glazed, then handed the bag to Val who extracted an enormous apple fritter.

"I can't believe you still eat like an adolescent," Zammi said.

"I can't believe you don't," Val said around a mouthful of fried dough.

Zammi bit into the fluffy, sugary torus, the taste reminding him of countless other times in this car. It was sweet – both the doughnut and the memory – and he leaned back to take in the view. They weren't traveling so fast that he couldn't make out the scenery, though they'd left the dome far behind and the landscape was mostly barren desert punctuated with blocks of greenery and small settlements. They were off the beaten path, quite literally.

As they zipped along, Zammi marveled at how much the planet had changed in the last few decades. The Martian sky was developing a blue tint to the brown, dust storms were an infrequent hazard rather than a regular nuisance. The major cities – Noctis, Deimos, and Tharsis – now had competition in the urban landscape with Cupola City growing steadily and some of the smaller habitats expanding rapidly. Mars was still a harsh environment, but progress had been made and it was clear that the planet was becoming more livable with each passing day.

The rover flew over the patch of greenery to the city's southeast and Zammi couldn't help but imagine what a terraformed Mars would look like from above. Rolling hills carpeted in green grass, streams of glistening water snaking through valleys, clusters of trees swaying in the gentle breeze, and brilliant orangey-purple sunsets. It was still a long way away, not something Zammi or even his younger students would ever see, but it was obvious what the future of Mars would be… assuming that everything went to plan.

When in the history of humanity, Zammi wondered darkly, had everything gone to plan?

The upgraded Oryx had a comfortable mesh mode driving speed of around 200 KPH, but it was still a thirteen-hour trip to the Arcadian Communities, and they wouldn't make it in one day. As darkness was beginning to fall, Val pulled into the dock at a small settlement owned by the Philares Corporation in Tithonium Chasma next to Noctis Lake, one of the two bodies of water that would one day become part of Lake Marineris. They parked, paid for a night's berthage, then walked through the airlocks into the small domed community. Zammi was surprised to see one of the prefabricated buildings designated as a traveler's inn.

"Things have changed a lot in the last decade," Val said, noticing his wide eyes as they ambled up to the door. "Remember when we were kids, half the places Mom took us to had never had visitors before. Now, I wonder if there's anywhere left on the planet that's like that." She tapped quickly at the screen at the door, ran a credit chip, and with a whir a pair of fobs dropped out of a slot in the wall. She handed one to Zammi, then passed her own over the reader. The building door opened and she walked into the dim hall. "You coming or what?"

Zammi nodded, though she'd already turned away. The hallway reminded him eerily of the miners' quarters on the asteroid, so starkly utilitarian as to be almost punitive. Val passed her fob over a door marked 118, and it opened with a pop. The room itself wasn't so bad, just a small table with two molded seats which doubled as storage, which obviously dropped into the floor to accommodate the pair of fold-down beds on opposite walls. There was even a faded print of an Earth landscape painting.

"Not bad," Val said, tossing her backpack on the table. "Not that we'll be here very long. We'll need to get an early start tomorrow."

Zammi sat on one of the seats, struggling to fit his long legs under the table. "You've seen a lot of places like this?" he asked.

Val nodded. "A few. My life is a lot like Mom's was now. The Mining Guild sends me wherever they think I'm needed, and usually it's the smaller settlements or newer work sites. I mean, it would be great to stay at the Interplanetary Cinematics resort, but something tells me that's never going to happen."

"Unless you become a media star."

Val turned her head to catch the light and struck a heroic pose. "And why not? Let's call that Plan B, shall we?" She laughed and grabbed her key fob from the table. "Last time I was here there was no restaurant or anything, but there should be a shared food prep space down the hall. They usually have some supplies on hand that you can buy. Let's go check it out."

"Sure," Zammi said, patting his pocket to make sure he had his own fob. They left the room and walked down the hall, the place either deserted or offering excellent soundproofing. At the end of the corridor was a large, windowed door with a sign reading, "Shared Kitchen – CLEAN UP YOUR OWN MESS!!"

Val pushed open the door to the small space, which was indeed clean, but also empty. She grunted but set about opening cupboards and trying drawers. Zammi wandered over to the sink, which had a rough lattice of packing tape covering the basin and a lock on the tap. A handwritten sign explained that due to rationing orders, all water had to be claimed from the community reserve stocks at the company store, and that a charge was implemented for all non-Philares employees.

"Is this normal?" Zammi asked, pointing to the sign.

Val came over, frowning. "No. I've never seen anything like this before. I guess we better find the shops after all."

The settlement was in a pop-up dome with prefab buildings, and the single dusty street made it easy to find the shop. It was near the far edge of the dome, and in the glow from the lights inside, Zammi could just see water lapping against the rocky shore of Noctis Lake on the other side of the barrier.

"Water water everywhere," he quoted, but Val either didn't get the reference or she was too busy scoping out the pair of people sitting on a bench outside the store. They looked to be a little older than she was, dressed in the comfortable soft clothes people tended to wear in their off hours when they worked in enviro-suits all day.

"Hi, there," she called out to them in a friendly tone. "Is this the shop?"

Zammi glanced at the large, extremely legible sign reading "Philares Company Store" on the side of the building, and sighed. He was sure that Val knew what she was doing, but why couldn't she just go inside, buy some water and meal packets, and leave like a normal person?

"Sure is," the woman nearest to her said without getting up. "You two new here?"

Val shook her head. "Just passing through. We stopped at the hostel but there's something about water rationing? That seems a bit…" she gestured at the lake less than a kilometer away, "strange."

"Strange is an awfully charitable way of putting it," the other guy grumbled, his eyes narrow. "Noctis." He said the name like it was a curse word.

"What about it?" Zammi asked, curiosity having gotten the better of his instinct to leave strangers alone.

"The city cut off our pipeline to the lake is what's about them," the woman said. "Said that they need all the water for the city, and since it's their lake it's their water."

"I'd spit but I ain't wasting the liquid," the guy added bitterly.

"Water is a communal resource," Zammi said, confused. "Surely they can't do that?"

The woman shrugged. "Probably not, legally, but injunctions take time and they control the pipeline. As long as there's a shortage, they're going to do what they want."

Zammi looked at the lake and imagined that he was almost able to make out the large dome of Noctis City on the far shore. Surely, they couldn't need all that water for themselves? What were the people here supposed to do?

As if reading his thoughts, the woman said, "We're trucking water in from the other lake out east. There's a daily ration for all the employees, but it's not much, and I can tell you that I don't know how much longer we're going to put up with it."

"Damn," Val said, her voice low. "I'm sorry to hear that. We'll try to take only what we need. We'll be out of your hair tomorrow."

The two workers nodded, obviously understanding that the situation wasn't their fault. "The store will charge you market rates, so it's not like you're taking anything out of our pockets. You take what you need."

"It's embarrassing," the fellow said. "This ain't the kind of hospitality we should be showing to visitors." He clucked his tongue against his teeth.

"It's no problem," Zammi assured him, "we're happy to pay our way." He only got a grunt in return, so he held up a hand in thanks then walked into the store.

CHAPTER TEN

The shelves were well stocked with clothes, entertainments, pouches of beverages, prepared meals and even some packaged ingredients for home cooking. Val made a beeline for the meals, and picked out an armload of something Zammi was horrified to contemplate. He grabbed a self-heating bean-based chili then walked over to the hastily installed water dispenser. There was a screen to enter an employee code, and credit scanner for everyone else. Cartons of flimsy three-liter containers sat next to the machine, and he picked up one of the flat-packed bottles.

"You think this will be enough?" he asked Val, unfolding the plastic then holding the container up for her to see.

She frowned, then said, "Better get two, in case it's like this everywhere."

"Surely not," Zammi said, then grabbed another bottle anyway. He swiped his credit chip, took a double take at the per-liter rate, then slotted a bottle under the spigot. "Surely not," he repeated as he started the precious water flowing. Careful not to spill, he filled one bottle, then the other, and made sure the caps were well secured, then paid for his chili at the main vending station.

"You get something for the morning, too?" Val asked and then repeated, "We should get going pretty early."

"Oh, yeah." Zammi scanned the options and selected a large tofu scramble, then paid for it. He hadn't really thought about the expense of traveling before they left and while he knew his accounts were healthy enough to handle it, he wasn't accustomed to spending so much. It felt wrong.

As they made their way out of the shop, Val nodded at the two locals who were still sitting on the bench.

Once they'd gotten out of earshot, Zammi asked, "So, when you're working, you're on the road a lot, right?"

Val nodded.

"Does the Guild pay your expenses, or what? This is really starting to add up and we've only been gone a few hours."

"They used to," Val said, "but a few years back they switched to a per diem. Lots of folks are happy to do it on the cheap – staying with family or camping in their rovers, bringing their own food – and it wasn't really fair to them when other people were eating in restaurants and staying in hostels."

"I guess," Zammi said, wondering about how fair any of it was. Not everyone had the luxury of a rover that could double as a safe place to sleep.

Val caught the furrow of his forehead. "I know it's not perfect, but nothing ever is. There's a distance and remoteness scale, and everyone knows what the compensation is going to be before they agree to the job." She shrugged awkwardly with her armload of groceries. "You've never done a job which ended up more work than you expected?"

"Well, sure..." Zammi said, his voice trailing off. His whole life had been spent with books and ideas, not shovels and maps. It didn't seem like the same thing at all, but he knew that intellectual labor was real work. Even so, he couldn't help but think of his office and separate living suite at the university, its faculty café and chandlery, even the ridiculous *Platonic Ideal*. He reminded himself how lucky he was to have everything he needed so conveniently. So many other people on Mars were more like the ancient homesteaders of Earth, making do with the little they could bring with them. It would be a long time before everyone lived as well – and as easily – as Zammi did.

They got back to the hostel and stowed some of their rations and one of the bottles of water in their room, then went back to the shared kitchen to eat. Zammi's chili was amazingly bland for something with a spice for its name, but it was filling. Val's green onion cakes and mystery meat skewers didn't seem much more impressive, but she polished them off quickly enough before unwrapping a slice of pie.

"You want a fork?" she asked, surprising Zammi. She'd never been a big sharer of dessert.

"Maybe one bite," he said, the scent of sugar and fruit undoing his resolve.

"A normal bite," Val said, a joking warning tone in her voice. "You could stick the whole piece in your mouth if you tried."

Zammi chuckled and took a modest chunk of the pie. "This normal enough?" He held up his fork.

Val paused as if inspecting it. "It's acceptable," she said, then pulled the pie toward her and leaned her arm on the table as a barrier. "You could have gotten your own pie, you know."

"You offered!" Zammi said, mock insulted.

"What could I possibly have been thinking?" she muttered, digging in. Zammi watched her eat. The obvious joy she took in what was, for him, mainly a biological imperative, was delightful and familiar. She'd always been like this, the only blip in her otherwise passionate embrace of everything life threw at her was when their parents had died.

She'd been a teen, barely more than a kid herself, and she'd stepped up immediately. Making sure Zammi got to school, had a decent lunch, had a shoulder to cry on. She'd always been so strong, and Zammi had been too young and too in need of her care to notice that she must have been hurting, too. By the time he realized what she'd given – for him, for their now tiny family – it was too late. Once Zammi was old enough, strong enough to care for himself, she'd left.

Zammi the adult, the tenured university professor, understood why she had gone. No one could keep that up, she needed to find someone or something that gave back to her. She'd obviously found that now with the Mining Guild, and it was wonderful to see. But the hurt little kid that still lived inside Zammi could never forgive her for abandoning him. It was a terrible contradiction, but he couldn't help feeling how he felt.

"Deep thoughts, eh, professor?" Val's voice broke into his reverie and Zammi's face heated as if he'd said aloud what he'd been thinking. Obviously, he hadn't, though, since Val wore a wry grin as she peered at him over the now empty plate.

"Just thinking it's been a while since we've done anything like this," Zammi said. "It's nice."

Val nodded soberly. "Yeah, there's nothing quite like company store ready meals in the tasteful ambiance of an institutional shared kitchen." She brought her fingers to her lips in an exaggerated chef's kiss. "Exquisite."

Zammi laughed. "As if fine dining has ever been on the menu for us."

"Fair enough." Val collected the detritus of her dinner and fed the various parts into the recyclers and compost mashers under the countertop. She gestured for a holo and squinted at a scrolling list of messages. "I need to check in with the Guild," she announced. "I might be an hour."

"Take the room," Zammi offered. "I want to go stretch my legs."

Val was obviously still distracted by her comms since she didn't crack a tall person joke, only nodded and made her way back up the hall to the room.

Zammi turned in the opposite direction from the store and walked up the narrow road. The scant illumination of the buildings allowed the deep purple of the sky to be visible through the translucent dome, and Zammi could even see the pinpricks of stars. The dome wasn't large, and it didn't take him long to reach its edge, where he saw that a footpath had been etched along its inside rim. They were still decades away from building an open city, and most everyone on the planet had developed the habit of going to the edge of a dome and looking at the horizon. Some people did it only once in a while, especially the people who lived in large cities, but one of the advantages of a smaller settlement was being closer to the real Mars.

Zammi didn't hurry as he followed the path that who knew how many Philares workers had forged in the dust, his head turned to the right to look out at the desert. At this side of the dome there wasn't much to see. Zammi knew that Cupola City was not far in the distance, but he couldn't make out its dome. He wondered what living on a larger planet, like Earth, would be like. No doubt he'd be able to see much further because of the bigger horizon. Everything must seem so small there.

As he walked, the patch of greenery that they'd driven over hove into view, its tenacious mosses and succulents clinging to life in the just below freezing environment. It wasn't a comfortable life on the open face of Mars, but it was life. Even humans could survive unaided on the surface now, if only for a few minutes.

He trailed a hand absently on the surface of the dome, its thin membrane the only thing that had ever allowed people to live and work on Mars. Zammi wondered how life would change when technology and engineering were no longer required to separate inside from outside, settlement from wilderness. When a person or family could choose a place to live without having to rely on the infrastructure of a corporation or community. He knew that this line of thinking was, in many ways, a fantasy. Even on Earth people needed each other, needed the security and facilities that society provided. Even in remote locations, people gathered in villages. But you could, even if only for a short time, get away. There was a freedom in knowing it was at least possible to be truly alone that Zammi, and everyone else on Mars, had never experienced.

He wondered how many people would take advantage of such liberty, once it was possible. Val would, he was sure. Would he? He didn't know.

As he circumnavigated the dome, the lake began to come into view, its surface reflecting the tiny light of Phobos as it glowed in the night sky. He didn't understand how water – something that was a necessity for life, just as much as a livable environment – could be controlled and rationed by one corporation. Surely no one could own the planet's water? He began to understand why Val was so committed to her work, why his parents had been the same way. The reason people were on the planet was to work on the terraforming project, but the reason for the terraforming project was so that planet could sustain the life of people.

Zammi soon found himself at the door to the hostel. He checked his holo and saw that he'd been gone nearly ninety minutes, so figured it would be reasonable to return to the room. When he got to the door and opened it with his fob, the lights were off, and the only thing he could hear was the soft sounds of sleeping. He quietly got ready for bed and slipped into his bunk.

When Zammi awoke, he was alone. There was no sign of Val's stuff and her bunk had been folded into the wall. Not again. Zammi's sinuses tingled, and he breathed deeply. He was not going to let her perverse need to take off get to him agai–

The door to the room opened and Val stood there, her backpack slung over a shoulder. "Rise and shine, Zammi," she shouted vigorously. "We've got a lot of ground to cover." She tossed him a pack of cleanser cloths.

"Yeah." Zammi struggled to realign his feelings with reality and swiped at his eyes. He grabbed the clothes and his bag and made for the washroom. "Won't be long."

He washed, then rummaged through his duffel for a fresh warm shirt and dressed quickly. When he left the washroom Val was holding out a steaming carton of tofu, veggies and potatoes.

"We can eat in the car," Val said.

Zammi took his breakfast, and a wave of nostalgia came over him. "Some things never change, huh?"

Val grinned, then turned to the main door. "You got all your stuff?"

Zammi nodded. He hadn't unpacked a thing.

This time, Val didn't bother with any dramatic pronouncements, just navigated out the dome's airlock then turned off the road and set a course in the console. The car lifted gently, then evenly set off, smooth as a commercial transport. Zammi tucked into his breakfast, while Val destroyed a burrito in as few bites as possible, as the Oryx chewed up kilometers of Martian desert. A while after breakfast Val asked if he was OK with her taking a nap.

"Sure," Zammi said. "The car's driving, right?"

Val nodded. "If anything happens the alarms will wake me up. Worst case scenario, here's how you'd brake." She showed Zammi the clearly marked controls on the console. Zammi had been too young for his mom to teach him to drive, and his dad had sold the Oryx shortly after she and Papi had died. Since then, he'd never had the opportunity or inclination to learn, but he'd watched his mom operate the car hundreds of times.

"Go to sleep," Zammi said. "I'll be fine."

Val had already dropped the seat down into a recline and was burrowing into her coat as if it were a blanket. A muffled noise came from within, but Zammi couldn't make it out.

Absolutely nothing happened for the next hour, though Zammi wasn't bored for even a second. The scenery was breathtaking. They were driving through a deep, undisturbed valley that would one day be part of the great Lake Marineris, but for now there were only two lakes – the now embargoed Noctis Lake on their right, and East Lake to their left.

It wasn't enough. Even a historian could see that.

And Zammi's knowledge of the history of human space settlement told him that this was exactly what happened when you left massive projects up to the whims of individual organizations. Sure, there would have been problems with trying to orchestrate a single, unified terraforming effort, but at least there would have been a plan.

A quiet, contrary voice in the back of his mind reminded him that if the terraforming project had waited for a single plan, they might well still be waiting. And what had been achieved was, indeed, remarkable. He and Val and countless others were Martian-born and bred. Humans who had never set foot on their once-home planet now lived and worked not only on Mars, but in the Rocks and on Luna, maybe even soon on colonies on Ganymede and beyond. Zammi knew that everything in life was a trade-off between competing options. Maybe it was better to do things a bit more haphazardly, but to actually do them.

That would be something for his students and his students' students to decide. History would judge them no matter what they chose. All they could do now was try to do the best they could for the most people.

That was what it seemed like Val was doing. Zammi realized that he was proud of what his big sister was accomplishing, following in their mother's footsteps. Helping people help themselves. What could be more noble?

A terrible screech sounded from the car's internal speakers and Val sat bolt upright, cursing loudly and creatively.

So much for nobility.

CHAPTER ELEVEN

"Stars-damned intake manifold…" Val grumbled as she shut off the alarm and scrolled through the Oryx's console screen.

"Are we in trouble?" Zammi asked, looking out the window and eyeing the extremely rocky and uneven ground beneath them.

"Nah," Val said, tapping quickly on the panel. "I just have to reroute the filtration to secondary… there!" The blinking warning light disappeared, and the console screen indicated that all systems were within acceptable parameters. "Phew, that was some wake-up call."

"Yeah," Zammi said, his hands still shaking. What would have happened if Val hadn't woken up? He knew he wouldn't have been able to safely control this thing, not unless they were on a smoothly paved road with no traffic. Even then…

"Hey, Val," he said once she was done with the console and was staring out the window.

"Yeah?"

"You think you can teach me to drive?"

She burst out laughing. "If anyone can, I can."

"OK, but will you? Maybe sooner rather than later? I didn't like that... not knowing what to do."

Val shrugged. "We were never in any real danger." She put up a hand as Zammi was about to say something, "But yeah, I can teach you. It's not as complicated as it looks." She peered out the front window. "I could use a pit stop anyway. You watch what I do, OK?"

"OK."

Val tapped at the console. "This icon brings up a topographical scan of the area ahead. It's a live feed, not a map, so it's accurate. See here, these green zones are safe. The red stuff, not so much. You can tell the car to stop here, like this." She tapped on one of the squiggly green lines, and a pop-up asked if she wanted to disengage mesh mode upon braking. She chose yes and the Oryx slowed, stopped, and then began descending. It felt like the wheels deflated. Soon, the engine quieted.

"That's... really simple," Zammi said.

Val nodded. "It's less simple on manual, but it still isn't rocket science." She laughed at her own joke. "Get it?' Cause it's a space car."

"Yes, I get it," Zammi said. "And you know jokes aren't funny if you have to explain them."

"Yeah, they are," Val said matter-of-factly, then grabbed a heavy coat from the back. She shrugged it on, adding warm gloves. "You need the john?"

Zammi sighed. He'd forgotten this part of traveling off the beaten path. "I'm afraid so."

Val nodded. "At least you don't have to do this in an enviro suit anymore. I'll go, then you." She popped open the door and stepped out into the Martian desert. A blast of dry cold slapped Zammi in the face, and he could feel it in his eyes and nose, then Val shut the door. Zammi had to clear the pressure from his inner ears and the chill stuck around for the few minutes it took Val to take out the portable toilet from the storage compartment and set it up a few meters away from the car. The compartment was a tiny version of the portable life support stations that had been used frequently at the beginning of the terraforming project – hermetically sealed with a small heater and air supply. This one also held a chemical toilet, which Zammi remembered with a shudder. He'd hated having to use it as a kid, but there weren't any other options. It's not like you could just go behind a rock.

Val returned in next to no time, and she clapped her cold hands together once she was back in the car. "You remember how to take it down?"

"Yeah," Zammi said. "I got it." He fastened his coat up to the neck and pulled up his hood, took a deep breath, and left the car. He knew better than to try to hold his breath, but it felt like he couldn't quite get enough air and he had to remind himself that it was fine, there was ten percent oxygen, he could be out there for several minutes. He walked briskly to the toilet tent and made sure to close the seal behind himself quickly. He waited a beat then took a breath. This felt like the air inside a dome, and it didn't even smell.

He did what he had to, carefully making sure the toilet had gone through its cycle and was in transport mode. He tapped the button to strike the tent, then exited. It collapsed into a tight package, which he secured with the attached loops, then carried back to the car. He stowed it in the rear storage compartment, trying not to think about the engineering of the thing. It was extremely clever, but also it was just plain gross.

He got back into the co-pilot's side, closed the door, and breathed deeply again.

"Better?"

"Yeah," he said, warmth creeping into his cheeks as he popped his ears.

"So, you want to drive?" Val asked, sliding the console over to Zammi's side of the car.

The terrain wasn't the easiest, but there was something to be said for learning to drive in the middle of nowhere. No traffic, nothing to hit, no one to stare as you lurched ahead or got left and right confused.

The console wasn't as complicated as Zammi had feared as he started in standard mode. Forward and reverse were easily delineated, the slider for speed was simple to use and there were a couple of options for steering. After some trial and error, Zammi learned that he preferred the analog joystick to the console's wheel or edge taps. He found the foot activated brake confusing at first, but after a few minutes he got the hang of it.

Val made sure they were still headed in the right direction whilst Zammi practiced, and after an hour suggested that he try mesh mode. "We're not going to make it before dark at this pace, and you might as well learn how."

"Uh, OK." Zammi was only barely getting comfortable with driving normally, but he knew Val was right about the timeframe. They'd hit a top speed of less than a hundred kilometers an hour and that had felt way too fast for him and he'd slowed quickly. He could see the map display and its estimated time of arrival just as well as she could.

"So all you have to do is engage the mesh mode. It's the green button near the top left."

"I just tap it?"

"Yup. You should be stopped, because the car doesn't like it if you're moving. Green means go!"

Zammi took a breath and tapped the button. The rover lifted off the ground evenly as the wheels expanded. He tentatively pushed the joystick and the car shot forward, the ride smooth and comfortable.

"Don't accelerate too fast or you'll topple the rover. Now, you can just keep driving manually if you want, same as before. The top speed is about 200 KPH, unless you engage the aftermarket override." She winked at Zammi, and he guessed that it might not be an entirely legal modification.

"No thanks," he said, "and this seems more than fast enough. But there's an autopilot, right? Might as well let the car do its thing."

Val nodded. "Even I have to admit that in mesh mode the car does a better job than I would. Just hit the auto button and it will switch over."

Zammi did and the console's background turned a pale yellow, with the word AUTOPILOT in place of the manual controls. He took a deep breath, feeling the tension that had built up in his shoulders slowly ebb. He looked over at Val.

"You admit that something can drive better than you do?" he asked, incredulously.

Val made a face. "Don't you repeat that," she said, "and it's only in mesh mode."

Zammi laughed. "Thanks, Val, this was… fun."

Val smiled, and Zammi thought he could detect a trace of wistfulness there. "It was. I kind of wish we'd done this a long time ago, you know? It's the kind of thing you should do when you're fifteen and reckless."

"Yeah, well."

There was an awkward silence, then Val broke it. "You did good, Zambo."

This time the annoying nickname felt less like a slap and more like a hug.

The car's autopilot put in a long day of work before they began to see any hints of civilization, and even then, it wasn't extensive. The Arcadian Communities weren't like most of the other settlements on Mars. They were a loosely connected group of habitations and services that were mainly independent and self-run. An alternative to the governmental or corporate communities, they weren't even co-located, but this area had the largest grouping of settlements in their network. According to Marius, the shipyard there was known to be a source of smaller, second- or third-hand shuttles that were more accessible and affordable for independent asteroid mining teams or local operations needing vacuum-rated vehicles. He hadn't actually used the term "black market" but Zammi couldn't help but get that impression.

Val peered at the console, which she'd pulled back to her side of the dash. "I don't think we're going to make the shipyard today," she said. "But there's a settlement about a hundred klicks that way where we can stop. I've been there before. It's nice." She pointed just to the left of forward and tapped the console. The car changed trajectory, and in a few minutes they were settling on the ground before turning onto a well-paved road. "You want to take us in?"

Zammi gulped. There was no one around, at least not now. Would there ever be a better time or place to practice? Probably not. He wondered how many new things he'd done in the past few days. More than he had in the past year, probably longer. Val was certainly an influence on him – for good or ill, who knew?

"Why not?" he said and pulled the console over.

He engaged the manual drive and felt the shot of adrenaline shrieking in his veins. He fought panic, and gently brought the speed down to something that felt manageable. He didn't even look at the readout, he just wanted it to feel like he'd be able to cope if something happened.

"You're doing great," Val said, just when he needed to hear it. The road ahead was gently curved, but he picked up the steering mechanism quickly. It almost felt like the car was still driving itself, and he glanced at the console to make sure.

Nope, it was him. He was driving on Mars.

The dome of the settlement came into view, and Zammi slowed further. As they approached the outer airlock, Zammi turned to Val. "Should you...?"

She shook her head. "You got this."

"OK." They rolled to a stop before the door opened, and Zammi nudged the car forward until they were in the lock. The outer door closed behind them, and in a moment the door in front of them opened. Zammi let the car roll ahead at a crawl, looking around for an indication of where to go. The road curved to the left, and he followed it, and soon saw a haphazard collection of other rovers and transports parked near the edge of the dome. There was no dedicated double airlocked vehicle hangar in a dome this small. He carefully pulled into an empty area past the last vehicle and stopped the car.

"Nice job!" Val said, pulling the console back to power down the vehicle. She stepped out and looked around at the abundant space between the Oryx and any other vehicle. "No one's going to ding us here."

She popped the rear compartment and grabbed her backpack and Zammi's duffel. He was still sitting in the passenger seat, his eyes wide. She dropped the bag next to the car and said, "Hey! You love it so much you want to sleep in the car?"

Zammi shook his head and opened the door, stepping out. His knees were shaking but he felt fantastic. "No, I'm good. Sorry. Thanks." He picked up his bag while Val laughed.

"Let's go find a couple of beds."

It was getting late and Zammi would have expected the community to be pretty quiet, most people having settled in for the night before the workday tomorrow. But on their way to the town's hostel, they saw a knot of people gathered around one of the buildings in what looked like an infrastructure section of the town, and Zammi could hear nervous chatter.

"I don't like the look of this," Val murmured as they approached. They stopped at the periphery of the group, quietly listening to the worried conversation.

"... I'm telling you, this is the third one this week. Once these seals crack, that's it, the whole system stops working. We can't compensate for it, the only thing we can do is reduce usage."

"What you're talking about is rationing," an angry voice from the crowd called out.

"Yes, some kind of usage allowance is probably the only way to cope," the first person said, obviously struggling to keep calm. "Even if we can source new seals somewhere on Mars, which I don't know that we can, it won't be tonight. Or tomorrow, or even the next day. We aren't the only ones with this problem and there just aren't enough parts to go around. We can't make water out of nothing."

"Well, not without working reclamators," someone called out.

There were a few chuckles at the attempt at levity, but the mood of the group was tense. Zammi glanced at Val, but she didn't look like she was worried about things turning ugly. She had her problem-solving face on, not her defend-the-little-brother face. Of course, Zammi hadn't been little in a long, long time, but that had never stopped Val coming to his aid. Luckily for him.

"Come on." Val elbowed Zammi and led him away from the group. "Looks like it's a good thing we got that extra water back at Philares."

"Is this happening everywhere?" Zammi asked.

Val shrugged. "I guess so. I mean, there's only so much water on the planet, right? Mining asteroids was fine when there were only a few thousand people on Mars, but now a whole cargo hold full of ice represents one city's usage for a few days.

The entire solar system's ice mining operation doesn't even come close to meeting demand. But I can't remember the last time anyone started a major aquifer project. It seems like all the corporations have been choosing to focus on habitation and oxygen production. That's the downside to there being no central authority, I guess."

Zammi was expertly conversant on the various economic theories underlying the governance of exopopulation settlements – whether small, like the orbital habitats, or as expansive as Mars. He hadn't realized Val was equally knowledgeable – and clearly more so when it came to the details about ice mining.

She opted not to continue the conversation, though, and walked ahead to a building that looked remarkably like the place they'd stayed the night previous. It was obviously a standard prefab design. Zammi wondered why he'd never seen one before. Of course, Tharsis City, where Mars University was based, was one of the oldest settlements on Mars, and there were few prefabricated buildings left. The ones that were had been upgraded, renovated, and redesigned so often that the original base would have been lost to history. And these were likely newer models that had never been installed at Tharsis. They certainly hadn't been around when he and Val had been traveling with their parents.

Val handed Zammi a fob and swiped her way into the hostel. Its layout was identical to the one in the Philares encampment, and their room was a mirror of the one they'd shared the previous night. Val dropped her pack on the central table and sunk into the near seat.

"Have you ever been to any of the Arcadian Communities

before?" she asked Zammi, who shook his head. He was starting to realize that since his parents' crash, he'd hardly been anywhere.

"They're kind of like tiny versions of Tharsis," she explained. "Independent, non-corporate. Folks here will be doing anything from small contract mining jobs, to making clothes, to custom rover conversion." A corner of her lips twitched upward. "There are a lot of artists and makers out here, but there are still engineers and scientists and builders. There's everyone out here you'd find in a Teractor or PhoboLog settlement, except maybe the corporate management folks. But they don't always have the right ratio of say, mechanics to cooks. There's no central office making sure the staffing fits the needs, so things can be a little hardscrabble."

"Yeah, I can see that." Zammi jerked his head toward the door, indicating the hubbub they'd encountered on their way in.

Val stood. "But the upside is that there's almost certainly a better option for dinner than ready meals from the company store. Come on, let's go see what's out there."

CHAPTER TWELVE

Out there was a haphazard collection of prefabs, home-built structures, and well-engineered bespoke buildings. It hadn't been random, exactly – more like organic – and while the settlement was small, it was large enough to be confusing to a newcomer. Val had a map on her holo and followed a trail through the winding footpaths as Zammi kept up. After a few minutes, he was thoroughly lost, though he knew he could use his own holo to get back if he had to.

He smelled their destination before he saw it: *Krayne's Bar and Grill.* The scent of fat and flame hit his nose, and while the thought of grilled meat didn't appeal, his stomach rumbled anyway, and he was certain they'd have something else on the menu. Right?

Val banged open the door and there was the low sound of a moderately occupied restaurant within. The place was large enough to host maybe fifty people, but about three-quarters of the tables were vacant. Val led the way to a spot in the middle of the room. "You're going to love it here," she said, a wicked grin growing on her face.

Zammi groaned. Was it going to be another meal of nuts and fries?

He pulled up the tabletop menu and did a double take. The place specialized in exactly what he'd assumed – burgers, chops, rotisserie, sausages – all done on a grill which they claimed emulated the taste of open flame cooking. But everything on offer was made entirely from plants. Not a cultured flesh or slaughtered animal to be found.

"You've got to be kidding," he said and looked at Val.

She spread her hands out. "I've missed a few birthdays. Seemed like I ought to make it up to you."

"Are… are *you* going to be all right here?" he asked.

Val laughed. "I know it may be hard to believe, but my tastes have expanded somewhat since we were kids. Honestly, the all-dressed hot dog is out of this world." She tapped in an order.

"Well, all right." Zammi struggled with the options, but eventually chose a plate of three different varieties of sausage, with grilled eggplant and peppers on the side.

"Get the potato fritters," Val said and Zammi made a face. "No really, trust me. Get them." Zammi shrugged and added them to his order, then sent it to the kitchen.

As they waited for the food, they glanced at the other patrons. A few were joking and laughing like you'd expect in a bar, but there was an overall sense of anxiety in the room. A sign taped up over an empty trolley explained that free water was no longer available, and Zammi noticed that everyone was drinking from their own containers.

"How long do you think this water problem has been going on here?" he asked.

"From the way people were talking, I'd say it's been more than a few days," Val said.

"How did they let things get this bad?" Zammi mused, but the thought was cut off by the arrival of their food. Everything smelled amazing – salty, oily, savory and slightly charred. Zammi cut into one of the sausages and took a bite. It was spicy and a little bit sweet, and he wasn't sure he'd ever eaten anything like it.

Val took a huge bite of her hot dog, the sausage completely invisible under the layer of grilled peppers and onions and sauce. She chewed, her eyes closed, then said, "Almost better than the real thing."

Zammi made an exaggerated surprised face, then went back to his own plate. They'd missed lunch and he was famished. Val had been right about the potato fritters. They were crispy on the outside, fluffy and creamy inside, with flecks of herbs generously dotting the whole thing. "If all potatoes tasted this good, maybe I could live off them after all," he said, then lifted another generous forkful to his mouth.

They were about halfway through their meals when the door opened and Zammi recognized some of the people they'd seen before enter the bar. They looked like the weight of Phobos hung from their shoulders as they dropped into chairs at a nearby table. None of them spoke as they entered their orders into the menu, then sat blankly staring at one another with the look of desperately tired people.

Eventually, an older woman with an air of authority said to no one in particular, "If only we had an old compressor or rover around. Then at least we could try..." Her voice broke off and she slumped back into her chair.

Val looked over at Zammi, her expression one he recognized. She had an idea and was not going to be shy in expressing it.

Oh no, what was she going to get them mixed up in now?

"Are you sure you can manage without it?"

The woman's name was Millicent, and she was the town's engineer. For the past several weeks she and her team had been working non-stop to try and keep their water reclamators online. The devices had been in full-time use since the town incorporated, but they had never been designed to last this long. The machines processed waste water as well as extracting humidity from the air in the dome, and they relied on a high-pressure system which functioned only with well-working seals.

Even Zammi knew that seals were consumable parts, and the town had been going through them faster than they could replace them. The material they were made from was difficult to source on Mars, you couldn't just print them from the resins and plastics that fabricators used. Millicent's connections on Mars were all out of stock – after all, they weren't the only settlement which was still relying on reclamators. But there was one option: older Martian vehicles had used the same material in their shock dampeners. Later technology had replaced the large, rubbery flaps with micro-controlled hydraulics, but the dampeners were still installed in some classic vehicles. Like the Oryx.

"It will make for a rougher ride than we're accustomed to,

but we can still operate safely," Val assured her. "And you need the seals a lot more than we need a smooth drive."

"I don't know how to thank you," Millicent said, the relief palpable in her voice.

Val's eyes glanced at the menu. "How about a beer?"

"We still have some of that," Millicent said with a grin. "The nearest mechanic shop is in the next settlement down the road. It might be a day or two…"

Val shook her head. "I can do it myself. You'll have your seals tomorrow."

"Are you sure?"

"Absolutely. I've had that car apart more times that I can count. I might need to borrow some tools, though."

"Anything," Millicent said, as a dozen pouches of beer arrived at the table. She passed them around, then held her own up in a toast. "Finally, we've got something worth celebrating."

An hour later, Val and Zammi made their way back to the hostel. "So, exactly how rough is rough?" Zammi asked as they walked.

"Depends on the terrain," Val said. "Honestly, anything other than mesh mode will be pretty uncomfortable."

Zammi made a face. He knew that Val was right to offer up the part, but he didn't look forward to *pretty uncomfortable.*

"But, we're using mesh mode almost all the time," Val reminded him. "The expanded wheels will create their own suspension."

"Oh, yeah," Zammi said, feeling foolish. "Of course."

"Still…" Val said, unlocking the door to the hostel, "where we're going, we do still need *some* roads."

Zammi groaned.

The next morning Val met with Millicent and several members of her team at the Oryx. Zammi watched as they set about dismantling the car. He'd never really seen Val in action like this before – taking charge, working with people, putting them at ease while getting things done. He'd always thought of her as wild, maybe even a bit irresponsible. His image of her had frozen in her teenage years when she'd been rebellious and independent… and angry. That young woman was still there, but there was so much more now. He couldn't help but admire the person she had become.

There was nothing Zammi could do but get in the way, so once they'd gotten stuck into the job, he decided to take the opportunity to catch up on his normal life. He found a small shop selling baked goods and sundries, and picked up a small fruit and oat loaf and some loose tea. He went back to the hostel, set up the table and brought up his portable holo.

He checked his messages – some updates on new students, a recently released paper from an Earth-based historian whose work he followed, a couple of increasingly curt queries from Fern. Fern! He'd completely forgotten to let her know that he wasn't going to be in the office for a while.

He checked the time, then called her holo knowing that she was likely to be on campus. She answered and her frowning face filled the space hovering over the table. In the small room, it was like she was glowering right at him.

"I'm so sorry," he started, then briefly explained that he was on an impromptu road trip with his sister on Marius's and the Committee's behalf. Fern quietly listened as Zammi spoke, her face softening as he went on. When he finally stopped for breath, she shook her head.

"If it were anyone else, I'd say that was the worst story I'd ever heard. But it's you, so it must be true. Did you say that your sister is currently taking your rover apart to give people water?"

"Not exactly, but kind of."

Fern shook her head. "I'd always thought those stories you told me about your sister were exaggerated."

Zammi grimaced. "If anything, it was the other way around."

Fern chuckled. "Well, it looks like she's a good influence. I'm glad to see you getting out of your comfort zone. I do wish you'd thought to mention it to me, though. I can't remember the last time two consecutive workdays have gone by without seeing you in your office. I've actually been worried."

She kept her voice light, but Zammi knew that she'd been truly concerned. Disappearing without a word was out of character to say the least.

"So, what have I missed?" he asked.

"Nothing great." Fern frowned. "We've had to close the baths. The steamers are still open, but we can't justify the pools when the city is contemplating water rationing. Luckily, it will only be a temporary measure, thanks to Factorum."

"What's Factorum doing?" Zammi hadn't been keeping up on the news since he'd been away – another factor of Val's dubious influence – and he hadn't realized that the water situation had become dire enough to affect somewhere as well-developed as Tharsis.

"They're bringing down a large ice asteroid, tomorrow, I

think. Up in the northeast, should create a good size lake. The corporation is branching out from its industrial roots, it seems." She shook her head. "And not before time, too. It sounds like things are getting desperate all over. There's water up in the far norther reaches, but it's too expensive and difficult to bring down here. Everything is hard and difficult for us."

"That's definitely how it seems out here. Living in Tharsis City it's easy to forget how tenuous living can be in the remote parts of the planet. Even now."

"I'd have thought that's something you of all people would remember." Her voice was kind, not chiding.

"It's different to know a thing intellectually than it is to see it – to experience it – first hand," Zammi admitted.

"That's certainly true. Hey, maybe you should institute some kind of field work for the History Department."

Zammi laughed. "As far as I know, time travel continues to be the stuff of science fiction. Most historians don't think of the current era as a legitimate source of study."

Fern grunted. "Well, I don't know about that, but it sure seems like this trip is doing you some good."

Zammi nodded. "I just hope we can accomplish something worthwhile out here. I mean, Val's doing that right now, but me… I kind of feel like I'm only along for the ride, at the moment."

"Oh, I'm sure Marius will take care of that," Fern said. "He's not going to let you come home empty-handed."

"Probably not. Speaking of which, I should probably check in with him, too."

"Aw, you called me first?" Fern said, "I'm touched."

"Well, Marius at least knows where I am," Zammi said, sheepishly. "I am sorry."

"It's fine. Just don't do it again."

"I'll try. See you in a few days."

"You bet. And, Zammi, you make the most of this, OK? It's not like this opportunity comes around every day."

"Yeah, I could probably stand to get out of the city more," Zammi said.

Fern waited a beat. "That's not what I mean, and you know it."

She ended the call, and Zammi was left to think about her words.

"Are you still going to be able to make it to the shipyard?"

Zammi thought the apprehension in Marius's voice was equally distributed between concern for his own safety and anxiety over his ability to complete the assignment.

"I think so." Surely Val wouldn't have stranded them here.

Marius nodded. "Well, Val would certainly know what the Oryx can handle. Check in again when you have an update. If the rover is out of commission, we might be able to requisition a shared transport. The Committee is not entirely without resources." Marius waved cheerily and ended the call.

Zammi headed back out to see how Val and the team were getting on. The car was nearly unrecognizable with its panels all removed and hydraulic lifts holding the main mass of the vehicle off the treads. A large, rubbery sheet was being carefully removed from the chassis by four people from Millicent's crew, then once it was free of the car, they quickly bundled it away.

"What's going to happen now?" he asked Val, who was taking a break with a pastry.

She wiped her mouth with the back of her sleeve, then said, "They'll use a cutter to fabricate seals that fit their reclamators. If they're careful, they ought to get a dozen or more out of that piece, enough to share with some of their other communities who are having the same problem. It will buy them all a little time, at least." She shook her head. "It's a drop in the bucket though." She chuckled at her own reference. "Literally, I guess."

"Yeah," Zammi said, unable to stop staring at the car – in pieces. "Uh, I hate to be so self-serving, but… What about us? The car?"

Val shrugged. "I'll put it back together and we'll be fine. I hadn't been planning on upgrading the shock system to the micro-controllers this soon, but it was on the list. Maybe the dealer I was planning to see has some of those in stock, too. This all might work out just fine."

Zammi nodded, unable to take his eyes off the unrecognizable rover. He'd never really liked thinking about the fundamentally fragile nature of technology, and how utterly dependent upon it everyone on Mars was. The domes, the rad-suits, even the way they communicated and paid for goods. All of them were nothing but pieces of material put together in clever ways, all of which could fail at any time. Technology had propelled humanity to the stars, but it was a life on the edge.

Of course, Zammi knew well enough that this had always been true. Even on Earth, human existence was mediated by technology – the cities where people lived, the mechanisms which allowed the many billions to be fed and clothed and educated. All of it, throughout all of history, had been precarious.

How could life be so tenuous yet also so tenacious?

CHAPTER THIRTEEN

"Are you freaking out about engineering, again?" Val asked.

Zammi waited for the smirk to appear on her face, but there was nothing but a look of concern. He contemplated waving it off, keeping his thoughts to himself, but decided that the two of them had done enough of that.

"Yeah. I don't like thinking about how fragile everything is, but…" He gestured at the pile of parts that had once been a nearly magical vehicle. Which would, hopefully, become that vehicle again.

"Mom and Papi. The crash," Val said. "I get it, you were so young. It's hard any time to learn that all the things you take for granted, everything that seems so solid and safe, are really only held together with duct tape and string. But when you're a kid and you need that stability, well, it must have been terrifying."

Val had never acknowledged any of this to Zammi before, and it was like a punch to the chest. He sucked down a breath and felt something open, tension leaking out of him like he was doing a deep muscle stretch.

"Yeah, it was," he said eventually.

Val just looked at him, letting the moment expand. Then she handed him the rest of her pastry and dusted off her hands. "I better get started on this." She jerked her head toward the disassembled car.

"I'd offer to help, but..." Zammi raised his hands in a "you know" gesture. Val cocked her head, then grinned.

"You don't need to know anything to help," she said. "Let's put those muscles of yours to some use."

They spent the afternoon working on the car. Val tightened bolts and directed Zammi, who mostly carried heavy things around and held parts in place. By the time they took a break for more food and a drink of precious water, Zammi's shirt was stuck to his back with sweat. It felt good, better even than a run on the treadmill or a session with the resistance weights. There wasn't much banter between the siblings as they worked, Val needing her concentration to get things done correctly and in the right order, and most of the time Zammi was working too hard to talk. The time went by in companionable silence and Zammi found that he felt better watching the reassembly process happen. It took a little of the mystery away, which for him was a good thing.

When Val was finally done and wiping the dust off the hull, Zammi leaned against one of the dome's bulkheads and marveled at what they'd accomplished. Val had done all the real work, of course, but they'd done it together.

"You want to take it for a shakedown?" Val asked.

"Me?"

"Sure. You can drive, now."

Zammi chuckled. Why not? He slipped into the driver's

seat, and Val hopped in at his right. Zammi wasn't sure if he was imagining it, but the seat felt harder. He ran through the start up, then slowly backed up.

They were hardly moving, but it was rough. Zammi thought he could feel every pebble the wheels rolled over directly in the muscles of his butt. He made a face.

"Yeah, I wouldn't want to have to go too far like this," Val agreed as they turned on to the ring road which circumnavigated the interior of the dome. "Most roads out there aren't anywhere near as smooth as this."

"Yeesh," Zammi said as a jolt went through the car when they drove over something. "You sure this isn't dangerous?"

"Nah, the rover can handle much worse. The shocks are only there for the fragile cargo." Val pointed to Zammi then to herself.

In a few minutes they found themselves back at the entrance to the dome, and the other parked vehicles. Zammi carefully pulled the rover into an empty space and shut it down.

"Boy, am I ever glad there's another way to drive this thing," he said, getting out and stretching. He needed a wash, then he needed dinner. They walked back to the hostel, got cleaned up and changed, throwing their grimy and sweaty clothes into the onsite laundry. They'd be sanitized and freshened by the time they got back from *Krayne's*.

The walk to the pub felt like it was seven times longer than it had been the previous night. Every muscle in Zammi's body was sore, and he wished he were back on campus so he could make a trip to the baths. Except the pools were closed. Which reminded him of the rest of his conversation with Fern.

"Oh, hey, did you hear the news about Factorum?" he said to Val as they approached the bar.

"What news?" she asked, but then a cheer from within *Krayne's* sounded, drowning out any answer Zammi could give.

They walked into the pub and saw that a huge holoscreen was showing the aftermath of a massive impact on what looked like a remote part of the Martian desert. An Interplanetary Cinematics News announcer's voice could barely be heard over the whoops and cheers of the patrons in the packed bar.

"… asteroid, creating what Factorum spokespeople say will become the largest lake ever on Mars." The visuals cut to a well-dressed older Black gentleman wearing a spotless white lab coat and standing before the bright orange logo outside Factorum headquarters.

"We are pleased to announce that this project should increase the total water on Mars by over thirty percent within a year and we should begin to see useable meltwater as soon as next week. Water rationing will become a thing of the past." He smiled widely, his remarkable good looks and ease in front of the camera drone made Zammi think that he was a public relations officer wearing a scientist's costume. It was tacky, he thought, but how the news was delivered didn't really matter all that much. If their projections were even close to the mark, this was going to make a huge difference in the lives of so many Martians. Maybe it was fair enough that the Factorum PR team made the most of it.

Certainly, any Factorum staffer who walked in the door of *Krayne's* would receive a warm welcome. The mood in the place had done a complete reversal since they'd been here last night. Val led the way to a table with several members of the team which had helped her take apart the Oryx. Jugs of beer were passed around, alongside carafes of the first fresh water from the newly repaired reclamators.

"I'm sorry about the timing," Millicent said to Val, handing her a foamy beer.

"Don't be," Val said, raising her glass in a toast. "I'm no hydro engineer, but I don't think a huge block of ice is going to melt overnight and, anyway, you needed those reclamators working today. I'm just happy I could help."

"Well, we are very grateful," Millicent said. "This should keep us going for a few more years. I do think it's time to have a conversation about priorities. The Communities' Council has talked about building an aquifer a few times, but it's always been voted down in favor of expanding our settlements. Maybe now is the time."

"I don't know," one of the technicians next to her said. "The crisis has passed, right? It's hard to get people to commit to a project that doesn't directly affect them in the moment. New domes, better habitations – we can see the results of those right away. But green spaces and aquifers are long-term resources that are shared among everyone, not just Arcadians. It's a lot harder to convince people to invest in those."

Zammi nodded. "That has always been true," he said. "Thankfully, there has always been a visionary or two who was willing to take the long view. I mean, let's be honest. We wouldn't be here if those first explorers from Earth hadn't thought about a future beyond their own lifetimes."

"You honestly think Earthers are more forward-thinking than Martians?" The voice came from the table one over and was thick with both frustration and inebriation. "Let me guess, you're fresh off the transport yourself, buddy?"

"Hey now," Millicent said, reaching a hand out to stop an altercation before it started.

"It's all right," Zammi said, and stood slowly. Martian-born people were taller and thinner than people who grew up in the higher gravity of Earth, but Zammi was quite tall, even for a Martian. He also worked hard on bulking out his naturally willowy figure. He towered over the seated patrons, his hands on his hips making his body especially imposing.

"I'm afraid you're wrong on all counts," he said gently. "As you can see, I'm Martian born and bred. Third generation, in fact. And, no, I don't think altruism is something that's confined to any particular group of people, thankfully. History is as full of people helping each other as it is of folks being self-serving. Of course, we all need to think of what we and our communities require for the immediate future, but we also have to consider the legacy we're leaving our descendants. This is the great tension humanity has contended with for our entire existence. The history of the human exopopulation is just another example of how this plays out. For instance, take the second lunar colony–"

Val groaned dramatically, cutting off Zammi's lecture and relieving some of the tension. "Cool it, professor. No one's enrolled in any of your classes, and you don't want to be giving that golden education away for free."

"Well, actually, there's no charge–" Zammi said, then stopped when he heard the laughter from the group around him. "Oh. Right." He sat down again, and Val draped an arm over his shoulder.

"Good job," she said to him quietly, as convivial conversation resumed around them. "If that had been me there probably would have been a mess." She glanced at the heavily laden tables. "And we can't afford to waste any of this." She lifted a glass to her lips and drained it. "Come on, let's get something to eat then head back to the room. I'm about ready to pass out."

Zammi nodded and they found an empty table in a corner and ordered rather a lot from the grill. As they ate, Zammi said, "I hadn't realized how much anti-Earth sentiment there still is out here."

Val nodded. "You probably don't see it as much in the city. But out in the remote areas, these days the only time anyone ever really sees people from Earth is some kind of UNMI inspection team, or an influx of greenhorns." She made a face. "And no one really likes either of those."

"I can't imagine there are many workers imported from Earth in the Arcadian Communities."

"Obviously not, but you know how it is with stereotypes. The incompetent Earther has been a joke on Mars for longer than we've been alive. It's not going to die out that fast."

Zammi frowned, but there wasn't anything to say. It may be wrong, but he knew that was how a lot of people thought about new immigrants on Mars. Now that more Martian citizens were planet-born than newly arrived, "Mars for Martians" was a popular view.

Once the food was gone, Zammi could feel his body crying out for rest. Val waved goodbye to the engineering team, which was deep into a well-earned night of revelry, then they both headed back to the hostel and their own well-earned deep and undisturbed sleep.

The next morning Zammi woke slowly, at first unsure of where he was, then he heard the soft sounds of Val's snoring coming from the bed across the room. He sat up and the aches in his back reminded him of the work they'd done the day before. He'd been worried about missing the gym while he was away. He chuckled at the thought now. He couldn't remember the last time he'd worked this hard.

He slipped out of the room and padded to the washroom, where he took his time with the cleansing wipes and shampoo powder. He pulled out his last clean shirt and dressed, then got his clothes from the previous day from the laundry cabinet and packed up his bag. The shipyard wasn't far but he wanted to be ready to go when Val got up. If he was going to get back to the university in time for the faculty meeting, they needed to finish what they were doing and get started on the return trip.

He went outside to wait for Val, walking over to the car and stowing his duffel. The dome was eerily quiet compared to the previous day, but Zammi chalked it up to the morning after the revelries the night before. The people here deserved a break after everything they'd been through. He was gazing out of the dome at the patch of greenery outside when he heard a noise. Was that someone crying?

He knew it was none of his business, but he couldn't help himself – the sounds of someone in distress compelled him to follow the muffled noises. He walked toward the nearby habitation building and turned the corner, where he saw a familiar form hunched over on a bench. It was Millicent, and she was obviously trying to keep the noise down, but she was sobbing.

He approached, making sure to scuff his feet in the gravel so as not to startle her. She lifted her head and stared at him, her eyes puffy. She wiped her face with the back of her hand and Zammi cocked his head.

"You OK?" he asked, the question sounding ridiculous but he didn't know what else to say.

"You haven't heard?" she said, then took a breath to steady her voice.

"Heard what?"

"That Factorum lake, all the water…" Her voice cracked and she cleared her throat, visibly working to regain her composure. "It's contaminated. Full of lead. All that water is poisoned. It's worse than useless."

CHAPTER FOURTEEN

They gathered in the meeting room of the water treatment building: Val, Zammi, Millicent and several members of her crew. A holoscreen glimmered above the table and all eyes in the room stared at the ICN announcer, whose delivery and expression appeared dour.

"... efforts to remove the affected material would not be worthwhile, as the remote drone analysis has shown significant contamination likely to be present throughout the entirety of the ice. Further analysis to confirm this is currently happening, with results pending. Treatment of the meltwater is a possibility, however a purification plant will need to be constructed onsite, and sources tell us that the necessary components may need to be brought in from Earth or Luna. A representative of Factorum has confirmed to Interplanetary Cinematics News that their analysis of the asteroid indicated no significant lead levels and that foul play has not been ruled out."

"Foul play?" One of the technicians who had helped Val the previous day scoffed. "What do they think, that bandits stole out to the asteroid in the dead of night and injected it with lead?"

"That's ridiculous," his colleague agreed. "I mean, it's not even possible. Either the whole thing was riddled with lead before it got here, or at least some of that ice would be salvageable."

"You think Factorum is just trying to shift the blame?" Val asked. "It wouldn't be the first time someone cried wolf to distract from their own mistake."

"That would be cold," Zammi said, "if they knew they'd messed up and still claimed that it was some rival's fault."

Val shrugged. "They wouldn't necessarily have to blame another corporation. It could be Martian separatists or rogue rock jocks or the classic disgruntled ex-employee."

"Surely none of those..."

"Oh, I don't think anyone like that did it," Val said, "just that they're convenient potential scapegoats."

"You don't have a very high opinion of Factorum," Millicent said.

"Not just Factorum," Val said, breezily, then added as if it explained her position, "I'm a union organizer."

"Well, none of this speculation is going to ease the water crisis," Zammi said.

"No, it isn't," Millicent agreed, then sighed and stood. "So I guess we'd all better get back to work."

Zammi was studying the map holo, trying to find a route to the shipyard which would involve the least amount of ground driving, when Val's communicator buzzed with an incessant notification that even Zammi couldn't ignore.

"Hang on," she said, getting up to find a quiet corner. "It's work."

Zammi found himself watching his sister as she spoke quietly and earnestly with a small holoimage that he couldn't see. She was so serious and professional sometimes, it was at odds with the way he remembered her – and how she still often made her way through life even now. She reminded him a little of Beryl Fernandez – fully committed to her work, but just as committed to enjoying life. Fern's balanced personality had been one of the things that drew him to her as a friend. Zammi's memory of his parents had been all about the responsibility they felt toward their work, but Val – the teenage Val of Zammi's young life, anyway – was the opposite. Fern was the first person Zammi had met who seemed to have achieved an equilibrium. A serious commitment to an academic vocation, combined with a zest for joy and adventure. Although now that he thought about it, apparently Marius Munro had more going on than Zammi realized. A passion for old rovers, at a minimum. Maybe that had been the case for his parents, too, and he had simply never had the chance to grow old enough to appreciate it.

How long had Zammi spent trying to emulate a singular focus that might not have even been real?

His ruminations were interrupted when Val returned to the table, her face screwed up in thought. "We've got a situation," she said, tapping at the tabletop menu for another cup of coffee.

"Oh?"

"That was my contact back at Guild headquarters, Sato. There's nothing official, but someone at Factorum has asked the Guild for help."

"What kind of help?"

Val pitched her voice low. "They really think it was sabotage."

"You don't buy that, do you?"

"Not tampering with the asteroid itself, obviously. But the data they used to make the decision. Factorum is the biggest industrial conglomerate on Mars, they'll have access to more engineers and data scientists to call on than anyone, so you know they'll have checked their records in triplicate. Apparently, their people are absolutely certain that it showed that the ice was clean, and they think someone fudged the numbers."

"Whoa." Zammi leaned back in his chair. That would be a way to ruin things for Factorum. But it was bad for everyone, not just a single corporation. Who would do something like that?

A server stopped by with a large mug for Val, who smiled gratefully and accepted it with both hands. She took a long drink, then set the cup down.

"I'm not sure exactly how this came down to me, but it's not official Guild business. Sato asked me to sniff around, I guess because I mentioned I was helping you ..." She trailed off and a smile spread across her face. "The Oversight Committee! This is exactly their kind of thing, right? We should call Marius."

Zammi blinked slowly. He knew they'd been going off the script for the past few days, but it wasn't taking anything away from their goal. It was one thing to help some people out along the way, but it was an entirely other thing to pick up a whole new mission – or whatever you wanted to call what they were doing. He was just supposed to be asking a few questions then he could get back to his real work, his real life. This was getting out of hand.

So completely out of hand that Val was talking to Marius right now, the small holo glowing just past her coffee cup.

"It's lovely to see your face, too," she said, her voice low and husky, and Zammi felt like he wanted to melt into the floor in mortification, but then Val went on, "but I'm afraid this isn't a social call." She paused, listening, and Zammi couldn't hear the other side of the conversation.

"No, no, Zambrotta's fine. He's here with me – look, why don't I put you on speaker." Val made a finger gesture in the air and the holo expanded to sit in the middle of the table between them. Zammi could see Marius's concerned expression fade to benign confusion when he saw Zammi.

"Everything all right?" he asked.

"Honestly, I don't even know," Zammi said, sighing.

"Oh, it's fine," Val said, then frowned. "We'll, *we're* fine, I can't say about everything else." She gave him a brief rundown of the situation they'd encountered in the two settlements they visited, and finished with Sato's request that she look into how Factorum's asteroid data might have been altered.

"Hmm…" Marius absently drew two fingers along the crisp waxed end of his moustache. "This water situation is dire," he admitted. "If someone is out there playing silly buggers and affecting new water production, that's going to cause a lot of trouble for a lot of people, who have nothing to do with whatever argument they've got with Factorum. And while those folks who died on that asteroid deserve answers, nothing we learn will bring them back." He continued to fiddle with his moustache, a sure sign that he was working through a tough problem. Zammi knew better than to interrupt the process.

"All right," he said finally. "I may or may not be able to get this Factorum business on the official roster of COC review, but regardless I think the two of you ought to pursue it."

"But the faculty meeting is only in a few days. If we run around chasing after this rumor who knows when I'll get back?" Zammi said, knowing he sounded like a petulant child, but he was past caring.

"There will be more faculty meetings in your career than you can imagine," Marius said, kindly. "You can miss this one. I'll make sure you catch up."

"But…" Zammi stammered, "what about the crash?"

"I can talk to the people at the shipyard," Marius said. "I'll work the investigation from here. We won't forget about them, I promise."

"Wait a minute." Zammi glared at his mentor, who glanced at Val, but she was looking steadfastly elsewhere. "If you could just have talked directly to the shipyard all along, then what are we doing all the way out here? This whole trip has been for nothing!"

"Uh, sorry, you're breaking up a bit there," Marius said, obviously faking a connection problem. "I'm going to go, but keep me apprised of how the investigation is going; I know the two of you will get to the bottom of it!" And then he cut the connection.

"What was that?" Zammi scowled at Val.

"Don't look at me," she said, hands in the air in a defensive gesture. "But it looks like we've got a new plan."

"No, we don't," Zammi said, still angry at being railroaded into some unsanctioned investigation into something that maybe didn't even happen. "We have nothing that remotely resembles a plan."

Val shrugged. "Then I guess what we have to do is make one."

For Zammi's whole life, all he'd ever wanted was to be an academic. As a kid, he read voraciously about schools and universities in books, both in fiction and in children's Earth history texts, then when he was twelve, he'd visited Mars University on a school trip and come as close to falling in love as he'd ever done since. Spending one's days in the pursuit of knowledge and understanding, living in an environment where sharing ideas and philosophies was not only allowed but encouraged – it seemed like an ideal life, and so unlike his current situation. Before the crash, his parents had been loving and attentive, but he'd only been a small child. And after, Val wasn't exactly interested in debating theories of the mind. Zammi never knew whether their dad would have shared his academic interests; he was so rarely home and when he was, he was so distant that he might as well have not have been there at all.

But to their credit his small family had done what they could to help him achieve his dreams. His father ensured he never had to worry about credits, and Val helped with his university application. He'd moved into the dorms as soon as his acceptance was final, and he'd never left. He sometimes worried that the reality would be unable to compare to his idealized vision of academic life, but it turned out that there was so much more to scholarly life than his young self had realized. The truth was that he'd never felt like anywhere was as much his home as that campus was.

And now, in his moment of finally achieving the singular thing he'd wanted his entire life, where was he? Not meeting his former mentors as peers for the first time, not preparing his lecture notes or outlining a new paper. No. He was in a barely functioning vehicle that was rattling his bones nearly out of his skin as it slowly drove out the airlock and into the Martian desert. And it was beginning to smell somewhat unpleasantly of Val's teenaged bedroom.

"What's eating you?" Val shouted over the sound of the Oryx's shaking.

Zammi turned away from the window and gave her an "isn't it obvious" glare, then resolutely looked away to stare at the receding Arcadian Communities dome. Val didn't push it, either because she recognized his need to sit with his sullen attitude for a moment, or perhaps because it was just too loud. She carefully maneuvered down the road, away from local traffic, then turned off the road, stopped, and engaged the car's mesh wheels.

A long, deep breath escaped from Zammi's lungs as he incongruously felt himself get lighter as the car rose above the expanded wheels. It was the tension leaking out of his shoulders now that they were properly underway – and it was finally quiet enough to hear himself think.

"You think going straight to Factorum is a bad idea?" Val asked after a moment.

Zammi bit back a sharp retort, then sighed. "No, it's not a bad idea. I just don't understand why I'm here. What do they need a historian for? At least when I was helping you put the Oryx back together, I could carry stuff. What does Marius even think I'm going to do?"

Val didn't answer right away, as if actually thinking through how best to approach it. "I guess it's the same for you as it is for me. Sato says, go check out Factorum. Sato's my boss, so that's what I'm going to do. I don't have to like it or want to do it, I just have to get it done."

"I don't get the impression that this was an actual work order," Zammi said, a little more harshly than he'd intended. "I kind of think you actually don't have to get it done at all."

Val raised an eyebrow. "Right. Like saying no to your boss, even when you technically could, is a great way to advance your career. Even you know that's not how it works. I mean, that's why you're here. Marius said 'go,' so you're going." She shrugged expansively. "Like Dad used to say, 'It's not rocket science.'"

Zammi had always hated when his dad had said that, especially since he actually was a fusion engineer. As if his work was so much more complicated and important than what everyone else did.

"Marius isn't my boss," Zammi said.

Val waited a beat. "Yeah, he kind of is, though."

"Since when are you such a loyal and obedient worker, anyway?" Zammi was reverting to the way they used to bicker just before Val left home, and he hated the petulant way he sounded. Somehow, though, he couldn't keep the words from coming out.

Val wasn't rising to the bait, however. "Since always. I mean, I've done a bunch of different things in my life and, sure, I spent some time bumming around and doing my own thing, but I've always been a good worker. Even the worst jobs – and I mean the absolute worst jobs, like mucking out a malfunctioning waste reclamation tank kind of worst job – I've always done it right, on time, according to protocol." She didn't sound like she was boasting, it was just a fact. When Zammi thought about it, he'd never known her to do anything halfway.

"Work hard, play hard," he offered with a weak smile.

"That's right!" Val tapped at the console and the small passenger compartment was bombarded with the strains of guitars and drums, the music nearly loud enough that it might have been heard over the rattle when they'd been on the ground. She waved her fists in the air to the beat as if holding invisible drumsticks and Zammi couldn't help himself.

He laughed. And then he sang along.

CHAPTER FIFTEEN

It wasn't as far to Deimos City as it would have been to go back to Tharsis, but it was still a long day of driving. They ate filled rolls and sweets they'd gotten at *Krayne's*, and they'd refilled those flimsy containers with newly filtered water, but they still had to stop a few times for comfort breaks, taking turns setting up the portable toilet. Zammi had somehow ceased being revolted by its presence, and he wondered exactly what that said about him.

Neither Val nor Zammi had ever seen Factorum headquarters but they expected it to be in one of the shining glass and chrome buildings in Deimos that had been modeled after the architecture of the last of Earth's megacities. Zammi preferred the connected squat buildings of the university campus, and Val confessed that she would happily live somewhere small and self-contained like the Arcadian Communities settlement if she had the choice.

"I'm always traveling, though," she explained. "So it always made sense to just use the room the Guild provides for me at

Tharsis. It's more like a storage locker than an apartment, at least how I use it."

Zammi nodded. His own rooms on campus were modest, but they were enough for his needs, especially with his private office and access to all the amenities the faculty were entitled to use. "No big family homes for either of us, then," he said, chuckling.

Val shrugged. "I wouldn't say never, but certainly not anytime soon."

"Oh?" Zammi's eyebrows crawled up his forehead. "Is the pitter-patter of tiny feet in your future?"

"Sure, why not?" Val said, then her composure broke. "OK, maybe puppy feet."

"They're called paws, I think."

"Har har, funny guy."

Pets were a new addition on Mars, and so far only a few people had imported domestic animals from Earth. Zammi thought it was a wasteful luxury to bring animals all this way, although now that there were a few different species already on Mars, homegrown cats and dogs might become more common.

"It's going to be too late to go to Factorum when we arrive," Zammi said, after a few minutes of companionable silence. "Do you have a line on a place to stay?"

"The Guild has an office and residence hall in Deimos," Val said. "They'll find us rooms."

"Did you say 'rooms' *plural*?" Zammi asked.

"It's wishful thinking, but I hope so," Val said brightly. "It's been fun hanging out with you, bro, but this is too much togetherness."

They both laughed, the moment almost easy. If only it could always be like this between them.

When they arrived at Deimos they had to disengage the mesh mode, and they chose the first free berth on the inside of the airlock – not just to save the credits.

"I don't care how far we have got to walk, I'm not riding one meter farther in that deathtrap."

"So dramatic. It's perfectly safe," Val said, shouldering her backpack and locking up the rover. "But you're not wrong about walking being better." They set off on the long trek to the exit of the vehicle hangar, then up the road toward a transportation hub to find their way to the Guild's residence. "I'm going to see about getting those micro-controllers installed while we're here. I can't imagine there's anything Deimos doesn't have."

"You think we'll be here long enough for that?" Zammi asked, as Val consulted the holo at the transport hub to figure out their route.

"Who knows?" she said. "The actual job won't take that long in a fully equipped workbay. I could probably do it myself in a day."

An auto-train arrived silently on its magnetic rails and the siblings boarded. The carriage was dimly lit but it was still easy to make out the occasional shade of graffiti long since removed. The train was clearly well maintained and obviously heavily used by the city's population. It was quite late, but even now they were not the only passengers headed toward the center of the city. The Guild's residence wasn't in the high rent core of Deimos City, but a few stops down the line they could transfer to the ring route which would drop them less than a kilometer from the door. Ground transport was available night and day, but after sitting so long in the Oryx, the walk sounded appealing to Zammi.

Their next train was equally efficient and when they alit at Outerbridge Station sensors detected their motion and soft lighting illuminated the many paths away from the hub.

"This way," Val said, pointing toward a walkway lined with greenery. It appeared to be flowers, but their buds were closed for the night.

"Decorative plants," Zammi commented. "I hadn't noticed at the time, but there weren't any of those at Arcadian Communities – or the Philares site."

"Yeah, that's pretty much a city thing," Val said. "Mars is still a frontier and the necessities are all you're going to get most places." She made a face, obviously considering the last few days. "If that."

It was a sobering thought and it made Zammi look at the city differently. He'd spent almost his whole life in Tharsis City, and it had become more and more comfortable over the years. Judging from these few blocks, Deimos was no different – if not even more luxurious. Buildings and homes of different, unique designs, public artwork, those frivolous flowers. There wasn't a prefabricated habitation unit to be seen. He understood why progress came to the cities first, and why remote areas had to start with the basics. But it seemed so unfair. Just because he had been lucky enough to be born in Tharsis City, why did he get access to fresh food or a bathhouse or the theater when some other kid who was born in a remote Arcadian Communities habitat got none of those things? Surely by now humanity had figured out a better way to distribute civilization?

"Here it is." Val's voice startled Zammi out of his thoughts and he took in the Guild's residence. It was the tallest building on the block, though it was on the more utilitarian end of the spectrum. Val swiped her microchip over the scanner by the door and it clicked open. Inside was a cozy atrium, with a pair of overstuffed armchairs next to a probably printed potted "plant." She pulled up a holo and made a few finger gestures, then Zammi's own communicator buzzed. He flicked up his own screen and saw an approved residence application from an official Guild account.

"We're preapproved for a week, but they'll extend it if we need it."

"A week?" Zammi's voice echoed loudly in the empty space and he flinched. He deliberately lowered his tone, then said, "We're not going to be here for a whole week?"

"Who knows?" Val said. "Besides, a week's the minimum." She peered over his shoulder at the screen. "Looks like we're on the same floor. Come on, I'm about ready to pass out."

They rode up the lift to the seventh floor, and Zammi was surprised to see that the decor of the atrium continued here. There was plush, rosy-colored carpeting and generic but attractive abstract art dotting the walls between the doors.

"This is me," Val said, as they stopped in front of the door marked 732.

"Have a good night," Zammi said as Val swiped her way into the room. "And don't leave without me tomorrow, OK?"

"I won't," Val said, stifling a yawn. "Don't you get me up too early."

Zammi nodded and found his way to his own room. The door opened to his implanted chip, and he shouldered his way in. The space was quite a bit smaller than his quarters back at the university, but it was clean, comfortable, and there was a private toilet. Also, there was a bed. That was the only thing he really cared about, and within ten minutes of arriving he was fast asleep.

Zammi's disorientation upon waking didn't last long the next morning and when he folded the bed up he found he had enough room to do some stretches. He had almost finished his usual routine when his communicator buzzed. It was Val, ready to get going.

He met her in the residence's atrium and found her dressed in corporate clothing. It wasn't the full suit and tie routine that the head of a department would wear, but the button-up collared shirt and pressed trousers would fit in at most offices. Zammi hadn't known she'd even owned clothes like that. She eyed his pullover and jeans and shook her head.

"If there was ever a time for the tweed jacket and corduroy pants, this is it, professor."

Zammi rolled his eyes. "No one dresses like that outside historical holos."

"Whatever," Val said. "But you'd better have something more suitable than that."

Zammi shrugged and went back upstairs to change. He'd thought twice about bringing one of his tailored tunics that was the current collegiate fashion for faculty, but at the last minute he'd rolled one up and stuffed it at the bottom of his duffel. Just in case. He shook it out now, the smooth fabric showing no signs of wrinkles or wear.

When he joined Val again, she nodded once approvingly, then set off toward Outerbridge Station. If it hadn't been for Zammi's long stride, he'd have had to scurry to keep up. When they'd seated themselves on the train, Val said, "They're expecting us at Factorum HQ. We're representatives of the Oversight Committee, by the way."

Zammi groaned. "I mean, that's technically true, in my case at least. But I don't have the training or the authority to be meeting with... wait, who are we meeting with?"

"I'm not sure," Val admitted. "This could go a few different ways."

"Oh?"

"If it's the media team, they're just going to want to find a good spin on the situation. If it's the actual scientists who made the decision to bring down the asteroid, they'll want to cover their butts. If it's the board, well..." She trailed off. "Let's hope it's not the board."

Zammi grimaced. He had no experience with any corporation's Board of Directors, but he was terrified enough of the university's board. He couldn't imagine Factorum's being less intimidating.

"Don't sweat it," Val said, cheerily. "You'd be surprised how many times I've done something like this."

"If it's greater than zero, you're right."

Val laughed, but conspicuously neither confirmed nor denied that she had any experience in this regard whatsoever.

They rode all the way into the center of Deimos City, its glittering towers and bustling streets overwhelming even to a city boy like Zammi. He had to stop himself from walking down the street with his eyes aimed up high to look toward the top of the buildings like a tourist. Val behaved like it was all in a day's work, so he tried to follow her lead, both figuratively and literally. The walkways were crowded with more people than Zammi had ever seen in one place, and it would be easy to lose his sister in the crush. He forced himself to pay attention to the ground beneath his feet. There would be plenty of time for sightseeing later. Probably.

Val led them to a silver building with orange accents, the Factorum name in its distinctive bubble letters over the wide double doors. They went inside and approached a desk with a human concierge standing behind it.

"How may I direct you?"

"Val Kaspar and Zambrotta Kaspar, with the Min– er, the Citizens' Oversight Committee. We have an appointment." Val did a pretty good impression of a corporate functionary, Zammi thought.

"Very good." The receptionist consulted a holo, nodded, then handed them badges on lanyards. "Please take the lifts up to the level eight meeting room."

"Thanks," Zammi said, grabbing the badges and following Val to the lifts. The badges were obviously more than printed plastic with their names on them, as they glowed briefly when they entered a lift carriage and the light for level eight illuminated without either of them doing anything.

"No unauthorized snooping around, I bet," Val said, waving her badge under Zammi's nose, and he just shrugged.

Level eight was one large meeting center, with a couple of smaller breakout rooms, an automated canteen offering both food and drink, and some comfortable chairs arranged conversation-style in the foyer. Zammi and Val shared a glance and then a nervous-looking woman in her late forties or early fifties strode toward them, her hand extended. Val took it and shook, Zammi followed suit, then she gestured toward one of the smaller rooms. She still had not said a word.

The room held two other people, both looking miserable, and like they'd been missing sleep for some time. Probably the ice asteroid team, then. The woman who'd collected them gestured to two empty chairs, where Val and Zammi sat.

"Thank you for coming," another, younger woman at the head of the table said. Her dark eyes were rimmed in red, but she was otherwise well put together in a tunic much more finely tailored than Zammi's. "I'm Krissy Huang, the team lead for the ice asteroid project."

Introduction panels hovered over the table in front of each team member, so Zammi knew to say, "You're welcome, Dr Huang. We hope we can help."

"At this point, we'll take all the help we can get," the older man next to Huang said. His holopanel read Mr Gabriel Kraev, chemical engineer. His tone made it sound like he didn't think much of Val and Zammi, but that in a crisis every extra hand is a blessing.

"It wasn't our fault," the woman who'd escorted them to the meeting blurted. Her panel read Ms Rose-Marie Jeuneaux, data analyst.

"Now, Rose-Marie," Dr Huang said gently. "I'm sure no one here is interested in assigning blame."

Val looked at Zammi, her face clearly indicating that she wasn't so sure.

"We're here to try to help find out what happened," Zammi said, diplomatically. This all reminded him a little of trying to coax an interesting analysis out of a reluctant student. That, at least, was something he knew how to do.

"The Committee is independent and impartial, beholden to no one, not even the UNMI," Val added, doing a remarkable job of parroting the COC's talking points, and the tension in the room eased slightly.

"Can you tell us what you know so far?" Zammi prodded.

Dr Huang nodded. She explained that the data they had received from the remote probe that had been sent to the asteroid clearly showed that there was no lead contamination in the ice. She provided copies of the analysis, and while Zammi couldn't make head nor tail of the numbers and symbols, Rose-Marie Jeuneaux nodded emphatically when Huang mentioned the point.

"There's definitely no indication of lead in these numbers," she repeated, jabbing a quivering finger through the holo spreadsheet. "The only way any of this makes any sense at all is if someone manipulated these figures."

Val leaned toward the holo, as if there was some answer to be found in the shimmering light and shadow that was rendering the data. "By *manipulated*, you mean…"

"We were sabotaged," Gabriel Kraev said, simply.

CHAPTER SIXTEEN

"Sabotage?" Zammi tried to keep the incredulity out of his voice.

"What else could it be?" asked Rose-Marie, her voice rising to a near squeak. "These data are all good, but the reality was… not good. Not good at all."

"You'll have to forgive us," Dr Huang said. "We've been working doubles trying to find the best way to decontaminate the lake. It won't undo what has happened here, of course, and the board…" She looked up briefly, as if she could see through the ceiling to the boardroom above. "They won't be happy no matter what we do now. But there's going to be quite a bit of water in that lake, and we will not let it go to waste."

"How long do you think that's going to take?" Val asked.

"Years," Kraev said, sounding grim. "Decades, probably."

"Oh." Val's professional demeanor cracked a little, as she realized that the immediate crisis was not going to be alleviated one bit by anything that Factorum could do right now.

"But it's still our number one urgent priority," Rose-Marie said bitterly, "because we have to be seen to be doing something in the wake of this… mess."

"Do you have any thoughts on who might be behind the sabotage?" Val asked, and Zammi looked at her, an eyebrow cocked. She couldn't really believe this story, could she? Zammi understood why the Factorum team would tell themselves whatever they needed to in order to get through the days, but surely sabotage was just ridiculous. The various corporations and organizations involved in the terraforming project had rivalries, of course, but no one would endanger everyone's lives to just get one over on the competition. That would be psychopathic.

Kraev made a sour face, while Rose-Marie said, "It could be anyone, couldn't it?"

Dr Huang added, "There's no obvious candidate. Our plans were well known, so anyone could have seen this as a potential attack vector."

Attack vector? Really? Zammi tried to keep a straight face but obviously failed.

"You have something to add?" Kraev asked tartly.

"I…" Zammi considered how to best phrase what he was thinking. "I've often found my colleagues in the sciences to have an advantage over those of us in the humanities. When I'm working on a paper, I'm dealing not just with facts, but with human motivations and complications. I'm often trying to maximize the complexity of a situation in order to make an interesting analysis. But in science, often you can use Occam's Razor. You know, look for the simplest solution and assume that's the case. Perhaps we should apply that here."

There was silence in the room. Only Val looked vaguely confused.

"You think we made an error," Dr Huang said simply.

Zammi shrugged. He knew this was a delicate matter, but it was the most likely explanation. He'd be remiss in his duties if he didn't at least try to get them to entertain the possibility.

"Do you really think we didn't make that assumption ourselves?" Rose-Marie said, her voice rising in both pitch and heat. "Obviously that's what we thought had happened. No one wants to think that a mistake like that could occur, but of course we checked the figures. It wasn't. Our. *Fault*!"

Zammi held up his hands, palms out, in a universal gesture of peacemaking. "You have to understand, I had to bring up the possibility."

Kraev shook his head. "What is the point of this exercise?" He gestured to Val and Zammi. "They've already made up their minds."

"No, *we* haven't." Val glanced significantly at Zammi. "I'll do some digging, and see if there's anything we can find about one of the other corporations. This kind of thing isn't going to leave no trace."

"Thank you," Dr Huang said, turning to face Val directly. "I'll make sure you have full access to all our materials." She glanced at Zammi, her face giving nothing away, but he knew he'd made no friends here today. "Thank you for your help," she said to Val.

"What in the galaxy was that?" Val hissed when they were alone in the lift.

"What do you mean?"

"You basically accused them of covering up a mistake."

"Now, come on." Zammi noticed the angry look on Val's face and took a step back. "I didn't say anything about a cover-up. I didn't even come right out and say that I thought they messed up. I just… you know."

"Implied it. Heavily."

Zammi shrugged, again. "Well, it is most likely what happened."

The lift doors opened, and they stepped out into the plush environs of the Factorum building's main foyer. Val looked at Zammi like he was an innocent, ignorant child. He knew the look well.

"You have no idea what the real world is like. You think everyone is the same as the nice professors and students at your university, but it's nothing like that out here." She rotated her index finger in the air. "This nice, clean office? It's a battlefield. It's war between these corporations, cutthroat competition. And even you know who loses in a war. Every historian knows. It's us. The people. So yeah, I don't think it's only possible that it really was sabotage. I think it's extremely likely that some corporation saw an opportunity to take down a rival and made the most of it. And why shouldn't they? It's what the other guy would do. Don't you get it? It's just a game to them."

"That's not true," Zammi said, but Val gave him a withering look.

"You can think whatever you want," she said. "Go ahead and look through that data and see if you can find an error. I'm not going to stop you. But what I am going to do is find out who really did this." She turned and stalked out the door.

Zammi stood in the foyer, the bustle of suited workers going past him so familiar from campus life and so utterly foreign to what the past few days had been like. He knew he was not sheltered, exactly, but at least he was living in a particular milieu at the university that not everyone shared. He had understood that long before this little road trip with Val. He wasn't naïve. But he refused to believe that anyone would be willing to put an entire planet's population – no, its entire *future* at risk just for some financial or reputational advantage.

Val simply had to be wrong.

As Zammi walked out of the building, he reflected that it wasn't as if Val was infallible. She made plenty of mistakes of her own. After all, she'd stomped off as if Zammi wasn't going to see her again, but they were practically next-door neighbors.

He sighed. It was going to be an awkward couple of days.

Zammi brought up a holomap of Deimos City and found a long but scenic walking route back to the Mining Guild's residences, and set off on foot down Central Avenue, toward the Plaza and then back into the suburbs of the city. He vaguely remembered that when it had first been built, the city's interior buildings had predominantly been brick-red, fashioned mainly from the natural resources of the planet. The ensuing century had seen an evolution in technology and materials science, not to mention creative people with good old-fashioned paint, and now there was hardly a clay-colored façade to be seen. Zammi imagined that the streets he walked down wouldn't look entirely foreign to a traveler from a city anywhere on Earth now. Those decadent decorative plants scattered about hadn't hurt, either.

He powered up the street, legs pistoning rhythmically. He'd always found that exercise helped him think, and he needed that analytical brain now. Val would do whatever she wanted, that had always been true. And for whatever reason, Marius wanted Zammi here with her. It didn't make any sense – he was a history professor, not some kind of private investigator. He was reminded of that thriller he'd read, but Zambrotta Kaspar was no Cherry Lazereyes. Still, he had volunteered for the Oversight Committee, and this was exactly what they did.

He turned a corner and his eye caught on a familiar-looking coat he'd definitely seen a few blocks previously – it was bright orange, hard to miss, and he had a momentary thought that the person was following him. He shook the notion away as Orange Coat turned into a small park and gave someone waiting a cheery wave. That book had really done a number on him. Deimos must just not be quite as large and anonymous as it seemed. He found himself glancing in the reflection of shop windows for a few blocks anyway.

After a while, the rhythmic pace of walking set his mind wandering. As it sometimes did, it ran to a place that he didn't really like, but he let himself sit with the dark thoughts. Finding out what happened to the Factorum data wouldn't clean the lead out of the new lake. It wouldn't provide clean water to the Arcadian Communities or the Philares worksite or anywhere else on Mars that was suffering. It wouldn't do a single practical thing that would make a difference. It was just curiosity, a desire to know what had happened. Like History. What was the real point of any of it?

As he got further away from the center of Deimos, there

were fewer other people out on the streets and the oppressive feelings began to lift. He found himself wondering about the crash that he was meant to be investigating. Real people's lives had been affected there, affected in the most significant way possible. Whatever it was that had gone wrong, whether it was an operator's error, a mechanical failure, or just being in the wrong place at the wrong time, it had been the most important thing to happen to the crew of that ship. But it was probably something small, something "minor" in the grand scheme of things.

Zammi knew from his studies that small decisions, minor events, created the catalysts for major moments in history. The history of worlds, of people, of planets. And of families. Tiny things, like a micrometeor, not much bigger than a pebble. That's what had killed his parents and changed everything. For him, for Val, for their dad. And subsequently, for everyone any of them had interacted with.

Small things mattered. Everything mattered. Everyone mattered.

It wasn't only curiosity. Knowing how things went wrong could teach you what not to do in the future. Knowing how things went right gave you a recipe to follow again. It wasn't about assigning blame or abdicating responsibility. The truth mattered. It had to.

By the time he arrived at the Guild's residence, he had a plan. But first, he needed to clean up and change clothes. That had been a long walk.

Neighbors or not, Zammi didn't see Val for the rest of the day, but that was fine. She wasn't the woman he needed.

"Fern!" He grinned at Beryl Fernandez's face in the holo, obviously still in her office. "How are things back on campus?"

"Oh, you know," she said. "Prepping for the all-faculty meeting in a few days." She squinted. "You're… not in Tharsis, are you?"

Zammi shook his head. "Marius has me on another side quest." Fern raised an eyebrow. "He's given me official permission to miss the meeting."

"Damn it!" Fern shouted. "Why do you get all the breaks?"

Zammi laughed. "Maybe you should join the Oversight Committee."

His friend made a face. "One committee at a time."

"Fair enough. Although, I could give you little taste of what it's like."

"Why do I get the impression that you're just about to ask for a favor?"

"I couldn't possibly guess," Zammi said with as much feigned innocence as he could muster.

"All right, out with it already."

Zammi explained the Factorum situation and quickly described the meeting he and Val had had with the team. He carefully elided the argument in the elevator afterward and didn't mention that Val had somewhat abandoned him. It wasn't exactly pertinent to the issue, and he didn't want to see the look on Fern's face.

"And so I was hoping you'd be able to give me a line on someone in your department who could look at these numbers. Someone who has a good background in… I don't know… ice asteroid science?" He gave her a hopeful grin.

Fern shook her head. "Ice asteroid science? Really?"

He made a "what do I know" gesture and said, "You know what I mean. Do you know anyone who might fit the bill?"

"Well, let me think. There's Hiro, but he's a mechanical engineer. And Leigh's got some time, but no – Leigh's a robotics engineer. Who could there be, who could there be…?" She actually drummed her fingers on the tabletop. Zammi had a sinking feeling and racked his brain for her speciality. All his life he'd been practically allergic to the physical sciences, his brain refusing to hold on to specifics. Was it – oh no.

"*You're* a chemical engineer," he said.

"With a special interest in geological extraplanetary H2O. So, you know, an ice asteroid scientist."

Zammi groaned. "I'm sorry I didn't remember. I don't suppose…"

"Just send me the files, you jackass."

"Thank you!" Zammi sent her an encrypted message with all the data that Factorum had provided. "I owe you one – no, I owe you several."

"And I'll make sure to collect, too," she said with a grin. Then her face grew more serious. "This is going to take some time. It won't be anything obvious or they would have caught it already, so I'm going to need to do a manual analysis myself. It's not going to be today."

"Absolutely," Zammi said, "take whatever time you need."

"Talk to you soon. Oh, and Zammi?"

"Yeah?"

"I hope you're having a great time with your sister."

Zammi gulped. "We've had some pretty good moments," he said. It was the truth, if not the whole truth. "Now, I better let you go. Thanks again!" He ended the call and let out a breath. If there was anything to be found in the files, he trusted Fern to get to the bottom of it but he knew she wasn't exaggerating about the time it might take. What was he going to do in Deimos until she got back to him?

That's when it hit him – Val had cut him loose. He didn't need to stay here. He could go back home, go back to his life. He might even make the faculty meeting. He pulled up his holo to look up the schedules for the Martian Rail passenger lines. Before he could switch screens, his eyes caught on a series of news bulletins, from all corners of populated Mars, but all with one common theme: water. Specifically, the lack of it.

Tensions were heating up between Noctis City and several nearby smaller settlements, as the city was continuing its embargo on the water from Noctis Lake. Emergency shipments of barrels of water were underway to several outposts in the north, and the much celebrated EcoLine Forest Project had been forced to go on indefinite hiatus. As a historian it was an occupational hazard to fantasize about what might have been, and Zammi was adept at not getting sucked down that path. But he couldn't help but wonder what all the ramifications of that contaminated ice were going to be in the end. It was like throwing a stone into a lake and watching where the ripples went.

In this case, it was a stone made of poisonous lead, and it had been embedded in the water all along, but the image still seemed apt to Zammi.

The Martian Rails passenger service to Tharsis City had already left for the day, so Zammi was stuck in Deimos

City for the night. He figured that he might as well take the opportunity for a little sightseeing along with dinner and was just leaving the room when a noise from down the hall caught his attention. Surely not…

"Hey, Zambo." Val leaned up against the wall next to the door of her room, her arms crossed and a vague smirk on her face.

"Val." He walked down the hall toward the stairs, and she slid into step beside him.

"I was going to see about some food," Val said as if nothing had happened. As if they were still working together. "Want to come?"

Zammi stopped abruptly and turned to face her. "What are you doing?"

"What do you mean?" Her tense face belied her relaxed act.

"I'm going back to Tharsis tomorrow. You and me…" He waved a hand between them. "We're done here."

Val shrugged. "Yeah, sure, whatever you say. We still have to eat, though."

It had always been like this. Whenever they fought, at some point Val would decide unilaterally that the argument was over and that everything should just go back to the way it was before. No resolution, no apologies. And Zammi had always just gone along, because he hated to feel like they were fighting. It was easier to just let it go.

Zammi sighed, falling into the pattern of a lifetime. "Fine. But I'm picking where we eat."

"You got it!" Val kept up as he hustled down the stairs and out the front door of the residence and up a few blocks to a tiny hole in the wall that was run by recent immigrants from

Earth. It offered a select menu of Latin American dishes, and Zammi ordered a plate of pupusas.

Val sniffed the air, and said, "Same for me."

They sat at a tiny table in the corner of the room and, as they waited for the food, Val said, "I talked to Sato and the crew at the Guild about..." Val dropped her voice. "The data we received from our contact."

Zammi frowned. What was with the cloak and dagger? There wasn't a soul in the restaurant but themselves and the staff of one.

"And?"

"And, this." Val flicked up a holo which looked like a complete list of the major corporations and non-corporate factions involved in the terraforming project.

"What am I looking at?"

Val glanced around her, then leaned in and whispered. "The prime suspects."

Zammi glanced at the list again, then barked a laugh. "That's basically everyone."

Val shrugged. "I didn't say it was useful information."

The shop's sole proprietor arrived balancing two heaping platefuls of food, the warm stuffed pupusas nestled under a blanket of crispy pickled cabbage.

Zammi dug in with a knife and fork, but Val just picked one up and took a bite, to the chef's approving smile.

"Mmpf." Val swallowed and wiped her mouth with the back of her hand. "Nice choice, brother. This is delicious."

"Beans, Val," Zammi said, with a mischievous smile. "That's beans in there."

Val wasn't fazed and finished her pupusa. "Dude, I'm not

fifteen anymore. I eat beans." She rolled her eyes, very much as she used to do when she *was* fifteen. "Anyway, this has been nice. But you should go back to the university, we don't have to be together to work on this Factorum thing. You've got your angle and I've got mine. You can go."

Zammi took a deep breath. He knew she wanted him to say, no, it was better to stick together, they'd work it out. But he was tired of being the one to bend to her way of thinking. He was tired of being the little sibling.

"OK, I will," he said, and stood. "See you around, Val." He didn't look back when he walked out of the restaurant and headed over to the Mining Guild's residence.

There, Zammi packed up his few things into the evening and was about to send a message to Marius letting him know that he'd be back at the university the next day, when there was a sharp knock on his door. He closed his eyes, forcing a deep breath down into his lungs, hoping that some measure of calm would join the filtered air. He stood and turned to the door, pressing the open button.

"Damn it, Val," he said as the door opened then his brain short-circuited for a moment. This wasn't possible.

"Hello, Zambrotta."

The face on the other side of the doorway was rougher, with a few more lines around the mouth than he remembered, but there was no mistaking it. He saw an alternate universe version of it every time he looked in the mirror.

"Dad?"

CHAPTER SEVENTEEN

"What are you doing here?"

Zammi stood up straight, hands balled into fists on his hips, completely filling the doorway. It was a small thing, keeping his dad standing awkwardly in the hall, and while he didn't consciously make the decision to block him from the room, the knowledge that the space behind him was his own private domain gave him a strange confidence.

"Can't I come see my kids?" Ivan said, a weak grin wavering on his face.

"Since when do you give a–" Zammi accused, then cut himself off. "How did you know we were here?"

Ivan shrugged and glanced down the hall.

"Val," Zammi surmised and managed to shoulder past his dad without making contact, then closed the door to his room and marched down the hall to number 732.

"Val!" He pounded on the door. "Val, get out here right now."

The door swished open, and Val peered out, bleary-eyed. "What the hell, Zam–" Her eyes widened as she took in the figure standing behind Zammi, his hand feebly aloft in a wave. "Oh. You made it."

"You did this?" Zammi asked, not turning to acknowledge his father. "You called him?"

"He called me, but whatever. It was before we... when things were still going good. I figured, why not make a real reunion out of it, you know?"

Zammi boggled at his sister. "You two talk to each other?"

"Yeah, every once in a while," Val admitted. "I mean, he's my dad."

At this, Ivan cleared his throat and Zammi wheeled around.

"Hey, kiddo, I know there's a lot of propellant through the pipes between us, but I got a long service award from Helion and it came with a bunch of paid time off. I couldn't think of anything else I wanted to do but see you and Val."

"Too bad there was no such thing as paid time off when we were kids," Zammi spat out, the sarcasm veritably dripping from the words. He hadn't spoken like that to anyone since he was an insufferable teen. Which was probably the last time he'd said this many words to his dad.

"Zambrotta–" Ivan began.

"Come on," Val interrupted, stepping fully out of her room and letting the door close behind her. "Zambo's heading home tomorrow and we're all here now. Let's go and get a drink or something, try to be a family for one night, OK?"

Zammi glared at Val. How could she take their dad's side in this? She stared back at him, and he could see something strange in her eyes, a longing maybe? The kind of hope you only see in kids who are convinced that if they just say or do the right thing, the adults in their lives will start treating them decently. Well, that never happened.

But Zammi didn't want to hurt Val even more. It was one evening. He could put up with one awkward night out with his dad. Surely.

There was a quiet neighborhood watering hole just down the street from the residences. On his long walk Zammi had noticed that every few blocks there was a commercial district with shopping, groceries, and gathering spaces, so that every home would be within walking distance of the basic amenities of life. It was a solid design, and Tharsis City was laid out in a similar way, but it reminded him just how different life in the cities was from everywhere else on the planet. A person could almost imagine that the terraforming project was complete in a place like Deimos, especially if you were deep enough in the interior that you couldn't see the dome. But there was still so far to go. Almost everything that was life-sustaining was reliant on the domes. With Ecoline's forest project having to be pushed forward another decade due to the water levels still not being high enough, they didn't even have outdoor trees.

The bar was called *Snickers* and when they walked in Zammi had expected a comedy club, but the place was a dimly lit classic old tap house, with a confectionary-themed decor. He didn't get it, but he wasn't here for the atmosphere. If he was honest with himself, he didn't know what he was here for at all.

Val led them to a square table near a darts board, then pulled up the tabletop menu and ordered. Almost immediately, a section in the middle of the table opened and a jug of beer with three frosty glasses arose from within. Val poured rounds for everyone and passed the glasses out. Zammi scowled over his. Val had chosen well, but it rankled that she hadn't even asked what he wanted. He felt like he hadn't had a say in anything that was going on right now, and he wanted to sulk about it. He knew it was immature and unhelpful, but he no longer felt like a grown human adult, a full professor at a prestigious university no less. He felt like the hurt and angry child he had once been.

"So, kids," Ivan said after taking a delicate sip and smacking his lips. "I had no idea the two of you were working together. How did this all come about? I bet there's a good story there."

Zammi fought the urge to roll his eyes.

"We just ran into each other one day," Val said, surprisingly vaguely, "then we discovered we had some side projects in common and it made sense to team up."

Zammi took a long drink of his beer. He was used to Val being cagey, but why now? Maybe she wasn't as buddy-buddy with Dad as it seemed.

"But, you're still at the university, aren't you, Zam? I'm sure I heard that you got tenure."

Zammi set his glass down. He was surprised that his dad knew about that. "Yeah, just in this last round. I'll have my first thesis students this semester."

"Good for you," Ivan said enthusiastically, spilling a little of his beer in his animation. Tiny robots swarmed out of the table's central aperture with absorbent pads, capturing every last drop of liquid for reclamation before disappearing back down into the table. "Mars needs good teachers, even if I don't really understand how studying history is going to raise the oxygen levels out there."

"Dad." Val's voice had a warning tone to it.

"Oh, I know it's important, I'm sure. I just don't get it. But I've been neck deep in a new project at work, I don't think I even know what the global parameters are these days."

"You can't tell me that anyone who works for Helion doesn't know the average temperature in every climate zone down to three significant digits," Val said.

Ivan shrugged. "Not anymore. We've done our jobs a little too well. A few years ago the UNMI officially asked us to slow down on heat production, so we had to diversify. My part of the company has gone back to our roots, you could say. I've been in half a dozen different roles in the past couple of years. I'm in the interstellar transport division now."

"Wait, did you say inter*stellar* transport?" Zammi said, forgetting his ire for a moment. "That's science fiction."

"So was this not too long ago," Ivan said, waving a hand expansively. "And with all the news of ThorGate's successful tests of its new warp drive, the board decided it had to make a move to stay competitive. So, they figured it was time to dust off the old solar sails for transport. That's how Helion started out, you know. Before all this."

Zammi barked a laugh. He actually had known that. "See, ancient history is useful after all."

Ivan joined him with a chuckle. "You got me there, kid."

"But you can't expect that we'll be sailing souped up space galleons to other star systems, do you?" Val asked, incredulous. "Yo ho ho and hoist the main, cap'n?"

Ivan shrugged and, ignoring her silliness, took the question at face value. "Why not? Once Mars is properly habitable you don't think we'll be content to just stop there, do you? Already people are talking about building a city on Ganymede, with homes and shops and schools and everything, just like this. The stars will be next, I'm sure of it."

Zammi shook his head, but it was in agreement. He knew that this clearly was the trajectory humanity was on, the exopopulation was poised to keep expanding as long as the technology to keep people alive kept pace. But were they even doing that now? This water situation had reminded him of just how precarious life was out here. Surely it was far too soon to be building interstellar starships.

"So, Val, you're not going to tell me that you've gone over to Zammi's side, are you?" Ivan said, changing the subject. "Academics were never your, uh, first love."

Val narrowed her eyes, and visibly chose not to rise to the bait. "No, I'm not at the university, Dad. I'm still with the Guild, fighting the good fight."

Ivan nodded, a mistiness clouding over his eyes. "Your mom and Papi would be so proud of you," he said, looking at Val, then turning to Zammi. "Of both you kids. You've done real well for yourselves. Real well."

No thanks to you, Zammi thought, but managed to keep his mouth shut. He caught Val's eye and was pretty sure she was thinking the same thing. If she was still angry at Dad, what were they all doing here? Pretending to be a family for a couple of hours in a tacky bar in a city where none of them even lived. To what end?

As if he could read Zammi's thoughts, Ivan said, "So, Val, you said Zam's going back to Tharsis tomorrow. Are you sticking around here? You two have some kind of divide and conquer scheme cooking up for this project of yours?"

"Hardly," Val said, then pursed her lips as if she could take back the word. She clearly didn't want to give their dad any of the details about what they were working on. That was strange – Zammi didn't think it was a secret. But this whole happy family routine had been Val's idea, so if she was keeping some things close to her chest, Zammi wasn't about to wreck it for her.

"There is no project of ours," Zammi said. "I needed a lift, Val gave me one, now I'm going home. That's all."

Ivan frowned as if he could sense the lie, but he let it go. "Well, it's none of my business, of course. I'm just happy to see the two of you getting along. You were always so good at butting heads over nothing. One of you would say stars and the other said planets and the next thing you'd know it was war." He shook his head. "For a couple of people who are really exceptional at understanding another person's point of view, you were both always so bad at that when it came to family." He looked away, something caught in his throat, then he took a sip of his beer. He looked at his two kids, who were both struck silent at this uncharacteristically parental lecture they had stumbled into.

"You are both wise enough to know that hardly any issue is easily rendered into two opposite positions. You'd do so much better to remember that when it comes to each other and put whatever it is that you're fighting about aside in order to solve whatever the real problem is." He drained his beer and set the empty glass in the center of the table, where it would be whisked away for cleaning by the automated system. He stood, not waiting for either Val or Zammi to say anything, and grabbed his jacket off the back of the chair and slipped it on.

"It was really great running into the two of you, and if you decide to sort out whatever this is," he waved a hand between the two of them, "I'm on leave for another ten days. You know how to reach me." Then he turned and walked out of the bar.

"What even was that?" Zammi leaned back in his chair after ordering another jug from the tabletop system.

Val just shook her head, filling her glass.

"I don't remember Dad ever giving us the business like that, not once," Zammi went on. "Not even when we were at our absolute worst."

Val was methodically working on her beer, and Zammi didn't blame her. It was something else to be getting one's first fatherly talking-to in one's thirties. She finally put down the empty glass, patterns forming in the foam on its edges.

"Making up for lost time?" she speculated, reaching for the jug. "I mean, he and I talk occasionally, you know, newsy updates every few months. It's not like the two of you..." Val had never lectured Zammi about his relationship with his father – or its lack. "Anyway, he let me know he was in town and it just seemed like a good idea. All of us in one place, when does that ever happen? I should have known better."

Probably," Zammi said, but without malice. "And it was actually going OK for a minute there. Then he has to go and ruin it all." Zammi could tell he'd already had more to drink that he usually did, but he didn't care. He didn't have anything to do tomorrow but catch a train. He refilled his glass.

"Right?" Val said, her words starting to slide around in her mouth. "He doesn't even know what we're doing, who is he to tell us how to do it?" She hiccupped once, then scowled. "I'm starting to understand why you don't talk to him. Ha! You see what I did there? Who's bad at seeing your point of view? If he could see us now."

Zammi laughed, a little too loudly. "He thinks he knows us so well, but he doesn't, not at all! How could he, when he was always working late or 'sorry, kids, I just have to finish this one project.' And for what? The UNMI to come in and tell Helion to stop?" Zammi thought about that for a moment. "Phew, that must have been tough. All those years, all that time, and then they say, 'it's all over!' If I were him, I'd be pissed."

Val frowned. "Me, too. But I don't think he is. He just moves on to the next thing. I guess it was never about the specific work, just… work."

Zammi looked at the walls of the pub, its weird slogans and blown-up pictures of old Earth candy bar wrappers reminding him of a storybook childhood he'd never had. "I wonder if it was just that it's hard to think about things when you're busy all the time."

Val nodded, her face giving nothing away. Eventually, she said, quietly, "He could have been busy with us, though."

CHAPTER EIGHTEEN

Zammi's head was pounding when he woke and he hadn't felt this terrible in years. He'd known full well that Val was a bad influence, so he only had himself to blame for allowing her to influence him. As he rummaged in his duffel with one eye open, he wasn't sure there was enough self-recrimination to account for this. He found a packet of painkillers and slapped a patch on, its immediate effect just enough to allow him to open his other eye. He flipped up a holo and... great. He'd missed the train to Tharsis. Again.

After a wash and a change of clothes he was just about ready to face the day, and hunt down some breakfast. He pounded on Val's door on his way out. She greeted him dressed and looking chipper.

"Hey, bud, you look worse for wear," she said, cheerily. "You want to go get some eats?"

He just grunted back at her but followed her down the hall.

The little café she led them to specialized in exactly what they needed – large portions of filling, comforting food. As

Zammi made his way through a second cup of coffee and a stack of hotcakes he started to feel like a human being again, enough that Val's rashers of vat-grown bacon started to almost look good. He made a face at the thought, and went back to the sweet, fluffy carbohydrates on his plate.

They didn't speak for a while, both of them methodically working through their breakfasts, but eventually Val broke the silence.

"Hey, I got some good news. There's a little custom mechanic's bay over on the west side of town called Sparky's that has some space for me, and they have the suspension microcontrollers in stock that I need for the Oryx. I think I'll even get the chance to take the starboard intake manifold apart while I'm there."

"That sounds great, Val." Zammi pushed his empty plate away and called for another cup of coffee. "You have enough to do here to keep your boss off your back for long enough to get that done?"

Val shrugged. "I'm still working that angle on our thing," she said, and Zammi couldn't help but chuckle at her deliberate vagueness. "I can do that anywhere, and it's possible the science team will want to see us… *me* again. The Guild is happy to keep me here for now."

Zammi nodded. "Well, I'm glad that's going to work out." It could have sounded sarcastic, but he meant it and he knew Val could tell.

"I'm going to take the car in after this," Val said. "You want to come?"

Zammi shook his head. "I'd rather wait until the suspension is back in place before I ride around in that rover again."

"Fair enough. What are your plans for the day?"

Zammi thought about it. He'd planned to be on the train back to Tharsis, where he expected he'd catch up on faculty news and maybe read that new Cristobàl paper he'd been saving. He realized he could do just that while he was here.

"I think I'll track down someplace to hang out and read," he said.

Val nodded. "There's a nice plaza in the center of Deimos, though you do have to put up with a very large, very tacky statue of Bard Hunter."

"Oh yeah, I've read about that," Zammi said, making an exaggerated cringey expression. "I probably should see it while I'm here anyway."

Val gestured at the plates and cups in a way that Zammi knew was her asking if he was done, and he nodded. She tapped at the tabletop and scanned her chip over the reader.

"Hey, I can get my own bill," he said once he realized what she'd done.

"Yeah I know, but I'm pretty sure I'm the only one on the clock here. Seems only fair."

She was really trying to make an effort, Zammi thought. Well. Two could play that game.

"Thanks, Val. But let me get the next one, OK? I'm making a full professor's salary now, remember!"

Val grinned. "You got it. Maybe tonight?"

"Sure."

Zammi wasn't quite up for the two-hour walk into the center of Deimos, so he caught the auto-train into the plaza. It was indeed scenic, as Val had suggested, with patches of greenery, those decorative flowers, and a central pond in the shadow of the large bronze statue of Bard Hunter, founder of CrediCor and one of the originating figures of the terraforming project. Or rather, the statue's shadow fell across the large, deep basin where a central pond ought to be. The pool had been drained, and a notice tacked up to the short wall surrounding it indicated that it was not to be filled in the foreseeable future and that the empty pool was unsafe. Zammi looked into the dry pond bed, the cracked, uneven painted bottom of its surface looking incongruously ancient. Of course, it had been constructed before even his parents were alive, but the idea that anything on Mars was *old* felt ridiculous. It was all relative, he supposed.

He found a bench at the base of the statue, with a lovely view of the gardens along the edge of the plaza. He stretched his long legs out in front of him, and pulled up a holo and began to read.

He'd been so engrossed in Cristobàl's interpretation of the Lunar Land Riots that over an hour had gone by. He'd still have been reading if his communicator hadn't pinged, startling him out of his focus. He was going to ignore it when he saw that it was from Fern. It was a text-only message, and he flicked his screen over to show it on his display.

Hi, Zammi. I suspect this isn't the answer you were hoping to get but I've checked the data twice and come to the same conclusion both times. According to the data you provided me, the asteroid Factorum brought down should have yielded clean, potable water. All the levels were well within tolerances. That ice should have been purer than most of

*the stuff we're shipping in from the asteroids. I don't know
what happened, but if this was the data upon which they
made their decisions, they chose correctly to bring it down.*

*Obviously, don't quote me on that. I don't know
where these numbers came from or who sent the probe
that generated the analysis, but off the record it wasn't
Factorum's fault. I know that gets you no closer to an
answer, but maybe it will narrow down the possibilities.
Sorry I couldn't be more help.*

Fern

That certainly wasn't what Zammi had expected to hear, and
a part of him that he didn't particularly like was annoyed that
Val appeared to have been right. But while he might not be
a scientist, he knew enough to know that in the face of new
information that contradicted his hypothesis, the thing that
had to change was his beliefs.

Zammi pulled up the map holo for Deimos City and tried
to remember the name of the place Val had taken the Oryx.
Dinky's? Stinky's? Eventually he just searched for "custom
mechanic west Deimos" and up it came. Sparky's. The transit
directions were long but not that complicated, and indicated
that if he left now he'd be there in thirty to forty minutes. It
was nearly twenty to twelve, but since some of that was on
foot and he was a fast walker, he figured he'd make it just in
time for lunch.

Zammi didn't know exactly what he'd been expecting, but
Sparky's wasn't it. It reminded him more of *The Platonic
Ideal* than a garage from Earth antiquity. It was bright and

airy, with decorative art on the walls and soft music piped in through invisible speakers. Before the work bays, there were comfortable-looking couches and a high-end food service machine offering drinks, soups, and other meals that could be rehydrated and heated. It did have an out-of-order sign hung on it, but it looked like that was a new addition.

There were half a dozen rovers in various states of disassembly in the bays along the far wall, and Zammi recognized the high gloss black of the Oryx in bay four. He wasn't sure of the protocol in a place like this, so he waited for a few minutes until Val emerged from the sunken pit under the vehicle.

"Oh hey, what are you doing here?" she called to him, wiping her hands on a rag.

"Thought you might want some lunch." He'd stopped at a sandwich shop on the way, and he held up a sack. He knew that once Val got her head into a project she could easily lose track of time. It was a smart bet that she hadn't taken a lunch break yet.

"What would I do without you, brother?" she said without irony and joined him at one of the tables by the defunct drinks machine. She rummaged in the bag and pulled out a large triple decker club sandwich. "You remembered!" She crammed a quarter of it in her mouth at once and chewed.

"So, I'm not just here to make sure you don't starve to death," Zammi said. "Long story short, I think you're right about Factorum after all."

Val stopped chewing for a moment, then went back to her lunch. She made a "go on" gesture.

"I had someone I trust look at the data, and Factorum

didn't just make an error. The numbers all show that the asteroid should have been good. So something went wrong somewhere, whether it's the probe that did the analysis, or the numbers they got, or – I don't know, they somehow got pointed toward the wrong rock? But whichever way, it stinks."

Val nodded, her sandwich gone. "Yeah, it does stink. Look, I don't like the idea that someone has gone out of their way to pollute the new lake any more than you do. I just don't put it past a lot of these organizations to do something like that."

Zammi looked down at his untouched sandwich. "You probably see a lot more bad behavior out there than I do," he admitted. "That's the trouble with history, it's easy to tell yourself that all the terrible things you learn about were in the past and that we know so much better now."

Val shrugged. "We do know better," she said, gently. "But we're all still human."

"So… you want a hand with your investigation?"

"You bet." Val stood up and looked at the Oryx. "I don't suppose you'd be willing to help out here, too? I bet I could get this done today with another set of hands."

"Why not?" Zammi said. "It would be nice to do something with a tangible outcome at the end of it."

At the end of the day Zammi didn't have a better understanding of how suspension micro-controllers worked or what the starboard intake manifold even did, but he did have a pleasant burn in between his shoulder blades and an equally warm sense of accomplishment. And the ride in the Oryx back to the rover bay in the vehicle hangar was as smooth as ice.

"I realize this might just be me misremembering," Zammi said, "but I don't think it was this nice before, was it?"

Val shook her head. "There's a reason everything shifted to micro-controllers." She patted the dashboard and murmured something under her breath.

"Are you talking to the car?"

"Are *you*?"

Zammi stared at her, the comeback complete nonsense, then burst out laughing.

"Some things never change, do they?"

"Guess not." Val pulled into an empty berth and shut down the car's systems. "So, I guess we better start looking over that list I got from the Guild." She didn't sound enthusiastic.

"Is there anything to even look at?"

"Beats me."

Zammi thought for a moment, then pulled up a holo. He reread Fern's note, then highlighted a line and blew the screen up to show Val.

I don't know where these numbers came from or who sent the probe that generated the analysis…

"Factorum got this data from somewhere," Zammi said. "Maybe *that's* where the bad information was inserted."

"Well, it's certainly somewhere to start. Even if it's just to rule someone out."

"All right." Zammi paused. "And how do we do that?"

Val smirked. "And this is why they told me to stay here. We go back to Factorum."

They didn't actually have to go back to Factorum headquarters, of course. Val simply sent Dr Huang a message asking for the sources of the asteroid data. She knew that it was probably under a non-disclosure agreement, but they had to try.

"So how are we going get around that?" Zammi asked.

"These agreements always have an out in them somewhere. We just have to try to make our use case fit the bill. I've thrown in an assurance any third-party information would be kept confidential and used only to exonerate Factorum, blah blah blah. Something something Citizens' Oversight Committee, you know. Spin a line. Hopefully it will be enough to get Huang to give over the goods."

Zammi looked at Val, dubious. But there wasn't anything they could do but try.

"We'll find out tomorrow if this works," Val said. "Now, you said something this morning about buying dinner, right? Time to make good on that threat, professor."

After the long day of manual labor and a heavy meal of freshly made pasta – Val's pick – Zammi was wiped out.

"You sure you don't want to come check out this band?" Val asked, waving a holo-flyer for a downtempo grindchamber trio in front of his face. "They're supposed to be the next BulaBula Noise."

"No, thanks. I don't like the original BulaBula Noise," Zammi said, to a dramatically shocked-looking Val.

"How are we even related?"

"Beats me," Zammi said, then yawned. "Besides, I'd probably fall asleep on my feet. I'm heading back."

"Suit yourself," Val said. "I, however, am not missing out on the opportunity to see what the big city has to offer."

"Tharsis is a big city, too, you know."

Val shook her head. "Not like Deimos," she said, then turned and disappeared into the night.

It was true. Deimos was the cosmopolitan capital of Mars and everyone knew it. Tharsis had the university, Noctis had more corporate headquarters than anywhere, and Cupola was so new that no one knew what it would be like. But for food, culture, art, music – there was nowhere like Deimos City. Zammi wondered if he'd regret not taking advantage of his time here, but who was he kidding? In his current state he wouldn't enjoy anything.

He plodded up the street and had the strange sensation that someone was following him, but when he turned to look there was no one there. He must just be tired. He slowly made this way back to the residence and its remarkably comfortable bed.

CHAPTER NINETEEN

Zammi was up early the next morning and fully intended to let Val sleep off whatever excitement she'd undertaken the night before, but when he returned from a quick run around the neighborhood, he discovered a message from her to meet. He quickly washed and changed then followed the directions to the meeting room on the second floor of the residence building.

"This is handy," he said as he walked in to find Val at one of the desks in the large space.

Val just nodded, engrossed in something on her holo. "Here," she grunted, and with a flick of her fingers, Zammi's communicator pinged. He opened the message to see that it was a forwarded response from Dr Huang. It was professionally worded and Zammi could tell she wished she could be telling them something different, but it was, in essence, no. She was bound by the NDA, and she wasn't about to break it, even if it could help her team.

"That's unhelpful." Zammi felt as if he were deflating. Now

what were they going to do? Val held up a finger though, and the shadow of a smile crept at the corner of her lips.

"Check this out." She flicked her fingers again and this time a large holo appeared over the table. There was no one else in the room, but Zammi looked around anyway once he realized what he was looking at.

"Where did you get this?" he hissed.

Val shrugged. "Anonymous source. Maybe Dr Huang herself, maybe someone else on her team. There's no way to know; that's what anonymous means."

It was an internal Factorum document, marked EYES ONLY, and dated about a year previously. It was the overview of the ice asteroid project, from the initial probe data to identify possible sources, the high-level analysis of the top three contenders, and finally the detailed composition of the asteroid they'd chosen. All with individual names from the sources of the data.

"These are just people," Zammi said, looking at the names. "It doesn't show which corporations supplied the probes?"

Val shook her head. "It won't be that simple," she admitted. "But these names are a good place to start. We'll just have to do a little digging."

They split the work, and Zammi soon found himself in the familiar comfort zone of research. A few of the names had been easy enough to track down – they were unusual enough and their bearers social enough to be easily found online. Perhaps because they were among the original organizations involved in the terraforming project, both the UNMI and CrediCor had publicly available employee directories, and a couple of the names were found there, although the

CrediCor employees had worked somewhere else when they'd been working on the asteroid project. After some social media mining and news searches, Zammi traced the CrediCor names to an arm of the research-driven Inventrix corporation that had developed inexpensive autonomous systems for charting nearby space objects. It was two steps forward and one step back, but by the time Zammi's stomach was rumbling, he was fairly certain that the UNMI and Inventrix had been the ones to supply the initial probes which located the asteroid that was eventually chosen by Factorum.

He looked up to tell Val what he'd learned, to discover that her workstation was empty. He blinked his eyes as if he'd somehow just missed her, but she was gone. He flicked up a holo and sent her a quick "Where are you?"

She replied with a glyph of a mouth taking a bite from an apple. Did that mean she was getting lunch for them both, or just herself? Why couldn't she just answer in words like a normal person?

Zammi's annoyance lingered even after Val appeared at the doorway, a bag in each hand. "I missed breakfast," she said, by way of explanation. She sat down, then said, "Hey, Zambo, you notice anything weird lately?"

"Like what?"

"There were a couple of well-built folks at the concert last night checking me out."

Zammi chuckled. "Oh, please. You and your admirers."

Val shrugged. "I don't think that was it. Well, I did think that last night, but not today. I didn't pay them much attention really – they weren't my type – but I'm pretty sure I saw them again today at the sandwich shop. When they were watching me, it didn't have a good vibe, if you know what I mean."

"No, I don't really." Zammi thought back to that feeling he'd had the previous night. Maybe it wasn't just fatigue. "You think someone's after us?"

"Could be. I mean this isn't exactly business as usual." She waved a hand to indicate their project.

Zammi contemplated mentioning the person in the orange coat he'd seen a couple of days before, but surely it was just a coincidence. "Great. Now I'm going to be thinking I see people following me everywhere." He laughed too loudly, and Val gave him a quizzical look. He reached over to the bag Val had passed to him, pulled out a container of a rather nice looking salad and busied himself with his lunch.

After a moment, Zammi put down his fork, and told Val what he'd learned about the source of the probes.

"Yeah, I had similar luck," Val said. "The data those probes collected was farmed out for analysis, and I'm ninety-eight percent certain that Cheung Shing Mars and Teractor both did some of that work, but there are half a dozen names I just can't place yet. And I really think this is the most likely point where someone could mess up the data." She pointed to the final line of the report, the detailed composition of the asteroid.

"Yeah, probably, but the team of *Smith, I; Chan, M and García, J* couldn't be more generic if it tried. This whole process feels like we're not doing much more than guessing," Zammi complained. "There has to be a better way."

Val shrugged. "There's no chance that any of these people are at Mars University?"

Zammi frowned. "I didn't check. Let me take a quick

look." He fired up the internal directory and ran a search, but while there was an Ines Smith in Literature, a Juan García in Mathematics and Morty Chan worked in the spa, they were clearly not the team he was looking for. "Nope. What about the Guild?"

"It was the first place I checked," Val said. "Nothing."

"Do we have any contacts at any other corporation we could check?"

Val looked at him.

"No," he said.

"We could ask."

Zammi sighed. "Not me."

Val held up her hands in supplication. "It was my idea, I'll do it." She pulled up her holo and tapped in some data. In a moment Ivan's face filled the screen.

"How great to hear from you," he said, the forced cheerfulness ringing out in the empty room. "Is… your brother there?"

"Yeah, I'm here, Dad."

"Oh, I'm so pleased you worked out your little spat," he said, real happiness in his voice now. "You're back on your, what was it, your side project?"

Zammi made an extremely immature face and Val had to stifle a laugh. "Yeah, that's why I called. You said that Helion had to pivot hard a few years back. They ever get into asteroid analysis?"

"Oh sure," Ivan said. "We did a little bit of everything. At one point I was helping Julika's team on something like that. It was all a bit loosey-goosey for a while, there. Helion had always been so well organized, a bit rigid even, you could say. But when the big restructure happened all that went out the window for – oh, geez, I'd say it was probably a couple of years, all told, before the new investment funds came in."

Val caught Zammi's attention, her eyes wide and pleading, as if to ask for help to extricate herself from what had all the earmarks of a very long, very boring story. Zammi laughed silently to himself and waved a hand, as if to say, "You did this. It's your problem."

"… all over the map in terms of the reshuffle. There were engineers in with designers, all doing mathematical analysis for some external contract work. We didn't know if we were coming or going. I think at one point I even ended up getting credited under some other name for some reason, Jones or Smith, in order to keep it from the Engineering Union." Ivan finally took a breath and made an "oops" expression. "I probably shouldn't have mentioned that to you, Val, given your connections, but it's all water under the bridge now anyway. Phew, that was ages ago, I haven't thought of Julika and Mohammed in yonks, I wonder how they're doing now? You know, I should look them up when I get back–"

"Hang on, Dad," Zammi interrupted, and Val sighed in relief. Zammi ignored her, and turned the holo to face him. "Julika and Mohammed *what*? What are their surnames?"

Ivan frowned. "Let me think… uh, it was Julika García and Mohammed Chen."

"Chen? You sure it wasn't Chan?"

"Yes!" Ivan clapped his hands together. "It *was* Chan. Wait, do you know them?"

Val's eyes were wide, and she shook her head back and forth vigorously. Zammi knew what she was trying to tell him, but she needn't have worried. He wasn't about to let on what they were doing.

"No, I just came across those names somewhere, it's no big deal. Hey, Dad, what do you say we meet up tonight at the arboretum? My treat."

Val was going silently apoplectic on the other side of the table, but Zammi kept a neutral expression. Barely.

"Oh, that would be great, Zam! A family outing, wow, it's been a long time since we had one of those. You don't need to pay, though, I'm doing fine. It would be great to take you out, the both of you. How about I see you at the Mining Guild residence at seven?"

"Seven it is," Zammi said, quickly. "Sorry, Dad, got to go." And he ended the call.

"What are you doing?" Val asked.

"I had to change the subject," Zammi said. "I figured that would work."

"Oh, it worked, but now we're going have to spend the evening with him!"

"So?"

"So," Val said, ominously. "You heard those names. Smith, García, and Chan. I. Smith – that was Dad."

Zammi paused, staring. "Yes, Val. I know."

"But don't you see? He's probably up to his neck in the middle of this sabotage business. And you want to pay money to go look at trees with him?"

"Come on. You don't think this is awfully coincidental?" Zammi asked. "I mean, Dad is a fusion engineer, not an ice asteroid scientist." He winced at the phrase again. Surely there was a real name for that job.

"No, what I should have thought was awfully coincidental is him turning up." Val smacked her hand on the table. "Here. *Now*. After how many years of nothing, *this* is when he's got a free vacation and just has to track us down and visit? It's a cover-up, Zambo, it has to be. They sent him here to stop us from finding out the truth."

"Val," Zammi said. "You sound unhinged."

She didn't say anything for a minute. "It is awfully coincidental, though. You said it yourself."

"Coincidences do happen," Zammi said, but even as the words were leaving his mouth he knew how flimsy it sounded. "So, what are we going to do?"

Val shook her head. "I haven't decided yet."

"Well, how about this for a wild notion: let's just ask him."

"You want to ask Dad if he participated in a hack job that could have disastrous effects on the entire planet, maybe even lose some people their lives?"

Zammi gulped. "I mean, maybe not in those words, but yes? Val, has it ever occurred to you that a big part of the problem – *our* problem – is that we don't just talk to each other? Not everything has to be a state secret, you know. We can talk."

Val stared at him as if he'd just revealed that he was a little green man kind of Martian. "Okay, Zambo, we'll play it your way." She started to pack up her stuff, and muttered to herself, "Those better be some great trees."

Seven o'clock was still several hours away, and Zammi had a nervous energy that he wanted to be rid of.

"There's got to be something that you can't get in Tharsis that you want to see or do," Val said.

"Well, there is supposed to be a really great art gallery by the Plaza," Zammi said and waited for Val to make a crack.

She just took a breath and said, "All right. You've helped me with the car twice now. I guess I owe you one. Art gallery it is. Let's grab the train."

Zammi would have laid money on Val never having set foot in an art gallery before, but he appreciated that she was trying. And who knows what she'd been up to in the last few years. She willingly ate beans now, apparently, so anything was possible. Even culture.

They left the residence and walked toward the train station, and after they'd gone a couple of blocks Val quietly said, "Don't look around but those people from this morning are still here."

Zammi stiffened, and all of a sudden became aware of his body in an extremely self-conscious way. "Where are they?" he whispered.

"Across the street and behind us a bit. See if you can maybe catch a glimpse in a window or something."

"What am I looking for? I just see people."

"They're two security types. They kind of look like you, actually. Except, if you were scary."

Zammi sighed, but as he scanned the reflections in windows, he saw what Val was talking about. There were two of them, big powerful people walking together but not talking, and he could make out their muscles even in their bulky jackets.

"Goons," he said.

"Exactly."

"You think they're from Helion?"

Val shook her head. "If Helion is on to us and they sent Dad, they wouldn't need security. And if they aren't on to us…"

"What if they didn't send Dad?" Zammi asked, then nearly tripped over one of the nearly imperceptible and utterly ubiquitous ground rods which helped tension the dome. He'd been walking like a champ for nearly thirty years but now that he knew that people were watching him, it was like he didn't know how feet worked.

"Easy, big guy." Val grabbed at his arm, and pulled him down an alley. "So far they haven't done anything but watch, but don't give them a reason to move to the next level."

"The next level?" Zammi's voice climbed up an octave. "What's the next level?"

"Calm down already, will you? It's just a figure of speech." She pulled him into the nearest building, a clothes shop which evidently catered to people more youthful – or at least more fashionable – than they were.

"Can I help you?" The shop attendant folding a sparkly green top turned toward them.

"You wouldn't happen to have a back door would you?" Val asked, turning on the charm. She glanced toward the front door of the shop, then said in a conspiratorial tone, "I'm afraid we've found ourselves in an angry ex situation."

"Understood." The shopkeeper actually threw them both a wink, then showed them into the back room and to another way out of the shop. As they were exiting to the street, Zammi looked down to see that Val still had a hold of his hand. He wrenched it free, then glared at her.

"Ew, Val, gross!"

Val shrugged. "It got us out of there, didn't it? Come on, I think we can cut back to the train station this way." She hurried along the walkway and glanced behind her once. "Move it, Zambo."

As he caught up to her, Zammi couldn't help but think that even a few weeks ago the notion that he'd be running away from some corporation's security officer would have been ludicrous. But at that moment, he wasn't even surprised anymore.

CHAPTER TWENTY

"We are not seriously still going to the art gallery." Zammi stood on the wide stone steps of the Deimos City Museum of Contemporary Art and stared at Val.

"Why not?"

"Because," Zammi waved his hands vaguely, "there are people who are chasing us."

"They didn't follow us here," Val said, confidently. "And what do you think we ought to do, go back to the residence and hide? That's the one place we can be sure they know about. We're safer anywhere but there. And this is most certainly not there." She pointed up at the double doors with their cheery signs welcoming visitors, the display cycling through several languages.

Zammi couldn't fault her logic, but it felt reckless. Like going to a holofilm in the middle of an apocalypse. But this wasn't the end of the world, and he didn't have a better idea, so he shook his head and trudged up the stairs.

"Okay, fine, let's go look at art."

•••

Val was surprisingly patient as Zammi led her around the gallery, his interests drawing them to the early modern Martian pavilion, then to a special exhibition of Lunar sculpture. He was examining a large bust in the shape of a twentieth-century Earth astronaut, carved from Lunar rock by LE Watanabe, one of the foremost artists of the first Lunar settlement.

"This is incredible. You can see the chisel marks," Zammi said, mainly to himself, but then he looked up and saw that Val was engrossed in a small holo floating before her face. A momentary flash of annoyance came over him, then he reminded himself that this was not an activity that she'd especially wanted to do, and her entertaining herself quietly while he enjoyed the exhibitions was more than reasonable. He was just about to move on to the next piece, when she looked up and caught him watching her.

"Sorry," she said, coming over to join him. "That was Dad."

"Oh?"

"I told him to meet us at the arboretum," she explained. "If I were those security officers I'd be staking out the residence."

"Good idea," Zammi said. "It's kind of putting off the inevitable, though, isn't it? We're going to have to go back there eventually."

Val shrugged. "We'll worry about that when it happens, I guess."

Zammi made a face. "You're not one for a long, complex plan, are you?"

"Sometimes I am. But we don't know enough to make any kind of plan yet. I mean, if they were going to grab us, they could have done it already."

"I suppose you're right. So what do you think they want?"

"I can't tell what they're up to," Val said, airily, "but if I had to guess, I bet they're working for whoever is behind the sabotage. Trying to find out what we know. They only seem interested in watching us at the moment."

"To what end?" Zammi asked, his mind going to scenes from thriller novels and action holos.

"Your guess is as good as mine, Zambo," Val said. "I just don't want to make whatever it is that they are doing any easier for them, you know?"

"No, not really," Zammi confessed. "I know you might find this hard to believe, but I've never been tailed by security officers before."

That made Val laugh, and the sound echoed in the high-ceilinged room. "Well, you're doing great," she said, and punched his arm hard enough that it hurt. "Come on, show me some more moon rocks."

They managed to spend the whole afternoon at the art museum and even Val found a few rooms that caught her interest. Zammi was surprised that she gravitated toward old-fashioned portraiture, but it was nice to see another side of his sister. After a tour of the gift shop, they caught a train at the gallery station and Val chose a labyrinthine route to the Deimos Arboretum which involved changing trains four times and doubling back twice.

"Just in case," she said.

Even with the roundabout trip, they were still a little early, so they hung around the main entrance with its grove of tall, leafy trees and extensive holopanels of information detailing the commissioning of this public green space by Ecoline back when the city was first constructed.

Ivan arrived a few minutes later, and the smile on his face when he saw the two of them was wide and genuine. Zammi felt terrible – he knew that even if Val held it together this was going to be a difficult conversation. What were the odds that Val was going to be delicate about this? About anything, ever? He blew a breath out and waved weakly.

"Zambrotta and Valentina," Ivan said, jubilant. "It is delightful to see you both, as always."

"Are you all right?" Val asked, suspicious. She mimed taking a glass and drinking from it, then cocked an eyebrow.

Ivan laughed. "I *am* on vacation." He poked at the interactive holomap and pointed at a short path marked out in red. Val glanced at Zammi out of the corner of her eye. Zammi lifted his shoulders slightly. They might as well get this over with. Zammi paid the entrance fee and they started walking.

"You know what we were talking about earlier," Zammi began, "that work you did on asteroid analysis?"

"Oh, yeah, that. Ancient history." Ivan made a shocked face. "No wonder you're interested in this!" He laughed at his own joke.

"Hilarious. So, was there anything weird about that job that you remember? You said it was a contract thing – do you know who the client was?"

Ivan shook his head. "No, they never told us much about those jobs, just what to do and when it had to be done by." He shook his head. "I have to tell you kids, those were not great days for the company. A lot of good people left. When they decided to go back to solar sails for propulsion instead of heat, that was when everything turned around. Ooh, should we sit?" They'd arrived at the arboretum's central mossy clearing and its picnic tables, benches, and a now-dry decorative fountain. A couple of kids were kicking a ball back and forth in the open space and a few families, couples and groups occupied most of the seats, but they found a free bench where they sat together awkwardly.

Zammi had forgotten how loyal his dad was to the company. So loyal, he thought, that he'd probably do anything his manager asked him to do without much question. But what if it was obviously unethical? Or worse?

Val sat rigidly, staring at Ivan. "You heard about the asteroid that Factorum just brought down?"

"Sure," Ivan said, confused at what appeared to be an abrupt shift in the topic.

"Well, that was on you. Factorum was your mystery customer. The asteroid that you did the analysis for all those years back is the same one they just brought down and discovered that it is contaminated with lead. All that water, water we desperately need, is poisoned, because your analysis didn't show the lead content correctly."

"Val." Zammi's voice had a warning tone, but his sister acted as if he hadn't said a word. She was ruining his plan.

Ivan frowned, his slow response indicative of a mind dulled by day-drinking and the weight of what his daughter was telling him.

"No, that can't be right. I remember clearly thinking what a shame it was that an asteroid in such a good position with so much ice on board was contaminated. I was glad it was a commissioned report for someone else, not a project Helion was counting on. The lead levels were definitely marked as dangerous on that report. I'm sure of it."

Zammi looked at Val and he could see in her face that she didn't believe Ivan. But Zammi didn't think their dad was that much of an actor. He'd never been any good at hiding his feelings which, now that he was an adult, Zammi realized was probably one reason why he'd spent so much time away from the kids after the crash. He must have been trying to spare them his grief. Of course, Zammi was sure that they would have been better off with a father who was present, regardless of how emotional he was, rather than the absent one they'd had. For one thing, they probably wouldn't be about to make a terrible scene in the middle of this otherwise lovely garden.

Val opened her mouth to kick it off, when something in the distance caught her attention and she stopped. Zammi followed her gaze and his heart thudded in his chest.

"How did they find us?" he asked, and even Ivan turned to see what they were looking at. It was the two security officers who'd been following them earlier, walking up the path and openly staring at them.

"Do you recognize them?" Val asked Ivan accusingly.

To his credit, Ivan looked carefully, then shook his head. "No, I don't think so. But there is something about them." He squinted, then a look of recognition came over his face. "Yes, those jackets. I've seen them before. They're Utopia Invest staff."

"I knew it wasn't Helion," Val said, and looked at Zammi with something that was close to an apology. "So, you remember all that mess at the mining site where we ran into each other? With the BeSADS?"

"I do, indeed," Zammi said, starting to put two and two together.

"Well, my presence there wasn't exactly welcomed by Utopia Invest management. That's why I had to hightail it out of there. I figured they might be looking for me."

"Like, 'have a chat on the holo' looking for you, or 'security goons with zip ties' looking for you?" Ivan asked.

Instead of answering the question, Val raised her eyebrows in answer: goons. Obviously it was goons, they were right over there, pretending to read the notice hastily tacked up next to a locked-off water tap.

"What is it with you?" Zammi asked, instantly angry again, the events of the past few days catching up with him. "Why does everything have to turn into a massive melodrama? 'Go on a little road trip,' Marius says. 'Spend a little time with your sister.' All I was doing was hitching a ride to go see someone about a ship and now I'm on the run from Utopia Invest security?"

"I don't think they really care about *you* in particular," Val said, defensively. "In fact, I suspect it's because you're around that they haven't picked me up."

"So you're using me as a shield now?"

Val just stared at him. She was right, he was being ridiculous, it was just that everything about this made Zammi's blood boil. He took a couple of long, slow breaths.

"I don't understand," Zammi said, still angry but cooling off enough to properly think now. "How did they find us here? They can't have a tracker on you or they would have caught up with us at the gallery."

A groan came from Ivan and both Zammi and Val turned toward him.

"I, uh, might have an idea about that. I told you that Helion got an influx of investment funds a few years ago, right?" he began, and Val made an impatient gesture at him. Zammi thought he could guess where this was going, though. "Well, the funds were from Utopia Invest. Ever since then the companies have been pretty closely entwined. Like this." He held up his hand, two fingers crossed. "The award I got, this trip…" He visibly flinched, then went on, his voice low. "It was bankrolled by Utopia Invest. They specifically suggested I spend time with my kids."

"Oh, Dad." Zammi dropped his face into his hands while Val shot to her feet.

"*You* did this," she shouted, obviously not caring about the Utopia Invest goons or anyone else who might be watching them. Which at this point was pretty much everyone in the immediate area. "You brought these people right to my doorstep. What is wrong with you? And you expect me to believe you had nothing to do with sabotaging the data that was sent to Factorum?"

"What sabotage?" Ivan sputtered.

"Come on, Val, there's no evidence…" Zammi began, but Val wheeled around to stare at him, her face twisted in anger as she pointed a finger at Ivan.

"He has always cared more about his position at that company than anything else on the planet. If they told him to jump, he'd ask how high. And if they wanted fake data inserted into a report, there is no one else that would be better suited to the job. You can't tell me he's not complicit in this, all of it."

"Now, Valentina," Ivan began, his voice wavering, but Val turned her back on him before he could continue. That was it. Something in Zammi broke, seeing her about to walk away. Again. She started to leave but Zammi's hand reached out to grab her arm. He wasn't even aware he was doing it until he felt her bicep tighten under his grasp. He relaxed his grip but he didn't let go.

"You think the two of you are so different, but you're exactly the same, Val. You've always cared more about yourself than this family," he countered, the words flowing out of his mouth without thought. "The minute you could leave, you were gone. Did you really think that just because I was sixteen years old that I didn't need you anymore? You left me, Val, just like Dad, and you didn't even have work as an excuse like he did. You just wanted more for yourself than taking care of a needy little brother. Well, fine. Fair enough, I guess. You had to live your life. But you do not get to stand on the high ground now and talk about who betrayed whom. Because you *both* let me down." Zammi pointed at Ivan, just like Val had done a few minutes before. "At least he has the decency to feel bad about it."

Val stared at him, and Zammi couldn't read her face. It was something new, something he'd never seen on her before. When she spoke, her voice was low and even.

"You have no idea what I feel bad about," she said, then stared right at the Utopia Invest team who just watched her as she turned and walked down a far path. They murmured to each other, then began to walk back the way they'd come. Zammi guessed they didn't want to make more of a scene by running after her, but it was probably just a matter of time before they caught up with her. Perhaps now the goons had changed directive from watching to interacting.

Zammi stood, his whole body shaking with the adrenaline left over from the fight. He needed to be alone. He looked around and said a loud, embarrassed, "Sorry," to the entire park before he stomped down the path to the entrance.

CHAPTER TWENTY-ONE

Zammi didn't see any sign of the Utopia Invest duo, or of Val herself, on his walk back to the Mining Guild's residence building. She'd had a decent head start, she'd be fine. *She was always fine,* he thought.

Once at the residence, Zammi didn't see anyone on the way to his room, either. It was probably for the best. He was in no mood to chat with a neighbor and he didn't trust himself to speak with his sister. Assuming she'd come back to the residence. Assuming she wasn't in some Utopia Invest cell somewhere… No. She was not going to do this to him again. She could take care of herself, as she'd always been so fond of telling anyone.

That had been the worst blowout he'd ever had with Val, worse even than when they had both been volatile teens, and of course it had to be in the middle of a public place. If he were any less angry, he'd be mortified, but as it was all he could think of was the image of Val walking away from him.

She'd always been so strong, so tough – whether it was

in the back streets of Tharsis City facing a pack of bullies or on some forgotten asteroid helping people get out of a bad situation. It was like she never ran away from anything, except her own family. Except for Zammi. What made it worse was that it seemed to him like it was the easiest choice she ever made: to leave him in her dust whenever he became inconvenient.

He should have known that this trip wouldn't work out, once it became obvious that it was going to take more than a day or two. It was as if there was a timer on their relationship, something in Val that compelled her to take off after a certain amount of togetherness had been achieved. Or maybe whatever it was came from him, that there was something about him that she couldn't stand to be around. If he was honest with himself, he was sure that was what it had to be.

Zammi went to the shared washroom and was about to run the tap to splash some water on his face, when he remembered that the faucets were disconnected and there was a sign taped up to the mirror reading *Water Rationing In Effect*. Of course. He used a cleansing wipe instead, but it didn't quite have the same effect. Still, it reminded him that there were bigger problems on the planet than one family's inability to get along. His issues were nothing in the grand scheme of things, and he'd do well to remember that. He strode back to his room, determined to get past this, like he'd gotten over it every other time Val took off on him. The best balm for any problem was work, and there was no shortage of things to do.

Val could take care of herself.

He pulled up a holo and saw that he had a message from Marius, simply asking him to call when he could. It was getting late, but still early enough for night-hawk Marius, so Zammi flicked the contact link.

"Professor Kaspar!" Marius answered quickly, his grin wide under his impeccable moustache. "How are you making out with Factorum?"

Zammi took a beat. He hadn't realized quite how much had happened since he'd last spoken with Marius.

"We've confirmed that it wasn't an error on the asteroid team's part, and think it might have been deliberate sabotage on the data long before the asteroid came down. Years ago, even."

"Whoa. That's not great. Any idea who's responsible?"

Zammi groaned. "Depends on who you ask."

Marius raised his eyebrows, but didn't say anything.

"Probably Helion. They were the ones who provided the analysis of the composition of the asteroid. The data Factorum got from them showed the lead levels as zero, so…" Zammi gestured as if asking Marius to make the inference himself.

"Hmm. Any chance you can talk to someone who worked on it?"

"Oh, no."

Marius said nothing, letting the silence jog Zammi to continue.

"We already did." Zammi's voice made it plain that the conversation hadn't gone well. "It was my dad."

"Oh." Marius's usual jocularity dissolved. "That's awkward."

"Yes, it was. Quite."

"And, did he shed any light on the situation?"

"He claimed that the figures they reported were correct. I believed him, but… well, *I* believed him."

"I see. Send me what you've got and I'll make some enquiries."

"Sure." Zammi sent Marius the files.

"Speaking of enquiries, I ended up learning rather a lot from the mechanic out at the Arcadian Communities shipyard."

"Oh, yeah." Zammi had completely forgotten about the crash that had gotten him involved in all this, and he was ashamed of himself. This was what fighting with Val did to him, it made him forget what was important. "Fill me in."

"So, the shipyard is actually a lot more like a scrapyard, but they fix up these old junkers to keep them out of the recyclers and to offer low cost options for the local community. You would not believe some of the models they get running down there. Orazio – that's the very nice mechanic I was speaking with, glorious head of hair on that man – anyhow, he told me they even had a Mark III, you know those generic satellite-guided ones from the days when there was only one fleet for all of Mars." He shook his head as if bewildered by how provincial it had once been.

"You know I don't share your enthusiasms here, right?" Zammi said, kindly. He didn't want to get bogged down in a conversation about old cars – or attractive mechanics.

"Yeah, of course. Anyhow, Orazio explained that they sell these old vehicles to all kinds of people for all kinds of reasons. But he remembered the *Lupa Capitolina* because it had been such an interesting ship."

Zammi's face must have shown his concern that this was going to turn into another dissertation on classic Martian vehicles, because Marius laughed.

"Interesting because in its day it had been a rather fancy

private mining ship, but time and wear had turned it into the cheapest spaceworthy vessel that could support ice boring equipment the yard had in stock. Which happened to be the exact brief they'd been given by this buyer."

"Oh. Who was the buyer?"

Marius's face darkened and he shook his head grimly. "That's the thing – they were just regular people. A team from one of the small settlements that are part of the Arcadian group. It turns out that one of Jocasta Rew's partners, Ethelbert Tipton, had a sister in the settlement, which was how the Starry Vistas crew got involved. They needed people to fly the ship. Tipton's sister, Edith, and two other people from the settlement joined them for the mission."

Zammi started to put it all together. The sketchy ship, the Utopia Invest mining site. The water shortage. The desperation.

"They were going to help themselves to some ice."

Marius nodded sadly. "I don't know if we'll ever know exactly why they crashed. Orazio was beside himself, afraid that he'd missed something on the safety check. But when I mentioned that they'd turned off their transponder and were flying on manual he got so angry he nearly punched a hole in the wall. Strong fellow. Anyway, apparently, he'd told them that the autopilot was a new upgrade and was up to current specs but the original navigation station couldn't be upgraded and shouldn't be used. He asked me why they would do that, deliberately ignoring his warnings, and I didn't know whether I should really explain it or not."

"He'll figure it out eventually," Zammi said. The autopilot would broadcast their transponder which would show any nearby station or ship who they were and where they were going. Flying on manual, a ship might be able to slip in somewhere undetected. Orazio would know that, and Zammi suspected it wasn't as if these were the first customers who'd been buying supplies for a robbery. The mechanic had to realize what they were up to, at least in the vague sense, even if he didn't want to admit it to himself.

"It wasn't that bad a plan," Marius said, wistfully. "The security for a mining site run by BeSADS would be more concerned about people leaving than unauthorized arrivals. They figured they could get on to that rock, grab a block of ice, and get out again before anyone on the ground even knew they'd been there. Once they got out, I bet they'd have been in the clear. I imagine it isn't impossible to trace the provenance of a particular piece of ice, but it probably isn't worth it either."

Zammi shook his head. Six people were dead, and the official COC report would show that it was because of their own misadventure. No one to blame but themselves. But he knew that those six people would absolutely still be alive if this water shortage were not happening. Who was there to blame for that? No one? Everyone? The system?

Zammi couldn't fight that, not in the short term. He knew that systemic change was possible, of course, but it took communities working together and it took years. Maybe this would be the beginnings of change, but it would only be that. The beginning.

Here and now, what could he do? Val was running from the consequences of her own actions, and there wasn't anything he could do to help her. Even if there was, he wasn't sure he should. If Ivan had been involved in the sabotage, he clearly wasn't about to confess to Zammi and if he wasn't then he didn't know anything that would help. There was nothing more for Zammi to do and he was more than ready to get back to his life.

"Thanks, Marius," he said. "I'll talk to you soon."

Marius looked like he had something to add, then appeared to think better of it and said good night. That was for the best. Zammi didn't need someone else telling him what to do. He'd made up his mind.

The Martian Rails station was at the northern edge of the Deimos dome, but it didn't take Zammi long to get there. The service to Tharsis was right on time and Zammi had just chosen a seat on the starboard side in the hopes of a view of Noctis Lake when they were underway. As they sped away from Deimos, they passed through the extensive grasslands between Deimos City and Noctis City, and Zammi marveled at what appeared from this height to be an ocean of green. He'd seen it before, but the waves of grasses somehow meant more to him now. All the sacrifices so many people had made to create this oasis in the stars seemed to be embedded in the cells of these tiny blades waving in the breeze of the train's wake.

Mars was beautiful. It always had been, before humans or even robots had ever disturbed its dusty shores, but Mars as it was now, with its visible patches of greenery, ice and liquid water among the rocks, seemed to him like a physical manifestation of the cooperation that had been required to get this far. So many people, from Earth and beyond, working together and separately toward this singular, difficult multigenerational goal. It was remarkable in history, Zammi knew.

Surely there had been issues like this in the past. There was no possibility whatsoever that an undertaking as lucrative and complex as the terraforming project had lasted several hundred years without some amount of grift and corruption. And Zammi knew that there were motivations at play that were less than entirely altruistic. But it had worked. It was working. All he had to do was look out the window at the lush field of grasses to see that. This water situation was entirely surmountable, they would get through it. They had to, after all. There was no other option.

The layover in Noctis City was long enough for Zammi to disembark and maybe even take in some of the sights of the old city, but he chose to remain aboard the train. He liked his seat and didn't want to lose it, but he also was exhausted. A six-hour journey with nothing to do but look at the landscape was perfect. Soon the train was leaving Noctis Station and beginning the long ride to Tharsis. The peaks of Ascraeus and Pavonis to the west were too far away to be visible, with Noctis Lake as the only notable feature behind them. Its surface shone in the midday light of the sun, and the hopefulness Zammi was feeling in the morning began to fade. As the train picked up speed and began to chew through the barren desert between Noctis and Tharsis, Zammi noticed that gnawing feeling in the base of his stomach, that there was something he ought to be doing. But he knew he couldn't solve all of Mars's problems himself and it was time to go back to the real world. The world of students and thesis papers and learning from the past. That was what he was good at, not running around chasing after ghosts.

He leaned his head against the seatback, stretched out his legs, and closed his eyes.

Zammi's rooms at the university were exactly as he'd left them. The automated cleaning systems had kept the surfaces dust free and the air recirculators ensured that there was no musty smell. The temperature was the comfortable 22°C he preferred. Even so, when he dropped his duffel on the floor the place felt cold, sterile even. He'd missed his solitude the last few nights, but now that he was finally alone, it felt odd. Uncomfortable.

He shook his head as if that would dislodge the thoughts. He just needed to get back to normal life, that was all. Once he was back to his routine, everything would be fine.

He was in his office early the next day, catching up on faculty memos and interdisciplinary gossip. He was about to head out for a mid-morning snack when he heard a familiar voice down the hall. He poked his head out the door to see Marius talking with a colleague. Zammi smiled as his mentor turned, but his grin faded when he saw the look of confusion then disappointment on the other man's face.

"Zambrotta!" Marius said, his voice booming in the small corridor. "What in the blue blazes are you doing here?"

CHAPTER TWENTY-TWO

"I, uh, work here?" Zammi offered weakly.

Marius frowned, the tips of his moustache twitching. "Very funny. Why aren't you tracking down that Helion data connection?"

"Because I am a history professor, not a data detective." Zammi took a breath. "Look, even if the Committee does have the right to dig around in a decades-old project, what can I do? I don't even have a badge to flash at someone to get them to talk to me. My hands are tied."

Marius sighed, then motioned for Zammi to follow him to his office. Marius waved him in and gestured for him to sit on the sofa, which Zammi did even though the low seat meant his knees came up to his nose.

"I'm sorry," Marius said. "I made assumptions which I obviously should not have. I take it that you and Val are–" He waggled his hands in a gesture Zammi interpreted to mean that he thought they were on the outs.

"Yeah."

Marius nodded. "I hadn't quite understood the, ah, complexity of your relationship. Still, things are coming to a head." He flipped up a large holoscreen and Zammi could read the headline of the *Deimos Times*: *Water Shortage at Unprecedented Level – Was the Factorum Asteroid Sabotaged?*

Zammi groaned. He skimmed the article, which didn't name Helion and stopped short of explicitly accusing anyone of anything, but strongly implied that *someone* had altered data which caused Factorum to bring down a contaminated asteroid. Without a doubt the team at Factorum – and its board – would have seen this article. Maybe they were even the ones who contacted the journalist – there was no byline on the Factorum sidebar, just a *Deimos Times* staff credit. Probably a lightly doctored press release, then. Val must have shared her suspicions with the Factorum team. Great. Trust Val to do exactly what made it all harder for the rest of them. At least that meant she was probably not sitting in some Utopia Invest detention facility.

"We don't even know that there was any sabotage at all," Zammi said.

"Exactly," Marius said. "And we need to know, whatever the truth is. You and Val are the only ones who've even come close to finding out what's going on. Regardless of whatever is happening between the two of you, it makes no sense to stop investigating now."

"Investigating what?" Zammi said, not bothering to keep the frustration from his voice. "It's all 'this person says one thing, that person says another' and there's no way to really know anything."

"There are always records," Marius said. "Primary sources."

"What do you mean?"

"You know as well as I do that Helion will have a kept a complete record of all the work they did on this project. Everything from the analysts' notes to the drafts of the final report. If they did send Factorum false data, there will be a record of it somewhere."

"Well, if they did they certainly won't just hand all that material over if we ask nicely."

Marius stared at Zammi, arching one eyebrow slowly.

Zammi closed his eyes. "You aren't seriously suggesting…"

"Desperate times, Zambrotta. I did a little checking, and Factorum keeps their private data servers at their head office in Noctis."

No one spoke for a long moment.

"You're actually proposing–"

Marius interrupted. "I know I'm asking a lot and, frankly, you'd probably be best advised to tell me to shove it. Obviously, this is well beyond anything you signed up for. But things are bad. If these accusations and retaliations escalate, they are only going to get worse. Someone has to do something."

Zammi took a breath. Marius was right, about all of it. But why did that someone have to be him? He sighed.

"And I was just there." The look on Marius's face made Zammi clarify. "Noctis, I mean. The train stopped there."

"Well, I hate to make you double back, but if you're going to make a move you need to do it now before they have a chance to hide anything."

"I have a feeling that you're not sending me alone."

"Certainly not. Val's there already."

The implications of Marius's sentence took their time sinking in. She must have given the Utopia Invest team the slip after all. She was all right. Zammi was surprised at the depth of his relief, and with the force of his anger once it had burned away the undercurrent of worry he'd been carrying since Deimos.

"Of course she is. Fine. I'll go back to Noctis. But then I'm done with this, and I'm done with her. I'll teach my students and write my papers and stay out of this Citizens' Oversight Committee. Understood?"

Zammi had never spoken to Marius like that, and he was surprised to see a flush of something like pride on his mentor's face.

"Loud and clear."

The train ride back to Noctis was not a repeat of the calm journey that Zammi had enjoyed the previous day. Even though the carriage was exactly the same, and the other passengers behaved no differently, Zammi couldn't find a way to get comfortable in the seat and the morning's ride felt like it would never end. He just didn't want to be doing this.

Marius seemed to think that he'd be able to saunter into Helion headquarters and simply ask them to hand over proof that they'd committed – what? Treason? It felt like that to him, but the more that Zammi thought about it, he wasn't even sure that faking data was a crime, per se. There were only a handful of offenses that were referred to the UNMI Criminal Board for adjudication, and from what Zammi could remember they all required that the injured party was an individual, rather than a corporate entity. Getting sued for breach of contract was probably the more likely outcome. A suit like that wouldn't be good for anyone, but especially not for a company that was already in enough trouble that they'd taken on Utopia Invest as a partner. Regardless, they weren't likely to confess just because he asked them to.

The train was well into the desert, the view outside Zammi's window nothing but ochre rock as far as he could see with the vague form of a mountain range in the distance. Once, this had been all there was to Mars, but to Zammi it seemed so strange for there to be this sea of nothingness. His Mars was the university, art galleries, libraries, all the trappings of human culture. And yes, mines and greenhouses and roadworks, too. His Mars was a human place, full of all the accomplishments humanity could achieve. It was a tenuous home, as he was becoming more and more aware, but it was a home. He struggled to imagine a time when it had been so utterly alien that no human being had ever stepped on its surface.

There was no going back to that now. Even if more projects failed, Mars would never be anything but a place humanity called home. Even if there was hardship and privation, even if people died, they wouldn't abandon the planet and its audacious terraforming project. And that was why it was even more imperative that they find a way to continue the work without hardship and privation. The people of Mars didn't need to suffer just to ensure that some corporation's terraforming rating remained within the tolerances of its shareholders.

If Helion had altered that data, that fact needed to come out. If it meant consequences for people – for Ivan – well, then, so be it. If people could put names and faces to the water scarcity, then public pressure would force the various factions to work together instead of trying to undercut each other. It was long past time for Mars to put aside its differences and focus its efforts. And it would start with Zammi.

"I didn't expect to hear from you so soon."

Val's demeanor was unusually subdued. Zammi knew he'd hit a nerve, and he was still angry with her. He took a breath, her image on the holo carefully neutral.

"This isn't about us. It's about finishing the job we were asked to do." He explained that he'd spoken with Marius, and that he'd convinced Zammi to remain onboard to help. He watched as Val's expression became more animated.

"Do you have an idea of what we might be contemplating?" she asked, cagey.

Zammi closed his eyes and nodded. "Yeah. This must end, and if it takes unmasking what Helion did, by whatever means, then that's what we have to do. I know what I'm getting into, and I'm in."

Val sucked in a breath then she began tapping rapidly. "OK. I'm sending you some directions. Meet me there when you get to Noctis."

"It won't be long now. We're almost at the station."

"Right. See you soon." She cut the connection and Zammi leaned back into the seat, his shoulders tight with tension. He was fairly certain that he did, in fact, know what he was getting himself into, and in the moment it seemed fine. The right thing to do.

He wondered if he'd still feel that way when this was all over.

The directions Val had given him led to a nondescript door in a basic prefab building. Noctis was the second oldest city on Mars after Tharsis, but unlike the university town it had struggled with modernization. Its city center was shiny and new, the streets and infrastructure kept up to date by council crews, but the outlying areas got less attention. There were several districts which had been historically more affordable, but also less likely to succumb to the lure of new fashions and technologies.

Zammi shouldered open the door and found himself in a space which could have been either a large open office or a small warehouse. There were no internal walls to break up the space, which had to be at least thirty meters along each of the four walls. In the middle of the room stood a large table with cheap holo boards flickering nearby, and a half dozen folding chairs rounding out the furniture compliment.

Val stood at the widest part of the table, gesturing to something on the screen that Zammi couldn't make out from the doorway. As he drew closer, he could see that the three other people in the room were watching Val intently, occasionally asking questions. Zammi's footsteps finally caught their attention and they turned to look at him. They all appeared vaguely familiar, but Zammi couldn't place them until the rough-looking man across from Val grinned.

"Hey, Big'un."

"I don't believe this. Rufus?" Zammi squinted, but it really was the old fellow he'd met at the Utopia Invest mine. The one who'd obviously been angling for a ride offsite. How had he gotten away? And what was he doing here with…?

Zammi looked around at the other faces. As he lived and breathed, the guy with the round eyeglasses and a paper notebook was *Milton, A*, his guide out to the crash site. And… no, it couldn't be. But Zammi would know those braids anywhere. It was Billie, Val's opponent in mess hall pugilism.

"Val," Zammi said, his eyebrows raised, "do you have something to tell me?"

"You don't think I abandoned everyone there on their own, did you?" Val looked incredulous.

"I…" Zammi had no idea what to think. So, he went for the easy question and pointed at Billie. "Weren't the two of you, like, mortal enemies?"

Billie laughed, the sound light and melodious. "Oh, that business in the mess hall? We weren't fighting. Well, I guess we were, technically, but it wasn't in anger. It was just a diversion."

"A diversion?"

Val chuckled. "While everyone was watching us, Karl was passing out the paperwork for officially becoming a registered union with the Mining Guild."

"Wait, are you saying that you did it?" Zammi asked. "You organized the Utopia Invest site?"

Milton nodded, his cheery grin infectious. "Sure did. That's how we got here. Paid time off, backdated."

"This is incredible." Zammi looked around the room. The faces that looked back at him were full of potential, their futures in their own control. It was no wonder he hadn't recognized them.

"Hang on," he said to Val, "why didn't you mention any of this?"

She shrugged. "We were kind of busy. Besides," she glanced away, "I didn't think you were all that interested."

"Oh, Val." Zammi pulled up a chair and sat. "Well, that explains how you're here. But *why* are you all here?"

"Well," Val said, "even I know better than to think that the two of us could pull off a job like this on our own. You meet a lot of interesting people in my work, and nowhere more so than at that Utopia Invest site. It seemed like everyone there had some untapped skills they might want to put to use someday."

"So this is our team?"

"You bet. Rufus here is the best systems analyst I've ever seen. He can get into an encrypted database faster than I can get into a bag of chips, and as you know Zambo, that's pretty zippy. Thankfully, Billie isn't that much of a fighter…"

"Hey!"

"…but I've never met anyone else who can open a locked door quicker."

"You're a lock picker?" Zammi asked Billie.

"Naw, I'm not a burglar," Billie said, giggling, "I'm more like a social engineer."

"So you don't break in, you talk your way in?"

Billie nodded. "Or, you know, create a distraction."

Zammi chuckled, then turned to Milton.

"Let me guess. You're the wheelman."

"Guilty as charged," he said. "Half the time with a job like this, getting away is the hardest part."

"I don't doubt it," Zammi said, then tried to combat the

tension starting to rise in his chest as the reality of what they were there to do caught up with him. "I have to confess, I've never done a heist before."

"Don't sweat it, big fella," Rufus said, slapping him on the back. "There's a first time for everything."

CHAPTER TWENTY-THREE

Zammi knew that what they were planning was of dubious morality and could potentially land any of them an all-expenses paid trip to the penal mines on Callisto. He tried not to think about that as they organized, focusing instead on the intricate details of the plan. When that didn't work, which was frequent, he thought about the people he'd met in those remote settlements, like the folks in the Arcadian Communities struggling with broken systems and relying on lucky breaks.

There were families out there, kids like Zammi and Val had been, kids who would grow up never knowing what it was like to just turn on the taps and have clean water come out. Kids who, if those settlements' luck ran out, might have bigger problems. Water was life, after all.

It took them a couple of days to get everything ready, between the supplies Milton needed to ensure their safe and speedy withdrawal from the scene, and the detailed schedules of the security team at Helion HQ. There was also a lot of time spent drilling each other on the minute-to-minute execution of the plan. It reminded Zammi a little bit of cramming for exams in his undergraduate studies.

As they worked, Zammi noticed the easy camaraderie between Val and the others. He realized that he had no idea how long she'd been at the Utopia Invest site. For some reason he assumed it hadn't been long, maybe a couple of weeks, but now that he saw them all working together with such practiced ease, he mentally revised that estimate. Of course, when she wanted to, Val could make friends anywhere she went, but this was different. It was as if they anticipated each other's strengths and struggles, lending a hand just as it was about to be needed or leaning into someone who would be able to shore up their weaknesses. Zammi was impressed and a little envious.

His role in the operation was crucial, but he couldn't pretend that he brought a particularly strong skill set to the event. As an academic, his physical stature was rarely relevant to his work, but this wasn't the first time Zammi had been given a job just because he was the biggest. It might not have been what he'd have chosen, but he knew his part was important, and he made sure to put his all into it.

On the evening of the first night, Zammi tracked down a motel in the neighborhood and was walking toward its location, when Milton appeared at his side.

"There's a decent noodle joint around the corner," he said, "if you're hungry."

"I am," Zammi admitted and he realized that he was famished. They found the place which was in an unmarked storefront, although the spicy, rich smell emanating from the open door did a reasonable job of advertising its wares. After Zammi was seated at a tiny table in the corner with an enormous plate of noodles, vegetables, and chunks of tofu all covered in a savory sauce, Milton joined him with a steaming bowl of soup. They focused on the food for a while, the bustling sounds of the busy eatery filling their ears.

Milton delicately plucked a dumpling from his bowl and set it on the spoon in his other hand. He contemplated it for a moment, then said, "You two are siblings, right? You and Val."

Zammi said they were and Milton nodded. "Me and my own sibs, we never did get along. One of them's a banker over in Cupola City, the other stayed on Earth if you can believe it. Just goes to show that even if you grow up in the same house, eat the same food, wear the same clothes half the time, you don't have to wind up the same, no sirree."

Zammi chewed something leafy for a moment, then said, "You noticed we're not exactly best friends?"

"Mmhmm. Don't have to be, of course. Not to do a job and not to be a family. Friends is its own thing." He popped the dumpling in his mouth and closed his eyes while he chewed deliberately. When he was done, he said, "Oh, I have missed this, I've got to say. Food was all right at the mine site, but it was a bit samey, you know? Anyway, what I was getting at is that we don't all have to be pals. But what we do have to do is trust each other." He looked at Zammi, his gray eyes intent. "That going to be a problem?"

It never even occurred to Zammi to simply say "no" without thinking. It felt like the kind of question that deserved contemplation. Val was frustrating and sometimes he wondered if she was being contrary just to make him upset. He didn't understand her or her priorities, not when it came to him or their family, but he was certain that in her work she tried to do everything in the best interests of the people of Mars. Maybe not just in work, maybe that was her version of Zammi's love of history. Maybe she loved a vision of the future, one where Mars was both prosperous and just.

"No, that's definitely not going to be a problem," Zammi said. "Val clearly trusts you all, and while I fully admit that there are some areas where I think my sister's reliability is…" he waggled his hand, "let's say 'suspect,' a job like this is not one of those, there's no one else I'd have more confidence in."

Milton nodded gravely. "Agreed. But sometimes those family feelings can obscure the truth a little. I needed to make sure we were all solid."

"We're solid," Zammi said, a smile creeping across his face at the use of the unfamiliar argot. It made him wonder if there was a paper in this experience: a survey of extralegal organizations from the Lunar Metropolis to Mars. It could be quite interesting, and he didn't think anyone had done it before. He knew that there was a robust black market operation on the Lunar outpost and of course there was that ridiculous rumor about secret societies operating in the shadows, but maybe that story was based on a real criminal organization…

He caught Milton's bemused expression and chuckled, embarrassed. "Sorry. Got a bit caught up in my head."

"Not to worry. You know, I could see the family resemblance there. Val looked like that quite often when she was helping us organize on that asteroid."

"Huh." Zammi didn't know quite how to take that. He'd never imagined that he was anything like his sister, not when they'd been kids and certainly not now. When he came to think of it, though, they were both adept at putting aside their differences in order to accomplish a shared goal. Because those differences were still festering between them. The whole time he'd been in Noctis, he and Val hadn't said one word to each other about a single thing other than this job.

The motel was a step down in quality and style from the Mining Guild residences, and even the travelers' hostels he'd stayed in on the road with Val had been nicer, but it was clean and inexpensive, and the bed was nearly long enough for him. Zammi turned in early and slept soundly, the intensity of the day's work knocking him out. In the morning he rose early enough to get in a quick run before meeting the team at the warehouse, where they double- and triple-checked their equipment in between rehearsing their roles.

Val and Zammi continued to have a perfectly functional working relationship and continued to avoid talking about anything else. Zammi was a little surprised that she hadn't brought up the very fact that he was here. It would imply that he'd come around to her way of thinking, even though that wasn't entirely the case. He had believed it when Ivan had said he hadn't had any part in sabotaging the data, but Zammi knew that even if Ivan was innocent that didn't mean Helion wasn't involved. And maybe that Utopia Invest security team really was just after Val for her work on the mining site, but maybe they were keeping an eye on Helion's interests as well. Zammi did think that all the evidence pointed to Helion being in this all the way up to their soletta, but there was just no way to know for sure without taking a look at the original data.

The night before the job there was no offer to go for noodles from Milton. Rufus and Billie disappeared as soon as the workday was done, so Zammi found himself alone in the warehouse with Val, the awkwardness palpable between them. She was carefully taking down all their materials, wiping the holos, and deep cleaning all the surfaces. Fingerprints and DNA, she'd explained.

Zammi nodded and grabbed a disinfectant wipe. They worked in silence for several minutes, then when Val bagged the last of the used wipes, she turned to Zammi.

"This is when I'm supposed to tell you that you don't have to do this." Her face was hard, but Zammi could detect a hint of real emotion underneath. He couldn't tell if it was fear or sadness or something else, but it was familiar and it worried him.

"I'm supposed to remind you that if this all goes sideways that it could ruin you. No more tenure, no more university. Prison, probably. If there's a particularly aggressive security guard having a particularly terrible day... well." Val looked away. "Worse than prison. And so, as your big sister, and as the leader of this motley crew, I'm supposed to give you an out. Let you know that you can walk away, save yourself from whatever happens tomorrow. And the thing is, Zambo, that's exactly what I want you to do. Just take off, get out of here, go back to your life. It's a good life, and it's what you deserve. Not this." She waved her hand toward the pristine, empty warehouse.

"But the thing is, we need you. This operation is brittle as hell. If even one of us doesn't turn up tomorrow, the whole thing is shot." She reached out for a nearby chair, then realized that she'd already cleaned it, and drew her hand back without touching it. She stood there, awkwardly, not looking at Zammi.

"Who knows? Maybe that's OK. Maybe this is a bad idea, and we should be forced to call it off. I honestly can't tell anymore if what I'm doing is the right thing or not. But I wish I could tell you to just beat it. I'm sorry I can't."

In that moment, Zammi knew what it was that he saw in her face. His military historian colleagues would probably call it the burden of command, but he thought of it as the weight of responsibility, and Zammi realized that it had sat on Val's shoulders nearly his whole life. That was why he hadn't seen it or recognized it for what it was – it had always been there. That constant fear that she wasn't doing enough, or was doing the wrong thing, or that something bad would happen and she'd be accountable. That something bad would happen to him, specifically. He'd seen this look in her face when their dad was away on some work trip or another, and the dinner they'd planned had ended up on the floor. He'd seen it when Zammi was studying so hard for his entrance exams and the power had gone out in their place. He'd seen it for the last two days, maybe longer.

What had it been like for her to carry that burden? Now, at least, she was a capable adult, able to make the choice. But when she'd first taken on that mantle of responsibility, she'd only have been a child. To Zammi she had seemed so mature with her friends and her stolen sips of beer, but she'd only been thirteen. He could never have done what she had at that age. How had he ever expected her to cope with all that? No wonder she left as soon as he was old enough to manage without her. He had thought she was so selfish, but she had never once had anything just for herself. And even if he'd known, what could he have done? He was a child.

Well, he was an adult now, and he was going to make adult choices.

"I know what I'm getting into," he said, working hard to keep his voice even and calm. "I know the risks. I'll be there tomorrow."

Val closed her eyes and if she'd been someone else, they'd have been wet when she opened them. As it was, she grabbed the bag of rubbish and cleared her throat. "Get an early night," she advised as she walked past him to the door. "Tomorrow is going to be a lot."

CHAPTER TWENTY-FOUR

The Helion building in Corporate Square had seen better days. Its yellow and gray logo was faded and the newer, brighter green Utopia Invest sign underneath it outshone the original, even if it was half the size. Zammi knew that once, Helion had been a star among the various corporations on Mars, its soletta array focusing sunlight toward the planet providing heat and power. But that was history, and in the present Helion was obviously struggling.

Its large foyer was well kept and tidy, the potted plants watered and fertilized, but the carpet underfoot was threadbare, and the large holo still showed images of its crowning glory, the soletta. As if nothing, anyone alive today, or even their grandparents had done, was worth mentioning.

Zammi stood before the holo, struggling to even pretend to be interested in its outdated promotional content. He'd arrived with Billie, playing the role of the partner or friend who is just killing time while the other person runs an errand. Staring at the holo incredulously fit his role perfectly. He shuffled his feet around as if bored, though really, he was maneuvering himself to be able to make sure that the reality of the floor layout matched the schematics they'd been studying. Yes, there was the main staircase, with the hallway to the maintenance center to its left. There was the centrally located camera with its panoramic view of the foyer. He allowed himself to meander toward the staircase slightly, until he could see the access panel in the ceiling in the corridor.

He couldn't be sure from this position, but he was fairly certain that someone standing beneath that panel would not be visible to anyone at the reception desk, and the schematics showed that there were no cameras in this hall. So far, so good. A light buzz in his implant told him that it was go time, and he casually wandered to his position in the middle of the foyer. He flipped up a holo and stood arms akimbo, taking up as much space as he could. It wouldn't completely block the view of the front door, but every little bit helped. Besides, the pair at the reception desk had their hands full, as Billie's voice rose in pitch.

"I sent in my complaint weeks ago, directly to the senior vice president of accounts, and I demand to see someone who can correct this error. I am absolutely not paying for even one second where I was without power."

Billie's litany went on and, as increasingly desperate-sounding soothing noises came from reception, Zammi heard the front door swish open. That would be Val, though he didn't turn to look. He saw her in his peripheral vision, dressed in a Robinson Industries – Logistics Division uniform, a large box in her arms. She walked to the corridor by the stairwell, completely ignored by everyone, and Zammi commenced his well-practiced slow shuffle toward her. He was moving so slowly that he'd be difficult to notice unless he was being watched, and no one was looking at anyone but Billie who was now insisting upon a personal apology from the board.

Zammi slipped into the corridor, and he turned to face Val. She had disassembled the box, which was a thin polymer rather than the strong, thick material used in real packaging, and she was able to fold it into a palm-sized parcel which she handed Zammi. He stuffed it in a pocket then waited. He felt like he could hear time passing, but finally his implant buzzed again, and he knelt and hoisted Val up on to his shoulders. She was heavier than she looked, muscle packed on her compact body, but his days in the gym and their practice sessions had prepared him well. He stood smoothly, his back straight, and Val could just reach the ceiling and its access panel. She quickly opened it, popping it up into the crawlspace above, then Zammi took one of her feet in each hand.

He whispered, "One, two, three…" then lifted her straight up into the ceiling space. Once she was slightly up, she was able to push off on the edges of the open panel, so it wasn't as impressive as it might have looked. Still, Zammi's breathing remained ragged even after Val had silently closed the panel behind her.

He sidled back into the foyer, where security had finally been summoned to escort a now-shouting Billie out. He joined the group heading toward the door, deliberately catching the eye of one of the harried receptionists.

"I knew this wouldn't work," he said with a shrug. "But it was the principle of the thing, you know?"

"It was three and a half credits," the receptionist said, shaking his head as they reached the door. "All this over three and a half."

Zammi made a *what-can-you-do* gesture and worked his way closer to Billie.

"All right, let's just go, OK?" he said, placatingly, and Billie smacked his shoulder, realistically hard.

"Don't you start, too!" The security team made sure they were well off Helion property, then moved with remarkable rapidity back inside the building. A couple of the more junior-looking guards were posted to keep an eye out that they didn't try to come back, but Zammi and Billie put on a good show of arguing before slowly heading toward the nearby tram station.

"How did it go?" Billie asked once they'd gotten around the corner.

"All went to plan," Zammi said. "It's onto Phase Two, now."

They strolled along the sidewalk, unhurried, to the next corner, then turned into a small walkway between the back of the Helion building and what used to be the Interplanetary Cinematics soundstage before they'd built their massive complex in Deimos City. The recording jammer that IC had installed to ensure the privacy of its stars while on company property was still working, even though the building was used as rental storage space now. No one could see them, in person or otherwise.

Billie and Zammi were just beginning to get nervous when Rufus appeared at the mouth of the alley, carrying a light but well-stuffed backpack. The three of them waited. And waited.

Surely something must have gone horribly wrong, so Zammi pulled up a holo to check the time and saw that it was only ninety seconds past the time they'd expected Val to appear. It had felt like an eon, but the maintenance door eventually cracked open and Val poked her head out. She gestured silently for them to enter, that it was momentarily safe for them, and one by one they each crouched through the square aperture and stepped into the bowels of the building.

The maintenance level of the building was basic at best – exposed girders, uncoated prefabricated wall partitions, even the odd patch of Martian dirt floor. This area was mainly reserved for the robotic staff that cleaned overnight, as well as housing the air filtration units and onsite water reclamators and waste processing. It was not somewhere most people would choose to visit, and therefore a perfect staging ground. Zammi flipped up a holo and took a quick 360° panorama image of the room.

Rufus dropped his bag and the three others pawed through it, revealing coveralls from a well-known cleaning drone maintenance firm, complete with tool kits. They all slipped the uniforms over their clothes, Billie adding a branded cap to the outfit. Anyone looking closely would recognize the irate customer from earlier, but there was no reason for anyone to look closely. Maintenance contractors were as close to invisible as a human could get.

Zammi grabbed a couple of bots from the charging rack, making sure to choose ones which were as depleted as possible, then walked to the human-size door that led into the main building. Zammi caught Val's eye and the urge to make a glib remark was nearly overwhelming. He knew it was just anxiety, and also knew that they needed to keep as quiet and unobtrusive as possible. This was only going to work if they could blend in. So he took a deep breath, held it for a count of five, then swung open the door.

The hallway was deserted, which the heat maps of building activity that they'd studied previously had indicated was likely. But you never knew if someone wanted to sneak out to make a personal call or needed the toilet. Still, they'd been lucky, and once they climbed the three flights of stairs to the IT department, they split into two groups for the next part of the operation.

Billie and Zammi headed left while Val and Rufus went right, deeper into the interior of the floor. They were making for the server closet, where Rufus was going to work his magic, apparently. Zammi was the lookout stationed within eyesight of all entrances to the floor. He popped open one of the hatches which housed the floor's cleaning bots, and Billie pulled out the fully charged units contained within.

"I'll get rid of these." Zammi swiveled his head and watched Billie head back to the stairs toward the maintenance level, making no haste whatsoever, just like a typical hired contractor.

He turned on one of the bots he'd brought with him, its low battery indicator blinking red. He popped open a small panel with one of the specialized tools and turned off the indicator. He did the same with the other bot, then placed them back in the hatch. He pulled up a large holo from a handheld tab which displayed cleaning bot schematics, but which also concealed a camera pointed over his left shoulder. A second holo from his personal tab sat just in front of him, showing the view from the camera: eyes in the back of his head. He sat on his haunches and waited.

He had known that this was going to be the hardest part. Rufus and Val were doing the hard work of a couple of rounds of break and enter, with a little light systems hackery at the end to copy the data. Performing any of those tasks was well beyond Zammi's abilities, but he understood it intellectually enough. So long as they didn't get caught, it would be fine. And it was his job to make sure they didn't get caught.

No pressure.

The traffic data they'd studied had indicated that this was the quietest time on this floor during a normal workday, when the motion sensors and heat detectors were turned off. It was the obvious time for them to make their move, and so far not a soul had disturbed Zammi at his post on the floor next to the cleaning bots. He'd started to think that maybe this was all going to go as planned, when a loud klaxon sounded, and some hidden red light began to flash. The hallway was transformed into a scene where the enemy was attacking our heroes' spaceship on some old science fiction show.

Zammi grabbed both cleaning bots, and quickly opened their maintenance hatches and connected thin cables to their access ports. He flicked a couple of screens on the large holo just as a pair of security personnel came out of the lift tube.

"Hey, folks," Zammi said, infusing his voice with embarrassment. "Sorry about all this. Looks like one of these guys hasn't been charging properly and lost its mapping. Seems like it tripped the alarm over in this section." He pointed to a schematic of the floor on his holo, a room in the northeast corner outlined in red.

"These bots shouldn't be in that area," the taller guard said in a grave voice, her face puckered into a frown. "They have their own units which never leave the secure zone."

"I know," Zammi said, lazily. "That's why we're getting the light show." He twirled a finger to indicate the still strobing red lighting. "I'm taking these in for repair. It shouldn't happen again."

The tall guard looked at her partner, who nodded, almost bored. "We'll have to check it out, anyway," she said. "Regulations."

Zammi stared at her for a moment. "Suit yourself," he said with a shrug. "You think you can turn this racket off while you're at it?" He went back to the holo, making one of the bots emit a forlorn beep. It was barely audible in the din.

"Yeah," the guard said, chuckling. "Will do."

"Thanks," Zammi said, not looking up but giving them a wave. "Have a good one."

The two guards walked down the corridor to the server room where Val and Rufus were hopefully no longer engaged in any nefarious activity. Indeed, Zammi hoped that he'd wasted enough time for them to make their escape, but he hadn't seen them go into the stairwell. The alarms shut off, and his heart pounded as he packed up the holos. He collected the two cleaning bots to take to the maintenance level, just in case the guards decided to check the hatch.

He was opening the door to the stairwell when the guards passed him, the tall one giving him a friendly nod as she continued to talk to her partner. Zammi couldn't make out what they were saying, but they had no one in custody and they didn't seem like they were on the lookout for anyone. He felt relief coursing through his body as he took the stairs three at a time down to the maintenance level.

Billie was gone when he arrived, but that was to be expected. He slotted the bots back in their chargers, then pulled up the image of the room he'd taken when they'd arrived and gave the space a once-over to make sure nothing looked different. Satisfied, he turned his coveralls inside out to reveal a stylish colorful pattern and put them back on. He stepped out the hatch to the back alley where the rest of the team would be waiting.

Except, they were not. The alley was completely deserted.

CHAPTER TWENTY-FIVE

I knew this all seemed too easy, Zammi couldn't help but think as he tamped down a moment of panic. But they had planned for contingencies, including the team getting separated, so he took off out of the alley, sure to keep his body language neutral. Just another Noctis City citizen going about his daily business.

Each of them had separate instructions and, probably because of his long legs, Zammi had drawn the longest route. He strolled over several blocks until he found a small specialty grocery that dealt in goods imported from Earth. He walked down a narrow aisle of cans and jars and kept going straight through to the shop's back room, where he turned left and opened a door to a set of steps. Noctis City had been built on a raised base, inside which was a series of tunnels, cables, and pipes. A few of the former had initially been used as a transport system for the builders and later for the teams that maintained the infrastructure. The stairs led to one of these, and a short walk away Zammi found Milton with what looked like a squat buggy, albeit woefully underbuilt for the Martian surface.

"All aboard," Milton said in a normal voice, and Zammi jumped into the backseat, where Billie was waiting. He turned to the open rear compartment with its slab seating and grinned when he saw Val and Rufus. Milton slid into the driver's bubble, and they trundled off, the small wheels hardly making any noise on the concrete surface.

"It's good to see you. I wasn't sure you made it out," Zammi said.

Val grinned, but Rufus said, "We didn't."

"What?"

"The alarm went off sooner than we expected," Val explained. "Rufus had only just accessed the data we needed and hadn't even begun the download. It was leave right away and abandon the data or…"

"Or improvise!" Rufus said. "You know how we couldn't find any way into that room through the ducts?"

Zammi remembered the blueprints clearly. While there was obviously air circulation into the server room, the ducts which fed into that space had been fitted with full width fans. Undoubtedly, they were designed to avoid just this potential vector for illicit ingress, as well as increasing the circulation in the stuffy space.

"Well, just because we couldn't get out that way, that didn't mean there wasn't enough room for a couple of people to get cozy up in there," Rufus finished.

Zammi looked at Val incredulously. "You were hiding in the air ducts while the security guards were in there?" he asked.

"Not only that, the data was downloading the whole time.

If they'd stopped and looked at one of those screens..." Her voice trailed off and she shook her head. "I really thought that was it. End of the line."

"Nah, we were golden. I bet Zambrotta could've had a fine career as a holostar in another life," Rufus said. "Those guards bought the story hook, line, and sinker. They didn't even try to look around, they were just ticking off a box on the to-do list then heading on back to their rounds. You know how it is."

Val nodded, but relief still shone all over her face in a thin sheen of sweat.

"So, you got it?" Billie asked, as the smooth concrete gave way to a tunnel that had clearly not been designed for driving, then they turned into what looked like an abandoned water pipe. The ride got a lot rougher as Milton expertly avoided jutting out sections of pipe and chunks of detritus.

"After the guards took off, we counted to five, then snuck out of the ducts. Grabbed the goods, cleaned our traces, made for the meet up."

"Yeah, we got it," Val said, holding up a data chip. "Looks like all that hard work and planning paid off."

After several minutes of driving in places definitely not intended for that activity, Milton pulled into a wide area, and they all piled out of the buggy. A rickety metal ladder was affixed to the wall, and Val immediately started climbing. Zammi looked at Milton, who made an "after you" gesture, so he put his foot on the bottom rung. It felt solid, though when he looked up it was too dim to see what was up above. Val had disappeared, so there must be something up there.

It wasn't that long of a climb to a round hatch which opened into an unlit room. He scrambled up into it, the darkness of the tunnels making his vision sharp enough to make out the small space with its single desk and chair. Val was at a wall panel, poking at some switches, then the lights winked on. She moved back to the desk, and fished out a power terminal which she hooked into a hand tab. She slotted the data chip into its port and began tapping on a keyboard.

As the others emerged from the tunnels into the room, Val's face became more and more pinched with frustration, until she turned to the assembling group.

"Rufus, I think I need your expertise, here."

He ambled over to the desk and shooed Val out of the seat then squinted at the text scrolling up the holo as his fingers flashed over the keyboard. He made a pensive noise at the back of his throat, but when Val asked, "What?" he said nothing.

"What's going on?" Billie asked.

"I think the file is encrypted," Val said, and Billie groaned.

"We planned for this, right?" Zammi asked.

"Sure. I was just hoping we'd catch a break."

"Hope for the best, but expect the worst," Milton said, with a philosophical air.

Disconcerting noises continued to emanate from Rufus who was busily working at the desk, but no one interrupted him. It was as if they feared that they would disrupt whatever magic spell he was weaving to coerce the file to give up its secrets.

After a period of increasing tension, Val finally said, "Do we need to settle in for the long haul, here? This place isn't set up for an overnight stay – or even a few hours."

For a moment it seemed that Rufus didn't even realize that she'd been speaking, but then he stopped working on the terminal and leaned back in the chair. It was as if he were a balloon which had sprung a leak.

"It's no good," he said, voice flat. "There's nothing I can do here."

To everyone's credit, there were only murmurs of the "you did your best" variety, although Zammi was certain that he wasn't the only one who was rocked by disappointment. He'd already tagged this day as "successful" in his mind, and having to reframe the situation was surprisingly difficult.

"Is there maybe someone you know who could…" Val started, gently.

Rufus shook his head. "I've done all anyone could do with these." He wiggled the fingers of both hands. "The trouble is that this data is secured by a physical token, made specially by Helion. If we had one, I might be able to recode it, if we got access to the schema they used, but as it is…" He spread his hands out in a gesture of surrender. "We're out the airlock without a spacesuit."

It took a while for the dejection to wear itself out, but finally they all agreed that there was nothing more to do here and the best course of action was to split up.

"I'll get rid of the buggy," Milton said, then disappeared back down into the tunnel along with Billie. Zammi didn't know if the old miner was going to dump it somewhere or break it down for parts. He wouldn't have been surprised if it were the latter.

Rufus left, offering another apology on his way out and making sure that Val had his contacts in case they managed to get a hold of a genuine Helion security token. It wasn't outside the realm of possibility, but Zammi didn't think any of them were up for another try. Not yet, anyway.

Zammi and Val found themselves alone in the sad little room, and given everything that had happened, Zammi just didn't have the energy to fight with her anymore.

"So, what now?" he asked.

"I don't know." That wasn't an admission she made often, and Zammi guessed that she was feeling as drained as he was.

"I guess we should split up," Zammi suggested.

Val nodded, obviously exhausted. "I'll take the car, you grab the next train. We probably should lie low for a bit."

"I don't even know what that means for me." Zammi walked to the only door of the room, then stopped at the threshold. "You take care, Val."

"Always," Val said, but she couldn't manage the usual swagger. "You, too."

Zammi didn't recognize the street outside, but that didn't surprise him. He hadn't spent much time in Noctis City, and he didn't have a terribly good sense of an internal map no matter where he was. He'd never missed it, always having access to the comms net and his implanted holo. Now was no exception, and he quickly pulled up an easy route back to his motel. As he followed the directions, he amused himself by thinking about the roots of the word "motel." Originally, it referred to lodgings where a patron could drive their ground car up to the door of each unit – a motor hotel. It was hard to imagine such a structure here on Mars; rovers and buggies weren't used inside the domes, so there would be no motor to drive up. Of course, one day things might be different, when open cities were possible and people might drive up to any building. What a strange world that would be, Zammi thought, as he slid into a seat on the tram.

He knew what he was doing, finding refuge in the trivia of history rather than thinking about how he'd just committed a crime for absolutely nothing. Rather than thinking about whether or not he was ever going to see any of his family again.

The power of ruminating upon odd little facts about the past wasn't quite enough, and Zammi pulled up the settings on his comm. He'd turned off notifications entirely for the last couple of days, thinking there couldn't possibly be anything more urgent than what he was doing. He took a breath, then flicked them back on, bracing for an onslaught of messages.

It wasn't as bad as he feared – Marius knew he was busy, so had left him alone to work. He'd never gotten a chance to let Fern know he was back in town, so she probably still thought he was on a roadie with Val. And Val… well, she had no reason to contact him. And so it was that all the missed messages, and there were over a dozen, were from Ivan.

Zammi wondered if he'd received as many messages from his father in his entire life as he had over the last few days. He didn't really want to know the answer, so he didn't check. They were all cheery vague versions of the same thing:

"Hey, kiddo, just checking in!"

"Hope you're doing well, I'm good."

"Feel free to call anytime! Day or night."

They were obvious attempts to keep the newly installed lines of communication open. It felt strange to be the one that he was reaching out to, but the way things had ended, Zammi struggled to imagine a scenario where Ivan would be trying to talk to Val. The bridge between his sister and father seemed completely broken.

Zammi had always thought of his father as someone who was oblivious to the inner workings of other people, but he knew now that it wasn't as simple as that. He still didn't understand Ivan's choices, and maybe he'd changed in recent years, but it was clear that now he wanted them to be a family, even if he didn't know what that looked like. Zammi had thought that was what he wanted, too, but now that it was achievable, he wasn't sure. Looking at all those messages, he couldn't help but wonder how his life would have been different if they'd come when he was ten years old, or twelve, or fifteen, or twenty-five.

But as much as he spent his life poring through the past, Zammi knew that time travel was a one-way ticket, one second per second into the future. What had happened could never be undone, but he could choose what he did now. If there was going to be a change, it was up to him to make it happen.

Ivan didn't answer immediately, but when he did pick up his face wore an eager expression, with only a hint of trepidation.

"Zambrotta! I'm glad to hear from you."

Zammi wondered how much effort it had taken his father not to mention how long it had been or that he'd been worried. He was grateful that Ivan had put in the work.

"Hey, Dad," Zammi said. "I'm sorry I didn't get back to you until now. We…" He stopped himself. Working with Val right now, after everything, was a complexity he didn't really want to have to explain. "I was on a job and I had all my notifications turned off."

"Of course, of course. Did it go well?"

He was just making conversation, Zammi knew, but maybe it was the stress of the past few days, or maybe the hope of renewed relationship with his father – or possibly it was just the loneliness of lying down in his rented room that made him actually answer the question.

"No, it really didn't go all that well," he said. "It went pretty badly, actually."

"Oh, I'm sorry to hear that," Ivan said, sounding genuinely concerned. "Is there anything I can do…" He bit back the rest of the sentence and visibly winced, and Zammi wondered if his father had been seeing someone. A counselor or therapist, someone who'd advised him not to try to insert himself into his children's lives even if that was what he most wanted to do. And if he was getting help, what would that mean? That this was more than just a free vacation and too little too late? Maybe Ivan was really trying to connect with Zammi, as two adult humans. Maybe there was hope for their family after all.

And maybe there was hope for more than just their family.

"Actually," Zammi said, "there might very well be something you can do."

CHAPTER TWENTY-SIX

"You did *not* tell our father that we broke into his place of employment and stole his bosses' secret data." It was technically a question, but the way Val was shouting, it was a statement. One to which Zammi, luckily, had the correct response.

"No, Val, I did not. All I said was that I wanted to borrow his data access token. That was it. He didn't ask why and I didn't offer."

"You don't think he's not going run off to those security goons as soon as he can and lead them right to us? Again?"

"Val, there were far too many negatives in that sentence, even for you, and no, I don't. I didn't get the impression that Helion even knows the data's been copied."

Val blew a breath of air out of her nose, and Zammi imagined that he could see steam. "And if you're wrong?" she asked, her voice dangerously calm.

Zammi looked away. He'd met Val at the place where she was staying – not another hostel or guild residence, but what appeared to be someone's apartment. Whoever it belonged to wasn't there, but it was unnerving to see his sister among the trappings of a home – stitched pillows on the chairs, worn blankets over their backs, pictures on the walls. Val had never seemed like a pictures on the walls kind of person to him. And she probably wasn't – this was not hers, that was evident by her own awkwardness around all its comforting knick-knacks. Zammi could sense that she was reining herself in. If this had been her apartment, he bet she would have thrown something at him when he arrived.

"Val, he's our father." He held up a hand to stop her before she went on another tear. "I know, he wasn't much of one, but he's still our dad. I refuse to believe he's just a shill for the corporate security goons." Zammi chanced a lopsided grin. "I mean, not for Utopia Invest, anyway."

Val stared at him, then chuckled. "You better be right about Helion not knowing about our operation, then," she said, the fight draining out of her.

"Yeah," Zammi said. "Just in case I'm not, Dad's on his way from Deimos now but we'll be meeting in a neutral, public place." He pulled up a map on his holo. "If any of the crew are still around, we could have a lookout up here." Zammi pointed at a twelfth-floor café with a large balcony on a building across the street from the square where he'd asked Ivan to meet. "Any signs of trouble, and we have a dozen escape routes." He pointed at the myriad ways in and out of the square.

"Not bad," Val said, and Zammi wasn't sure if she meant to say it out loud. "You're getting pretty good at this stuff."

Zammi shook his head. "Don't get any ideas. I cannot wait until I'm back being a boring history prof."

Val chuckled. "I doubt you're *that* boring." She punched his arm, hard enough that it hurt. "All right, I guess we'd better get ready."

Billie was set up at the café early, with a view of the activity below and an open voice channel to both Val and Zammi.

"All clear so far."

"Thanks," Val answered, then scanned the sparse crowd.

"The train has only just gotten in," Zammi said, checking the time on his holo. "He'll be a few minutes."

Val nodded but kept up her vigilance. She clearly wasn't looking only for Ivan. Her tension was seemingly contagious, as adrenaline flooded Zammi's body when he caught sight of a pair of security personnel heading toward them. It took much longer for the fight-or-flight to dissipate once he recognized the triangular logo of Mons Insurance on their jackets. Jackets which were nothing like the boxy uniforms of the Utopia Invest team that had been following them back in Deimos.

"This is ridiculous," he muttered to himself, but shook his head when Val asked him if he was talking to her. He couldn't believe that his own father would sell them out to Utopia Invest security – or even to his beloved Helion – but then why was he so jumpy? Was he as certain as he thought?

His stomach tightened when he caught a familiar face in the crowd, his father's wavy salt-and-pepper hair loose at his shoulders, giving Zammi a possible glimpse into his own future. He could do worse, certainly, though he'd lose the three-day stubble. For as long as Zammi could remember Ivan had cultivated a grizzled appearance, so at odds with his bookish sensibilities. Ivan did appear nervous, but he wasn't glancing about him as if there were any others among the crowd who were relevant to the meeting. His eyes were locked on Val and Zammi, and when he noticed them looking at him, he raised a hand in a tentative wave.

A beat passed, then Billie's voice came over the comms, even and calm. "No sign of anything."

Val glanced at Zammi, who raised his eyebrows then took a step toward Ivan.

"Hi, kids," Ivan said, awkwardly. "It's good to see you."

"You, too, Dad," Zammi said, while Val stood there rigidly.

Ivan glanced between the two of them, then his shoulders drooped. It was as if he'd decided to abandon the carefully cultivated demeanor that Zammi was increasingly certain he'd been advised to maintain.

"I'm pretty sure I wasn't followed," he said, directly to Val. "I mean, I'm not as good at this kind of thing as you are, but I was paying attention. This time." A look of chagrin crossed his face and Val seemed to soften for a moment. It didn't last.

"OK," she said, coldly. "You have the token?"

Ivan nodded and fished in his bag. He pulled out a small, yellow and gray disk, and handed it to Val. "I don't know what you two have gotten yourselves into, and I don't need to. But I do know what these tokens are used for, and how they're tracked. If you use this, it will be logged. And it will be traced back to me. There's no faking it with hackery, either. There's a set of biometric data stored in here, and the token has its own connection to Helion's network."

Zammi looked down at the token in Val's hand. Ivan had given it to her before he'd explained what that meant for him.

"Can't you just report it lost?" Val asked.

"Sure," Ivan said, with a wry smile. "But you know that biometric data I mentioned? Well it's not just to prove the token is mine. It's also part of the token itself. I expect the two of you would be able to use it just fine – they warned us that the matching algorithm is wide enough to pick up blood relatives. So, sure, I could say I lost it or whatever, but what do you think the odds are that they wouldn't take a stab in the dark and guess it was you two, especially since you're already on Utopia Invest's radar."

Val looked at Zammi. "Well, that's not great."

Ivan laughed. "So here's the thing. If you use that, I'm up to my neck in whatever you're doing. And that's fine. I've already made my peace with whatever consequences are coming for me. But I'd really prefer you fill me in on what I'm about to get in trouble for. You don't have to, and I'm not going to push. But it's what I'd like. So what do you say?"

Val held out her hand, the tiny disk seeming like it must have weighed a kilogram. She looked at Zammi and he nodded.

"OK," Val said, handing the token back to Ivan, "remember when I accused you of sabotaging some data?"

They explained it all: Val's undercover work at the Utopia Invest mine, Factorum's bad data, the heist at Helion. Zammi added in what they'd seen at the remote settlements, the struggle those communities were facing without access to water.

"It's going to get worse," Zammi said, and saw in Ivan's face that he not only agreed, but that he really understood what that would mean.

"I was telling you the truth when I said we didn't falsify any numbers," Ivan said, and Val nodded, though she refused to look him in the eye. "But that doesn't mean that no one in Helion sent bad figures to Factorum. If it was us…" He stopped talking then, as if he'd just heard what he'd said. "If it was Helion, then they need to be held to account. Whoever did it, and whoever was part of it. No matter where it goes."

Val turned toward him then, something not dissimilar to pride in her face.

"You know what this means," she said, "for you? There aren't too many scenarios where this ends up with you keeping your job."

Ivan nodded. "I've been a Helion man nearly my whole life. I gave everything to that company, and I know now that it was probably too much. But I didn't devote my life to them because I loved the work as much as it was something to fill the hole left by…" His voice caught and he turned away. Then it was as if he remembered something and he turned back to face Val and Zammi. Tears were falling freely down his face and he let them see. Zammi didn't think he'd ever actually seen his father weep before.

"I gave my life to the company because the people I wanted to give my life to were gone. But that was a mistake. The two of you reminded me of them so much, I couldn't handle it. But I was wrong, and that life… I should have given it to you." He held his hand out to Val, the token she'd returned still in his upturned palm. "I know it's too late, but you should have this, at least."

Zammi could barely see for the tears in his own eyes, but he could make out Val staring at their father.

"It's not too late," she said, reaching out and instead of taking the token, she held Ivan's hand.

"Let's do this together," Zammi said, putting his arm around the older man and feeling the tension of twenty-two years break and flow out of him.

The three of them stood there like that for a long time. After all those years, it wasn't long enough.

Val found another one of the Mining Guild's seemingly ubiquitous drop-in co-working spaces, and they waited until it was well into the evening and no one else would be there. Ivan literally looked around shiftily as Val signed into the room, and Zammi couldn't decide whether to laugh or slink off into the darkness. Really, they didn't even need privacy for what they were about to do – if Ivan was right, the jig would be up by morning at the latest.

Val slotted the data chip into a terminal and the now frustratingly familiar phrase *Place Token Near Reader* was centered in the picture. Ivan's hands were trembling, but only slightly.

"Dad, wait. You don't have to do this–" Val began, but in a fluid motion Ivan slapped the disk against the reader and held it in place. The text on the holo disappeared and it seemed as if time stopped. There was nothing – no warning, no klaxons, no data file.

And then, after what had likely been only a second at most, text and numbers began to scroll up the screen. A whooping noise startled Zammi out of the tunnel vision he'd found himself experiencing and he turned to face Val and Ivan, who were both grinning widely.

"OK, we did it," Ivan said. "Now let's see what it was that they were so busy hiding."

"If I'd wanted to spend my life poring over spreadsheets I would have made different choices," Val complained, not for the first time. There was a lot of information, and while it was well organized and searchable, the system presupposed that the user could articulate what they were looking for. For some reason, "evidence of malfeasance" wasn't a search term that the database understood.

"If we start with the information from the report I worked on, we can at least eliminate everything before that."

"Good idea, Dad," Zammi said, flicking his fingers in a practiced move to slice the data.

"Whoa," Val said, watching. "How did you do that?"

Zammi shrugged. "You get pretty good with gesture shortcuts when you're going through centuries of primary sources."

"Well, this is better, but it's still a lot," Ivan said. "We need to narrow it down to find the figures relating to the asteroid."

"I've got this," Val said, delicately waving the holo controls over to her chair. She began entering a series of search terms – minerals, metals, water – along with ranges in percent.

"How do you know what numbers to expect?" Zammi asked as Val typed figure after figure, never once stopping to look up a number.

She glanced up at him. "I'm in the Mining Guild, remember? You don't get past junior apprentice without knowing this stuff like you know your name."

"Huh." Zammi noticed Ivan's smug smile as he leaned back

watching his two kids. So it took a global crisis and some minor larceny to get them all to work together – maybe it was a small price to pay.

"All right, I think I've got a manageable data set here," Val said, flicking the holo so they could all see it. There was still a lot to get through, but at least it seemed possible now.

"I guess we break it up in chunks and each take a third," Zammi suggested to murmurs of agreement, and in a couple of finger flicks it was done. Each of them sat with their own holos and for several hours there was nothing but the taps of fingertips on the tabletop as they each made notes or copied files. The sunlight reflected from Helion's own soletta was beginning to brighten the dome outside when they came together again, Val passing around cups of coffee and tea from the credit-operated machine.

"Let me see it all together," Ivan said, blowing on his tea absently. He squinted at the numbers and rapidly moved things around, then frowned. He rearranged the data again, then sorted it in a new order. "Hrmph," he grunted.

"What?" Val asked impatiently, and Zammi shushed her. Ivan was obviously on to something, and there was no point in trying to rush it.

"I don't get it," Ivan said after another few minutes. "This is the data that was sent to Factorum from our report, and it hadn't been tampered with. You can see here that there hasn't been an update since it was originally filed." He pointed at the system-generated timestamp.

"Couldn't that have been altered after it was sent?" Val asked and Ivan shrugged.

"I'm no programmer, so maybe? But I don't think so." He

spread his thumb and first two fingers wide to enlarge the image. "This is the file that was sent to Factorum – you can see the network path there." Zammi was familiar with the long list of nodes a message took from sender to recipient, and it looked legitimate.

"And see here, this is exactly what I remember." Ivan manipulated the image to show a single cell of data: the column was labelled "Pb lead" and the contents read "Dangerous."

"So you're saying that everything here makes it look like Helion sent the full and correct data to Factorum." Val leaned back in her chair. "The data they gave us was definitely different." She pointed to the image. "That was a zero. What gives?"

Ivan stared at the text and digits. "I have an idea," he said, cryptically, "but I'm going to need a copy of the Factorum files." Val nodded and sent him the data. Ivan nodded to confirm that he got it, yawned widely, then took a sip of his now-cold tea. He grimaced.

"I'm not up to these all-nighters any more, and I can write a script to see if what I'm thinking is right. It'll run for a few hours while I get a little shuteye then I'll get back to you." He stood up and stretched.

"So, Dad," Zammi began cautiously. "How long do you think we've got before Helion comes looking for us?"

"I don't know," he admitted. "I mean, there's nothing incriminating here, so they might not care about this data at all. But I also wouldn't be surprised if the fact that I accessed it from an offsite location flags something. I guess we'd better keep our eyes open."

"Where will you be?" Val asked. "You going back to Tharsis?"

"Nah, I'll stay here for now, grab a bunk in a hostel or something. I'm still on paid vacation, remember?"

Zammi almost made a crack about how Ivan better make the most of it, but the thought that his father might be losing his job over this took the fun out of it, and he said nothing.

As Ivan left it occurred to Zammi that losing a job might be the least of their concerns.

"Should we be going into hiding or something?" he asked Val.

She shrugged and said matter-of-factly, as if going on the lam after a heist was the most normal thing in the world, "Probably."

CHAPTER TWENTY-SEVEN

In an abundance of caution, Zammi checked out of the motel and met up with Val at the rover lot by the south airlock.

"Dad's not the only one who could use a nap," he said as he threw his duffel in the aft compartment.

"We both slept in here loads of times when we were kids," Val reminded him, jerking her head toward the Oryx. Zammi raised an eyebrow, then looked pointedly down at his body.

"Some things have changed since then."

"Makes up for being able to reach the top shelf, I guess," she said as she opened the rover and crawled into the backseat. "Front's all yours if you want to give it a try."

A full-body exhaustion was threatening to take over and Zammi was willing to fold himself into some kind of origami if he had to in order to get a little rest. As it turned out, if he stuck his legs on the passenger side dash, leaned the driver's side seat back, and lay on his left side, it wasn't that bad. Or at least it was comfortable enough that he dropped off to sleep in a few minutes.

He woke to an incessant vibration from his implant, and when he sat up, he had forgotten where he was and knocked his head against the door jamb.

"Where's the fire, Zambo?" Val's muffled voice came from the backseat where she was completely hidden under a pair of jackets.

"It's Dad."

Zammi's bleary eyes took in his father's face, a sheen of excitement visible in the grainy image.

"I figured it out!"

They met at a public park near the budget hostel where Ivan had slept, Val with the hood of her jacket up, and Zammi with his hair shoved under a knit cap and wearing a pair of oversized polarized goggles. They were terrible disguises, but they might fool an automated facial recognition system. Hopefully.

"Not a number," Ivan whispered excitedly.

"Come again?" Val blinked at him in confusion.

"The data we sent showing the lead figures for the asteroid. It was not a number. It was text, you know, the word 'Dangerous' but I guess Factorum's system was expecting a number, and when it couldn't parse the word, it threw an error. 'Not a Number.' The data was probably set to null at that point. Then, when that data was converted to a human-readable document, that null got turned into a zero, and…"

"And dangerous lead levels became zero parts per million."

"Exactly."

"But how come no one noticed?" Val asked. "I mean, any human eyeball reading the word *dangerous* would know that something was wrong."

Ivan shook his head. "That's the problem. There was no human eyeball, not at that part of the process. All these reports just get sent to different systems and machine processed into useful material. Labor saving, you know. I don't think a single human being in Factorum would ever have seen the word 'dangerous' in these files."

"But how could this kind of mistake happen?" Zammi asked.

"Probably a better question is why it doesn't happen all the time," Ivan said. "The terraforming project has been an incredible experiment in cooperation and competition. We've achieved great things by working together and we've pushed ourselves to amazing heights by challenging each other. But we're still a loose collection of individual entities, each of us doing things our own way. Every corporation has its own data systems, with its own templates and defaults. There's only so much interoperability, which, as we see here, isn't enough."

"It wouldn't be that hard to standardize this, would it?" Zammi asked and Ivan shook his head.

"Not that hard to create, but probably tough to implement. Everyone's got their own ways of doing things, and no one wants to change for someone else."

"Yeah, but no one wants to die of thirst either," Val added.

"So I guess we need to get back to Dr Huang at Factorum," Zammi said after a minute.

"I'll contact Krissy," Val said.

Zammi narrowed his eyes. "Krissy?"

"What? It's not a crime to know someone's nickname. She's genuine. I wanted to help her. I'm allowed to have a friend, you know," Val insisted.

"Still. You told her we suspected Helion, didn't you?" Zammi asked. "That's where the information in that *Deimos Times* article came from . It came from you."

"I…" Val looked down. "I might have mentioned a thing or two. I definitely never said we knew anything for sure."

"Oh Val," Ivan said, but he couldn't keep the smile from his face. "Don't ever change."

"Well, you'd better get on the horn and make sure she knows what really happened," Zammi said. "Before real accusations fly and things get out of control."

"Whatever you say, boss," Val said snidely, but she was grinning as she walked a few steps away to deliver the news.

"You see what I see?" Ivan asked in a low voice, awkwardly keeping his head in place while swiveling his eyes toward a spindly stand of trees. Zammi followed his gaze, trying for surreptitious, when he spotted them. At first he thought it was the same duo who'd been following them back in Deimos, but they didn't walk the same way. And the jackets were different, gray with yellow piping.

"Helion," he groaned.

"We should probably make tracks," Ivan said, moving casually toward the tram stop.

"I'll get Val. We'll head out a different way." Ivan nodded and stepped toward Zammi as if for a hug, then caught sight of something over his shoulder and stepped back.

"You see them?" Zammi asked.

"Take care, kiddo," he said, "I'll talk to you soon." Then he briskly took off toward the tram stop. Zammi didn't have time to contemplate when was the last time he'd embraced his father, and instead walked toward his sister who, by the look on her face, had moved beyond the professional part of the conversation. Zammi mouthed the word "security," and Val quickly ended the call. She fell in behind him as they strolled toward a different train station.

Val nodded curtly. "Goons," she half-whispered, "hired goons."

Zammi frowned. "Surely not hired. No one uses contractors for security anymore, not since the Lunar uprisings. They're almost certainly salaried employees."

Val shook her head and chuckled. "Oh, Zambo. Don't you ever change, either."

They took a circuitous route back to the Oryx, and piled in.

"Do these windows open?" Zammi asked, wrinkling his nose.

"This is a classic Mars rover, Zambo. What do you think?" She blinked her eyes slowly, her face deadpan. "No, the windows do not open."

"Ugh." Zammi kept the passenger side door open as long as possible, and wafted his hands from the inside out to try and circulate the stale air around.

"Try the door," Val said, then demonstrated by rapidly pulling it almost closed then pushing it away. Zammi did the same and soon the car smelled, if not better, at least less bad.

"Humans are disgusting," he said when they finally closed up and the car pulled out of its stall and on to the road heading out of Noctis City.

"Oh, it's been way worse than this," Val said, cheerfully as they waited for the airlock to cycle. "One time I was living in here for a couple of weeks and the portable toilet crapped out. Ha ha, see what I did there?" She turned to him and grinned.

Zammi shook his head. Val was doing a very good job of being disarming. This was how she always won in the end – she turned on the charm, made people laugh, and they just kind of forgot about all the things she'd done to infuriate them. Maybe it wasn't people in general, maybe it was just Zammi. But he'd been down this road before and he was tired of it.

"Val, stop."

"I can't. The airlock is on an automated cycle."

"That's not what I mean," Zammi said, exhausted.

Val shrugged and kept on driving. "OK."

She didn't say anything, just kept her eyes on the road ahead. Zammi wasn't sure if she understood what he'd been saying or was just shutting up because it was easier than talking. Either way, he found the silence an awkward relief.

Once they were off the road and the car was on auto, Val shifted around in her seat, poking at the console. In a moment, music blared out of the speaker, but Val turned it down without being asked. Something from Papi's collection of files, ancient Earth music by the sounds of it, but at least it was something Zammi didn't mind. Not BulaBula Noise or any of their imitators.

A couple of songs later, Zammi took a breath. "Val, I don't want to fight. But I also don't want to have to keep pretending like everything is fine when it's not. It's so, totally, not."

She didn't respond, and for a minute Zammi wondered if she was ignoring him, but then she said softly, "Yeah."

What did that mean? Zammi didn't know, but it felt like an opening.

"I don't think he's going to say anything, but you remember how you accused Dad of being part of a sabotage that, as it turned out, didn't even happen? Are you planning on dealing with that at all? And, honestly, where did that even come from? Talk about leaping to a conclusion!"

"You probably never see this with your nose stuck in a dusty old book, but I deal with corporate malfeasance every day. You want to talk about Occam's Razor? The simplest explanation is someone saw a way to make a credit."

"Seriously, Val," Zammi said after a beat. "You can't really think that about Dad. He's not perfect, boy do I ever know that, but this…"

"OK, thanks, Zambo, I get it. I messed up. You don't have to beat it into the ground." There was tension visible along her jaw and Zammi realized he had hit a nerve.

"Yeah, sorry," he said gently. "I really would like to know where that all came from, though."

Val stared out the window, the plain beneath them almost like a carpet with its grasses and moss finally taking root and spreading. But there were already a few patches that were beginning to dry out, turning brown due to reduced irrigation.

"You have always had a hard time with Dad," she said to the window. "I knew it, he knew it, everyone did. He never knew how to deal with you, with all that quiet anger simmering inside, hiding behind your books and good grades and academic ambition. So I had to be the bridge, the one who kept up with each of you, the one that kept it all together as much as I could. Even after I left, that was all still up to me. Until this whole business, when was the last time you'd talked to Dad?" She didn't wait for an answer. "It was always me, Zambo, keeping this family together. But you can't really believe that I wasn't mad at him, too? That I didn't hate him for basically abandoning us after Mom and Papi died? I know now that he'd gotten lost in his grief, I kind of even knew it then, but we were just kids. And all that sadness and loss, it happened to us, too. We needed him and he wasn't there so I had to do it." Her voice caught and she was quiet for a moment.

"I guess I wanted something real I could blame him for," she said.

"Something you could be unambiguously angry about?"

"Yeah, that." She finally turned to face Zammi. "You know, I was always a little envious of you for that. How you got to just be mad at him, with no complexity. I always thought it would be easier."

Zammi laughed without mirth. "That's really what you thought it was like for me?"

Val shrugged.

"I knew that Dad wasn't some kind of villain. I always did, even when I was little. Back then I wasn't even angry, just vaguely convinced that somehow it was all my fault. Dad turning away from me – from *us*, I guess. You were there, though. I thought you'd always be there, but then…" This time it was his turn to stare resolutely at the Martian horizon. "Then you left me, too, and I couldn't pretend that there wasn't a single common element to it all. Me. Everyone was leaving me."

"Zambo…" Val began, but then her voice trailed off.

"It's OK, I can see the childishness of that analysis now. But it felt like that for so long, you know, it's hard to just turn it off.

And the only way I ever knew how to manage that hurt was to push you both away. So I poured myself into school and then work, and that wasn't a bad choice. I love what I do. But for so many years I told myself the story that I didn't need family, that I was better off on my own… it is so hard to throw that fiction away. Even if I know it's the right thing to do."

They both sat in silence for a moment, then Val reached over and squeezed Zammi's arm.

"Is this that thing I've heard of," she asked, "it's called maturity, I think."

Zammi laughed. "Yeah, maybe. I'm not sure I know anything about it."

"I don't know, it seems like we're becoming experts in it," Val said, then frowned as a notification buzzed on her comm. She looked down at her holo and her eyes widened. "And it's a good thing, too, because I fear we're going to have to teach that concept to a whole bunch of people."

"Oh?"

She turned to face Zammi. "You know how we said we'd better get the news to Factorum before things get out of control?"

"I do, and we did, right?"

"Well…" Val made that fake, awkward smile that indicated that things had not quite gone to plan. "We did and we didn't? I got a hold of Krissy – and told her that it was all just a data mistake, and she went to pass it on to the board, but…"

"But *what*, Val?"

"But the board already voted to take matters into their own hands."

"What does that even mean?" Zammi asked.

"I'm not sure but I don't think it's something as simple as taking them to court." Val flicked the holo message up to the car's console screen and Zammi read it.

Come quick! The board's about to retaliate and I'm worried people are going to get hurt. Or worse.
KH

CHAPTER TWENTY-EIGHT

"I can't believe this has gotten so far out of control." Dr Krissy Huang hung her head over a steaming mug of tea, her long dark hair creating a curtain over her face as she rested her forehead in her hands. "And it's all my fault."

They were in a little hole-in-the-wall teahouse far from the corporate center in Deimos City. Since they'd arrived in Deimos, neither Zammi nor Val had seen any more Helion security officers on their tail, but that didn't mean anything. They might have wised up and changed into other uniforms. Or maybe they just hadn't caught up with them yet, there was no way to know. Either way, Zammi was jumpy, and Val's eyes couldn't stop darting back and forth between entrances and exits, and the pair planned to stay as far away from Helion as they could.

"Just take a breath and start at the beginning," Val said, unusually gentle.

"Remember when you asked for the original data on the ice asteroid, and I said I couldn't give it to you? Because of the non-disclosure clause?"

Val nodded and Zammi wondered where she was going with this. Obviously, Val had gotten the files from Dr Huang, Zammi had figured that out even before he knew they'd been talking. But now he wasn't so sure. The look of naked curiosity in Val's face certainly implied that she didn't know where the data had come from.

"I didn't just say no right off the bat. I really wanted to give those files to you, so I put in a formal request to suspend the NDA. It took a while, longer than I expected, really, but finally I got back the answer – no. It was disappointing, and I really did think about just letting a datachip fall out of my pocket or something, but I'm too much of a stickler for the rules."

Zammi frowned. "So, if you didn't give us the files…"

Krissy shook her head. "Apparently, my request went all the way to the board. And you didn't hear this from me, of course, but the current board is not exactly a united front these days."

"Oh?" Val leaned in toward her.

"The rumor mill says that everything is a fight right now. There's a group of newer directors who want to take Factorum in a much more aggressive direction, high-risk, high-reward kinds of projects."

"OK," Zammi said, still not following. His confusion must have shown in his face, because Krissy leaned back in her seat.

"I guess you don't follow the terraforming ratings, do you?"

Zammi shook his head. The rankings of the various organizations building Mars held no interest for him. He didn't even really understand what would be the point of quantifying their contributions to the project. It wasn't like you could win at something like terraforming Mars.

"Well, the board does pay attention to the ratings, quite

closely. It's perhaps one of the few concerns all the directors share. As of the last rankings, Factorum was third, and it was a very close third. The number two corporation is only a point ahead of them."

Zammi's eyebrows shot up. "Oh." He might not understand why anyone would be competitive about making the planet livable, but he did understand competition. The new lake would have put them into second place, easily. As it was, they were probably going to have to fight to keep from dropping in the ranks.

"I don't get it," Val said. "This makes it sound like they'd be perfectly happy to give us whatever information we needed to find out what happened to the asteroid."

Krissy made a face. "Yes and no, and that's the whole issue. Apparently, the newer directors thought just like you said, and wanted to suspend the NDA. The old guard, though, are still very much of the school that we should take care of this kind of thing in-house. They were absolutely livid when you two were called in, but by then it would have been a public relations disaster if they'd made a stink. Honestly, I'm expecting the board to self-destruct any second now."

Zammi took a beat to think about what Dr Huang was telling them.

"So, you're saying it was someone from this new part of the board that leaked the data to us."

Krissy nodded. "I don't know that for sure, but it stands to reason. Especially considering what's happening now."

Val groaned. "What's happening now?"

Movement from across the tearoom caught Zammi's attention and he reached below the table to poke Val in the leg.

"What's happening now is we're going to quietly and carefully vacate the premises," he said, softly. "Helion's here."

The tearoom was a popular spot for young Deimosians, and they'd purposefully chosen a time when it would become crowded. There was now a crush of people between their table and the door, which was exactly what Val had been counting on.

"Let's go," she said, dropping to a crouch to hurry toward the hallway where the bathrooms were located. Zammi followed suit and Krissy made to join them when Val hissed, "No! You stay here. You haven't done anything wrong and you don't need to get caught up in this."

"But—" the Factorum engineer started, but Val gave her a hard look.

"No," she said. "I'll be in touch. It's better that you don't know where we're going. You know, just in case." Then she winked at Krissy and took off toward the bathrooms. Zammi followed, standing up straight once he was in the hallway and taking off at a run to follow Val into the restaurant's back room. Val lifted a hand to wave at the kitchen staff, who she must have sweet-talked or paid earlier to effect this exact getaway strategy. They burst out the backdoor and Zammi was half-expecting to be met by a team from Helion, but there was nothing but a tight passage used for deliveries. They sauntered out of the alley and jumped on the first tram that came by.

"Now what?"

Val looked up at Zammi, a glint in her eyes. "Now we check out the seedy side of town."

There wasn't really a seedy side to Deimos City, but there

were some neighborhoods which were at the more affordable end of the spectrum, including a few places where the zoning between commercial and residential spaces was treated more like a suggestion than a rule. After another of their now-typical labyrinthine transport routes, Val led them to the unmarked door of a nondescript warehouse, which she opened with a physical key.

"I didn't know they made those anymore," Zammi said, as she pocketed the anachronistic object.

"There will always be folks who need anonymity," Val said, lifting her left hand with its embedded ID chips and waving it in Zammi's face. "This is convenient, but it's anything but anonymous."

The interior of the warehouse had been bisected by prefab walls, and they found themselves in a utilitarian foyer. The resulting units were obviously not rated for residential space, and Zammi could clearly make out the sounds of competing music being played in a couple of the rooms. Elsewhere someone was having a loud voice call and someone else was playing an old holomovie.

"Yeah, this will do," Val said, leading Zammi down a narrow hallway. One of the doors about two-thirds of the way along was open and she walked inside. It was surprisingly well furnished, with a permanently fixed bed and a table with two comfortable-looking chairs. Val closed the door and slid the bolt, then sank into one of the chairs.

Zammi tested out the bed and it seemed solid enough, then stood up to inspect the walls for a fold-down cot. After determining that such an item was distinctly lacking in this space, he flopped down on the bed again.

"How long do you think we're going to have to stay here?" he asked, looking at Val dubiously.

She looked pointedly at the single bed. "Don't sweat it," she said. "I expect we'll be gone by tomorrow, and I don't plan on sleeping here tonight."

"Do I want to know?" Zammi said.

Val laughed. "I like the way your mind works, Zambo, but sadly that's not the plan. I have another one of these spots scoped out, and I figured that for once we're better off splitting up."

"Oh." Zammi discovered that he didn't relish the idea of being left alone with Helion security staff on his tail, but Val was right. It would be harder for Helion to catch them both if they were separated.

"OK, I guess that's fine. So, what's the plan for now?"

"Now, we see if we can figure out what Krissy was talking about."

There were several outlets that specialized in analysis of the terraforming ratings and even a couple of bookmakers taking odds on future changes. Anyone who'd shorted Factorum would have made a bundle after the asteroid debacle. Zammi and Val split the sources and they scanned the news and speculations for anything related to Factorum.

"You find anything?" Val asked.

"We only just started," Zammi complained. "Reading takes time, you know."

Val grunted. "What is with these people and their obsession with trying to guess what some other corporation is going to do?" she asked, idly.

"A person could ask the same about those folks who, say, like to fix up old rovers," Zammi said.

"That's different! At least you can drive an old rover."

"Well, guessing right about what projects will get funded next can be pretty lucrative," Zammi said, showing her the bookmakers' odds on ThorGate demonstrating a working warp ship capable of carrying freight and passengers within the next decade.

Val snorted. "Warp drive. What a waste of time and energy. Why don't we focus on making sure the planet we have right here is habitable before we try to take off to new ones?"

Zammi stared at her. "That's kind of an old-fashioned perspective you have there. In case you didn't know, it was a pretty common view on Earth back before we went to the stars, before anyone even dreamed of coming here."

"And they were probably right, too," Val said, hotly. "We're already here, so obviously we have to make the best of the situation we're in. But we don't have to make things worse. There are too many people whose eyes are fixed so intently on the next big thing that they can't see the suffering that's going on right in front of them. You think ThorGate cares about the water situation in those remote communities? You think the people staking their fortunes on these bold explorations give a wit about the individuals breaking their backs to make it possible?"

Zammi said nothing for a moment, then sniffed. "I can't believe you'd have such a selfish, narrow-minded view. If no one thought about the future, we'd all still be living in mud huts."

"And if no one cared about what's going on right now, there

would be people starving to death while others live in luxury. Oh, wait, that's exactly what happened on Earth. Surely, we can do better here."

They sat in surly silence. Zammi tried to read what was on his screen, but he couldn't seem to focus on the words. "Obviously, you're not wrong," he said, after a moment. "Addressing the immediate issues we have now is vital, of course it is. But it doesn't have to be an either-or situation. Humans as a whole have never been content with merely persevering through the status quo. We're curious, we're hungry for new opportunities. The inherent spirit of humanity is to explore, to pursue new experiences, and those aren't negative impulses. It's just a matter of finding the right balance between the needs of the present and the vision of the future."

"Is that from one of your books?" Val asked, clearly trying to keep the sarcasm from her voice, if not succeeding entirely.

Zammi laughed, though. "Not verbatim," he said, "at least, I don't think so."

"Hang on," Val interrupted, her entire demeanor changing as she flung the screen she was reading up to the larger holo. "Check this out."

Spotted along a quiet trade route, someone appears to be preparing to aim a ball of ice toward our fine red planet, sources tell MarsWatch. A thorough perusal of the project timelines of all the major players reveal nothing in the line of cometary activity, but there are clear signs of rockets being installed on a small icy comet on the edges of the Rocks.

Our in-house trajectory nerds confirm that it is likely to
be en route to Mars, probably to expand an existing lake.
Not a moment too soon, say we at MW, after the Factorum
misstep earlier this quarter.

"That Factorum reference isn't anything new," Zammi pointed out. "This could be anyone."

"Yeah, but what about this?" Val pulled up the original Factorum data that Ivan had worked on, and found the executive summary. "Back when they first planned to bring down that asteroid, they'd done one of those studies to determine the viability of the project. The original proposal had been to aim a comet at the planet; this asteroid project was just a backup until…" She grimaced. "Until it looked like the ice on the asteroid was so pure."

"So you think they've just gone back to Plan A?" Zammi asked, doubtful. "It's a stretch. And why all the secrecy? It's a perfectly valid project."

"Maybe it's not an official Factorum project," Val suggested.

"The rogue faction on the board."

"Could be."

Zammi scowled in thought. "Let's say this is it. So what? A big block of ice would be great for everyone, not just Factorum. And wasn't Dr Huang worried about people being hurt or something?"

"Yeah." Val's fingers flicked rapidly through the MarsWatch article, until she pulled up a projected trajectory for the mystery comet. "Oh no. We're definitely on the right track." She pointed to the likely impact zone, a small lake in Shalbatana Vallis.

"I don't get it," Zammi said. "That's a great spot. There's nothing around for kilometers."

Val shook her head and pointed at a section just to the southwest of the lake. "This is the site of a new settlement that's planned to open next year."

"Oh," Zammi said, "how do you know that?"

"I get around," Val said, vaguely. "It's been a long time since a new settlement was global news. As these MarsWatchers probably know, you find out more by actually going around and talking to people than reading any number of reports."

Zammi's experiences of the past few days had forced him to agree, so he figured Val knew what she was talking about. He couldn't help but imagine the impact of a comet crashing into even a small lake. Anything on its shore would be subsumed under the resulting tsunami. "That's not ideal. Do you know whose settlement it is going to be?"

Val looked at him, her mouth a hard line. "It's Helion's. It's not just going to cost them a future settlement. There are staff onsite now. If that comet comes down while they're there…"

Zammi's imagination took over again and he grimaced. "Right. That's no good. So how long do we have?"

Val's eyes darted to the article and then she literally counted on her fingers. "If this article is right, the comet is already on its way."

CHAPTER TWENTY-NINE

"How long do we have?" Zammi repeated, this time with urgency.

"A couple of days, a week at best," Val said.

Zammi let out a breath. "You don't think it's a coincidence, do you?" he asked. "A Helion settlement destroyed by a Factorum comet after we basically accused Helion of sabotaging their asteroid?"

"No, I don't," Val said, miserably. "And using the word 'us' there was kind of you, but not accurate. This is my fault. I'm the one who told Krissy about our suspicions, and I had to know she'd pass that on. How could she not?"

"But they know by now that it wasn't Helion," Zammi said. "That it was all just a misunderstanding."

Val shrugged. "Do they? I mean we haven't exactly had an opportunity to present a report. I told Krissy, but she said the board hasn't met since before this all went down. I honestly have no idea who knows what anymore."

Zammi put his head in his hands. What had they done? And what were they going to do about it now?

As if reading his thoughts, Val clapped her hands together and said, "Right. We've got two angles of attack here. One, try to reach the people behind this comet and get them to scrub the project."

"They wouldn't have to abandon it completely. They could just redirect landfall to somewhere safer," Zammi suggested.

"Yes!" Val said, excited, "of course, that's a much easier sell. That's step one. But we should also get a hold of the people on the ground at that Helion settlement and help them to evacuate."

Zammi raised his eyebrows. "Are we not avoiding Helion right now? You know, that whole 'we stole from them and they're a little mad at us' thing?"

"Yeah, well, there are people whose lives are at risk, Zambo. And I'm not confident enough about getting Factorum to listen to us, not enough to put people in danger."

She was right, of course. And it wasn't as if they were blameless in this. Val could try to take all the responsibility on herself, but Zammi had been just as much a part of it. They had to do what they could.

"All right. What's the play?"

"I'll take the Oryx to the settlement," Val said, and Zammi immediately protested. Val ignored his complaints. "It's the only way. If I try to go through proper channels, I'll almost certainly end up in a cell and there's no way to know for sure that the people on the ground will get out in time. If I actually go there, I know I can convince them to get to safety."

"Val, you'll be putting yourself in the path of the comet,"

Zammi said, hardly believing that they were even having this conversation. "We don't know for sure when it's going to hit. You could…" He was unable to finish the sentence.

"I know." She sounded grim. "But it has to be done. You go to Factorum and convince them to do what we both know they have to do."

Zammi felt a heat in his sinuses, like a sharp spike heading for his brain. His vision swam and he struggled to breathe. Then the tears spilled down his face. He hadn't felt sorrow and fear like this since he was a child. Since his parents had died.

"Val," he croaked and she walked into his embrace.

"I'll be fine, Zambo," she assured him, baselessly. "You do your part, I'll do mine, and in a week we'll be having a laugh over a couple of beers, right?"

Zammi held her, saying nothing. It was the biggest lie in the solar system but they held on to it as if it were a tether and he'd just been ejected into vacuum.

Val left to get underway as soon as possible, and Zammi sat in the small room, numb. He knew he had to reach out to Factorum, make them change the course of the comet. At that moment, though, it all felt impossible. Who was he to tell a board of directors what to do? Even if it was only a part of a board.

He blinked and shook off the unnerving sensation of knowing that some amount of time had passed without him noticing. He'd been staring at the blank wall and now he forced himself to focus. Val was putting herself in real danger, the least he could do was make a convincing case to Factorum.

Surely all those years of writing argumentative essays would be good for something.

He punched in the contact details for Dr Huang, but stopped himself just before he connected. Val had been trying to insulate her from them – guilt-by-association wasn't legally enforceable, but her career could easily suffer. And, of course, the last time he'd seen her he'd been running from Helion security, so it might not even be in his best interests to get in touch right now. He needed a connection with Factorum, though.

He didn't literally smack his hand against his forehead, but it wouldn't have been unwarranted. A few taps later and the familiar face of Marius Munro filled the holo.

"Well, if it isn't the fugitive?"

Zammi's heart thudded and panic must have shown on his face.

"Don't worry," Marius went on genially, "the last thing I'm going to do is dob you in to Helion security." He made a disgusted face at the last two words. Marius was well known for his opposition to the wide latitude corporate security departments were given – an authority he believed should be reserved for a police service that was beholden to the citizens of Mars. "I assured the so-called officers who talked to me that I'd be in touch if I heard from you, but obviously I was lying. Those jackbooted thugs will get nothing from me."

From anyone else it would have sounded absurd, but Marius meant every overwrought word. His own thesis had been on the abuse of authority leading up to the Lunar Land Riots.

"Thanks," Zammi said, his heart rate ebbing. "As I guess you know, I'm not exactly able to come and go as I please right now, but I really need to reach someone high up in Factorum. Do you have any ideas?"

Zammi explained what he, Val, and Ivan had found and their belief that the incoming comet was at least partially meant as retribution against Helion. Marius's usually jovial face took on a sterner and sterner mien as Zammi spoke.

"Hmm," Marius mused once Zammi had gotten it all out. "I don't know anyone at Factorum, but I have no problem cold-calling them on your behalf." His face jerked up and he snapped his fingers. "Hang on, you know who does have a connection at Factorum? The head of Engineering, Beryl Fernandez!"

"Fern?"

"Yes, the two of you are friends, aren't you? Isn't one of her siblings something big at Factorum?"

Zammi searched his memory. "It's a cousin, and he's an executive assistant, but yeah. Fern might be able to help me out. If it doesn't work out, I'm going to hold you to those cold-calls, Marius."

"I'll get the charm warmed up and ready just in case," he said, with a wink. "Good luck, Zambrotta."

Toni Rafael was Fern's mother's sister's second husband's kid, and he was now the head of executive scheduling, as it turned out, but he did have access to the Board of Directors at Factorum. And he and Fern got along pretty well considering that her extended family was enormous enough that it had about as many factions as Mars itself did. Once she'd made the introductions, Toni told Zammi that he would help as best as he could.

"My job is basically to manage all their calendars," Toni explained. "It's unnecessarily complicated, especially now since getting the matter and antimatter in the same place at the same time is… inadvisable."

"I'm not sure I follow," Zammi said.

Toni laughed. "Sorry, I forget that not everyone is as well acquainted with the board as I am. The two factions that make up the board oppose each other on basically everything. Indra Patel and Yan Michaels are the two who've been on the board longest and are trying to maintain the old ways of doing things. Alex Jardine-Lund and Casey da Silva are the new blood, and they are eager to make names for themselves, and the company. Honestly, I feel bad for the CEO. She has to be the tie-breaker and the referee, both. She gets paid an obscene amount, of course, but right now she's earning it."

"I'm pretty sure I only need to speak with Jardine-Lund and da Silva," Zammi said. "They'll be the ones who are behind this comet."

"I can make that happen, though I can tell you that they won't be pleased to be caught out before their plan bears fruit. Is there any chance you can make the meeting worth their while?"

Zammi contemplated. He was fairly certain that their scheme was as much about sticking it to Helion as it was about increasing the water levels. There were plenty of other options where the comet could make landfall that would provide similar water results, but this was the only location that would affect Helion.

"Can you set things in motion and let me get back to you on the sweetener?" Zammi asked.

The holo wasn't the clearest picture but Zammi recognized the dubious look on Toni's face.

"Give me an hour, OK?"

"OK."

"Hi, Dad."

Ivan beamed at Zammi when he picked up the call, but he could detect the signs of stress on his father's face.

"Zambrotta! It's good to see you. I ... uh, trust that you are keeping safe?"

Zammi nodded. "Yeah, so far. Look, I have a favor to ask and you're not going to like it. It's probably going to put in you a bad position. Career-wise."

Ivan sighed then visibly re-composed himself and managed a wry chuckle. "I'm not sure things can get too terribly much worse in that department."

"Oh?"

Ivan looked away, then said overly casually, "Yeah, Helion caught up with me, and dragged me in. Human resources, not security, so that was all right, I suppose. But, I've been fired. Not a big surprise, really, and given ... everything, I suppose I got off easy. No charges or anything."

"Oh. Right." Zammi had somehow forgotten what Ivan had already lost by getting mixed up in this business he and Val had found themselves in. Could he really ask his father for more?

"So, what is it you need, Zammi?"

Zammi explained about the rogue faction of the Factorum

board, the incoming comet, and Val's insistence on putting herself in harm's way. Ivan's face was a journey as he listened, and at one point Zammi wondered if he was doing the right thing in telling all this to his father. It was bad enough that he had to worry about Val – and everyone else on the Helion building site – did his father need to know about it, too?

His question was answered when Ivan, in an uncharacteristic cracking of the calm and even demeanor he'd been lately cultivating with Zammi and Val, said, "When were you planning on getting around to telling me this? I am your father, Zambrotta, and you do not keep it from me when your sister has run off to put herself in the path of a falling comet!"

Zammi was stunned silent, then couldn't help himself. He laughed. "Oh, Dad, why are we all like this? Val's going to do what she does, and no one is going to stop her. Not me, not you, not anyone. I'm starting to realize that you and I are no different. It's just that we're less likely to run in front of a comet, so it's not quite as obvious. But maybe we should put this family's stubbornness to good use and make the Factorum board listen."

"Not just Factorum," Ivan said. "Helion are still after you and Val, even when she's ..." His breath caught, but he carried on. "Even when she's putting herself at risk to save them. They all need to know."

Zammi nodded. "I have an idea. How fast can you get to Deimos City?"

Ivan glanced around him, as if checking for eavesdroppers. "I'm already here. I came back ... you know ... after."

Zammi nodded. "Good. Hey, do you happen to have a nice suit with you? Something that says, 'executive suite?'"

Ivan stared at Zammi. "Have you ever once seen me wear something that says, 'executive suite'?"

"No, I suppose not. Well, how do you feel about doing some shopping?"

"Are you certain that you want to do this?" Toni asked when Zammi called him back.

"Not even a little bit, but I can't remember the last time I was sure about anything," Zammi said. "You think they'll agree to meet with us?"

Toni whistled low. "Oh yeah. A Helion defector with information about the botched ice asteroid? They'll meet. They'll probably have a security detail with them, of course, but they'll meet."

Zammi shrugged. He already knew that he was probably going to be referred to the Martian Criminal Board for his part in the break-in at Helion. He couldn't tell if he'd resigned himself to his fate or if it was a superhuman feat of denial. As for Ivan, well, there wasn't anything that Factorum could actually pin on him. Helion could, probably, but they'd already chosen not to refer any of the possible charges to the MCB. It might be an uncomfortable conversation, but Ivan would come out of it all right. Zammi had to believe that.

"Can you get us in today?"

Toni's face took on a grim countenance. "I understand the urgency, but that would be impossible. First thing tomorrow is the best I can do."

"OK. And thank you," Zammi said. "I owe you one and I owe Fern one."

Toni gave Zammi a lopsided smile. "I can't speak for my

cuz, but there's no debt from my side. My work isn't exactly life-altering on a daily basis, but there's no way I could sit back and do nothing if people are in danger. I'm happy to help."

"All right. Thank you," Zammi repeated. Those two words were so little. If this went sideways, Toni would pay for his help with his career. How many people's lives and livelihood were going to get trashed in the wake of all this, Zammi wondered? If he had anything to say about it, no more.

Toni sent him a meeting invitation a few minutes later, with a copy sent to Ivan. It contained instructions for accessing the executive level of the Factorum building and included an electronic ID badge which should allow them both to bypass the onsite security desk.

Zammi looked around the dinky room Val had found for him and tried not to think about his sister. She was undoubtedly burning up the Martian desert, pushing the Oryx as fast as it would go to reach the Helion site. She was probably driving nonstop, catching catnaps on the way while the car's autopilot drove. It was probably grossly uncomfortable, stressful, and at least a little bit terrifying. And what was Zammi doing? Contemplating his wardrobe as he dumped his duffel out on to the bed.

Did *he* have something that said, "executive suite?"

CHAPTER THIRTY

Zammi slept poorly and awoke early, the adrenaline shakes already starting to set in. He forced himself to eat something, got cleaned and dressed in the same tailored tunic he'd worn on his last visit to Factorum headquarters. He called Val, for the fourth time since it had seemed late enough in the morning to make calls, but there was still no response. He tried not to read anything ominous into it – she had probably turned off the communications to conserve all the energy she could for the rover's drive system. The settlement itself didn't have a public comms link, Zammi had looked for that too. Besides, even pushing the Oryx to its limit, Val couldn't have reached the settlement by now, and the comet had only just appeared on the orbital sensors. She had time – they all had time.

Zammi kept telling himself that.

He packed up his gear and made sure to leave the room spotless. He didn't think he was capable of the kind of thorough cleaning that would defeat a full forensic scan, but he just needed to buy himself a few hours. He started on the now-familiar roundabout transit and walking tour of Deimos City to get to the Factorum building without being spotted by the Helion agents he assumed he still had on his tail. It had become second nature now, taking the long way round, checking exits and entrances, his eyes attuned to that pairing of yellow and gray. He hadn't spotted them once, and he thought ruefully that he'd gotten rather good at this cloak and dagger stuff.

As he found an aisle seat near the door on a tram going the wrong way, Zammi reflected on that trip to the Utopia Invest mining site. He'd been so skittish, so naïve back then, it was as if it were an entire lifetime ago. And yet it hadn't taken all that much to break Zammi out of his staid and secure professorial life, and while he wished heartily to return to it, he couldn't help but feel like there was something special about living on the edge like this. He didn't like the feeling of being on the run, and he certainly didn't relish the thought that his life of freedom might have mere hours remaining, but he was making a real difference. He was helping people, just like his Mom and Papi had done. Like Val did.

Maybe it was in his genes.

The thought returned nearly an hour later when he arrived at the Factorum building to find Ivan waiting for him. There were no Helion agents visible as far as Zammi could see, but his luck was bound to run out eventually. So long as they made it to that meeting room, it didn't really matter what happened.

"Let's end this," Ivan said by way of greeting as he strode purposefully through the double doors and into Factorum's decorous foyer. Zammi followed, wondering if he'd ever seen his father with such conviction. Perhaps it wasn't the genes. Family was more than just DNA, of course.

The executive lifts were where Toni had directed them, and Zammi keyed in the long code they'd been provided to the typepad by the doors. A cool tone sounded and one of the doors silently opened, and they entered to find a carriage with no obvious buttons, scanners, or keypads. The doors closed and the weighty feeling of upward momentum told them they were on their way.

No one was there to greet them when they reached the executive level, but a lighted panel on the floor directed them to a meeting room. They followed it and took seats at a small table. No one else was there yet.

"I guess we're early," Zammi said, resting his hands on the tabletop, then dropping them to his lap.

Ivan reached over and laid a hand on Zammi's shoulder. The touch was warm, comforting. Zammi struggled to stay composed. "It's going to be OK. They'll listen to us, they have to."

With that, the door opened and two people in late middle age wandered in. Somehow Zammi could tell by the quality of their haircuts that this was Alex Jardine-Lund and Casey da Silva.

"Kaspar and Michelson?" the shorter of the two asked, consulting a crisp holo.

"I'm Zambrotta Kaspar and this is Ivan Michelson."

Both heads swiveled to look at Ivan.

"We understand that you're here to confess to altering data purchased by Factorum from Helion," the taller one with the deep mahogany suit said.

"I…" Ivan took a breath, then stood, his head high. "I'm here to inform you that Helion had no part of falsifying anything and that, more importantly, the comet you are currently hurtling toward Mars is aimed at living people. One of whom is my daughter."

The two board members glanced at each other, then stood.

"I see this has been a waste of time, Case. Let's go," the short one, evidently Jardine-Lund, said.

"I'll call security," da Silva said, flicking open a holo.

"I don't think so," Zammi said, standing up to his full height and blocking the doorway. He couldn't believe that they were seemingly unconcerned about the danger. His anger grew. "You need to see this, or it will be the two of you and whoever else is involved in this comet project that will be going with security."

Ivan flashed him a grin, then pulled up several screens over the table.

"I'm afraid we don't have the time for politeness, so I'll be direct. This data here shows that no one, including Helion, tampered with the data you used to bring down the contaminated ice asteroid. It was an error, pure and simple. It will probably take you longer than we have available to verify this information, but I've sent it all to your engineering team. By this afternoon at the earliest they'll be able to confirm what I've said.

"But that's not the important thing. This is." Ivan enlarged a rendering of the incoming comet, its trajectory shown with a bright yellow line heading to the lake in what appeared to be more or less empty territory. "By my reckoning, this comet will make landfall in about three hours. We have less than twenty-two minutes to make course corrections with any accuracy. So I'm telling you now, you need to change this comet's heading." He enlarged the picture, which switched to one of the public feeds showing a ten-minute delayed satellite view of the surface. "As you can see, this site is well within the tsunami zone of your current trajectory. And, as you can also see here –" Ivan zoomed in again, to pinpoint a half-dozen individuals moving around a makeshift worksite, their faces blurred out by the privacy filters. "– this is not an uninhabited area. If you let that comet come down, you'll be responsible for these people's deaths."

The two board members stared at the image, as if trying to figure out how or if it could be faked. Then da Silva said, "We'll just call them. Tell them to leave. You said they have three hours."

Ivan shook his head. "You think we didn't try that already? No one answered. It's a remote site, and they likely only have a central communications station. That's why my kid is risking her life to go out there and tell them in person to get out. Look, we don't have time for you to decide if the risk is worth the reward. You need to do what's right, and deal with the consequences after."

Jardine-Lund's face was sour, but she turned to da Silva. "The alternate landing point is still viable," she said, then consulted an ancient analogue timepiece on her wrist. "But we'd need to get the remote rocketry team on it now."

Da Silva nodded once, then tapped on a holo. "There's no response. They probably aren't in yet."

"I'm a propulsion engineer," Ivan said, flicking the record of his degrees and commendations up on a screen. "If you give me access to your remote system I can program the new trajectory."

Both of the directors eyed Ivan suspiciously.

"It that what this has all been about?" da Silva said. "Some overly complex ploy to give a Helion spy access to our systems? What's your plan? To redirect the comet to Noctis City and let the blame fall on us?"

"That's enough," Zammi shouted, banging a fist on the table hard enough that everyone in the room jumped. "You don't trust us. All right, fine. Bring in whatever security you want, have anyone come in and watch us. If you're worried that we're going to… I don't know, weaponize your comet, well, protocol means you've got a remote detonator on there. And the planetary defense grid could shoot it down if that fails. But the whole point is that you don't have to lose this comet. You can still get what you want out of this. Plan B is a really good option. And the truth is that you only went with this site because of a misunderstanding. And it was a misunderstanding between computers, not even between people. If a single human being gets hurt because of that, well…"

The enormity of the situation hit Zammi, and he staggered into a nearby chair, the wind knocked out of him.

"Please. Just let us help you."

The meeting room originally felt oversized for the four of them, but it was cramped now. Two staffers who were described by Jardine-Lund only as "computer nerds" flanked Ivan as he sat at the table working a holoscreen filled with numbers. Several Factorum security officers clustered around Zammi, whose earlier door bouncer impression had convinced them that he was the muscle of the operation. More fools them, he thought to himself wryly. The muscle was somewhere in the Martian desert, hopefully convincing a bunch of site engineers to get the hell out of there.

"Like I said," da Silva repeated as if it were a nervous tic, "even a hint of funny business and we shut this whole thing down." The two Factorum staff who Zammi assumed were some kind of systems specialists nodded nervously at the director, who continued to pace around the limited space left in the room.

"I have the new coordinates locked," Ivan said.

"Confirmation?" Jardine-Lund asked.

"I'm not trained in planetfall trajectory mechanics," the young woman on Ivan's left said, a tremor in her voice. "All I can confirm is that the landing coordinates loaded here are the same as the ones you provided."

Jardine-Lund looked as if she were sucking on an underripe slice of lemon. "What about you?" She pointed her chin at the older gentleman on Ivan's right, with his large holotablet and stylus.

"The math looks correct to me," he said, "but like my colleague here, this is not my field of expertise."

"I am well aware of our limitations; if the rocketry team were available this would not be happening." Jardine-Lund waved a hand dismissively, indicating the entire process occurring in the executive meeting room.

"If I may," Ivan interrupted. "We have a limited window of opportunity to effect this correction. Like, extremely limited."

"Obviously, in theory, we would all prefer ample time to

study the options," Zammi said, struggling to keep his anxiety and anger in check, "but in reality, making hard decisions under pressure is surely why you are all here."

No one spoke, then the computer analyst at Ivan's side cleared her throat. She stood and addressed the two directors in a startlingly clear and confident tone. "I understand that you're afraid that we're being tricked here. And if we are, well, that would not be ideal, but I believe it would be manageable. But if they are telling the truth, and we do nothing… Well. That's not something of which I have any interest in being a part." She reached over and tapped a rapid string into the console and then a yellow progress bar appeared on the holo, along with the large words "Course change in effect – system locked."

All eyes in the room were aimed at the screen, when da Silva broke the silence. "What's your name?"

"Harper Griznowski," she croaked.

"Well, Harper. This is an important day for you. In a few minutes you're either fired, with a possible civil suit on its way, or you're in for a big promotion. It's kind of exciting not knowing which, isn't it?"

Everyone, including Alex Jardine-Lund, stared at Casey da Silva. "I think we might need to revisit our alliance, you and I," Jardine-Lund said to her fellow director, then turned away to watch the live feed of the comet's trajectory.

It was a tense ten minutes, the three scientists in the room the first to let out relieved breaths. Soon after, everyone could see that the comet had clearly overshot the original target and passed the Helion site overhead. An incredibly long minute later the comet exploded into the lone lake in the middle of Valles Marineris. The image was soundless, and it was oddly beautiful to see the column of water rising from the point of impact, then falling back to Mars, creating a massive ripple effect, the enormous wave radiating out all three hundred and sixty degrees, blocks of cometary ice bobbing on its surface.

There really was nothing around this lake but empty Martian rock, and as they watched the satellite image, they could see the chaos the comet had wrought slowly coalescing into the one thing Mars had been crying out for – a vast lake of sweet, pure water.

"Well, that sure is something," one of the security guards said, wiping what looked like a tear from his eye.

Ivan grabbed the controls for the camera feed and the image blurred then refocused on the original landing site. He panned the area until a dark, shiny blob seemed to catch his attention. He focused in until Zammi recognized it.

"The Oryx," he breathed, then squinted. "Is that … ?"

There was a figure leaning against the side of the rover, a slim enviro-suit showing off her familiar figure. She was in agitated conversation with three people in matching yellow and gray suits, gesturing wildly. There was some discussion, then all four made haste toward a large vehicle at the edge of the screen.

"She's OK," Zammi said.

"They all are," Ivan added, relief evident in his voice.

The sounds of notification pings and buzzes interrupted them, as everyone's communicators came to life.

"I see the word is out," Jardine-Lund said, bringing up a holo with the breaking story. It was on every news site, every industry publication – Factorum's triumph in the face of adversity.

"So anyone with money on promotion is a winner, then," da Silva said to a stunned Harper. "Congratulations." The director swept out of the room and Zammi raised an eyebrow toward Alex Jardine-Lund, who simply shrugged in response.

"So, what now?" Ivan asked.

The remaining director looked around. "I suppose I have a press release to update. There's a very nice canteen on this level, you're welcome to get lunch. On us, of course."

Ivan glanced at Zammi, who was struggling to wrap his head around the fact that it was over. They'd won. He noticed that his vision was beginning to blanket around the edges, and he was starting to get the shaky feeling he sometimes experienced after a hard workout. The crash.

"I could eat."

Ivan slapped him on the back and the security guards stepped back to make space for them to leave the room. They were on their way down the hall when a loud voice from behind them shouted, "You can't go in there!"

They turned to see a harried Factorum security staffer chasing after four large people with determination on their faces, wearing gray and yellow Helion security jackets.

"Ivan Michelson and Zambrotta Kaspar. You're under arrest."

CHAPTER THIRTY-ONE

"You can let them all go, Riley."

Alex Jardine-Lund issued the instruction to the breathless Factorum security officer, who glanced around at the two strangers being detained by this gang of foreign agents and stepped out of the way. This whole mess was obviously operating at a much higher pay grade.

"You're really going to let them take us?" Zammi said to Jardine-Lund as he was being frogmarched to the lifts.

"You've been a great help to us, I won't deny it. But whatever this is, it doesn't have anything to do with Factorum. We can't stand in the way of another corporation's lawful detainment."

Zammi's eyes narrowed. He was fairly certain that plenty of interference had occurred many times between all the corporations over the years, but he knew that if the director didn't want to put herself and her organization on the line, it wasn't going to happen.

He gave her another pleading glance, but there was nothing

but cold efficiency in her face. It wasn't going to happen. The Helion goon on Zammi's left tightened her grip.

Maybe this was the right way for it all to end. They'd managed to avoid a potential catastrophe, and even helped Factorum increase the usable water on Mars by nearly a third. The days of water rationing were over. It was a clear win – for everyone. But even winning came with consequences.

Zammi had always been a staunch believer in the power of a well-regulated legal and economic base for humanity's excursions to the stars. The wild days of early exploration where every organization was out for their own glory and screw anyone else had nearly broken the dream of space before it even really began. Only coordination, cooperation, and the rule of law had allowed the terraforming project to succeed. He knew that the law had to apply to everyone, and so it was right that he should face the repercussions of his actions. Everything he'd done had been for a good cause, but he really had committed burglary and theft. That shouldn't go unanswered.

When the lift reached the ground floor, Ivan and Zammi were marched out the front door, to the nakedly curious stares of Factorum staff. For a brief moment, Zammi had a flash of what Marius would make of this situation. Doubtless, if it were him in Zammi's place, he'd be wriggling like an eel, trying to break free of the guards' iron-like grip, all the while shouting something about never letting the bastards take him alive. The image made him chuckle, which earned him a scowl from the right-side goon and a yank toward the door.

On the path outside the Factorum building sat one of those small motorized carts that Zammi always assumed were only used for infrastructure maintenance, though he now realized were also employed by security and medical emergency staff.

"Michelson. You're free to go." The two security agents escorting Ivan had released his arms and had stepped back toward the cart. They turned to Zammi and their colleagues. "You're going to have to come with us." Without delay, Zammi was shoved into the back of the cart, his long legs barely making it inside.

Ivan's voice sounded like it came from a long way away. "No."

"What?"

"I said no. That's my son you have in there. You are not taking him without taking me, too."

"Dad, don't do this. You're not in trouble, you should just go. I'll be fine."

Ivan wormed his way through the stunned security guards and slipped into the rear seat next to Zammi. "I am not leaving you to deal with this on your own, Zambrotta. Not this time."

As the security agents piled into the cart and it trundled away, Zammi couldn't have spoken even if he did know what to say.

Once he'd regained his composure, Zammi remembered the advice Marius had once given him that he always assumed he'd never need: "If you ever get nabbed by the cops, keep your yap shut." It wasn't difficult advice to follow in the current circumstances, the cart being a surprisingly noisy conveyance. Every bump or crack shook the vehicle and made the wheels squeak. He understood why you didn't see many of these out and about – no one would drive one given any remotely reasonable alternative.

After a teeth-grindingly long ride, they finally alit at a regional Helion branch, the storefront office decked out in bright and cheery new-looking co-branded signage. A result of the Utopia Invest money, no doubt. The security guards hauled them out of the cart, not affording Zammi a moment to stretch his cramped limbs. He half-hobbled into the office, the guards nearly dragging him inside.

They were led to a dingy back room, the cosmetic upgrades not having made it quite this far yet, where Ivan and Zammi were left alone while the security team went to check in.

"Dad," Zammi leaned over to Ivan across the table. His father shook his head, eyes darting up to the corners of the room. There was nothing to see but they had to assume there were cameras and mics.

"No, Dad," Zammi insisted, "I don't care who hears this. You do not need to be here right now. I get it, I really do, and you don't know what this all means to me. The last few days, all of us together – really, I don't know if I even care what happens to me now."

"Zambrotta." Ivan clearly intended it to be a fatherly rebuke, an admonishment for Zammi to keep quiet. But it didn't come out quite like that, and the years of longing for a relationship with his son that Ivan had just never known how to create was all that Zammi heard.

The moment was lost when the door banged open and one of the guards who'd picked them up tossed a portable holoprojector on to the table. She turned to Ivan and gruffly said, "You're still free to go, you know. I can't be sure that will still be true when Ljunggren gets here."

"Ljunggren?" Zammi asked, and felt Ivan's foot graze his shin in a "shut up, already," kick.

"The boss," the security guard said. "Won't be long now. If you're going to go, you should get gone."

Ivan shook his head and the guard shrugged.

"Whatever." She turned to Zammi and switched on the holo. "I assume you know why you're here."

No one had to tell Zammi anything this time. He sat still and silent. The holoscreen lit up and the image of Factorum's main entrance appeared. Zammi was pretty sure what he was about to witness. Ah, yes, that was Billie at the reception desk, definitely making a nuisance even with no sound. And that was quite clearly Zammi in the background, looking for all the worlds like a bored person waiting. There was nothing remotely incriminating here, he thought, and began to relax. Then the picture flickered, the timestamp on the lower right corner advancing a few minutes, and the image changing to the view from a hovering microdrone as it entered a narrow corridor. None of the schematics they'd had said anything about microdrone cameras. Zammi guessed his heart could be heard by anyone in the room, as he and Val walked into the frame, and he watched as he boosted her up into the ducts, looked around guiltily, then left.

"We've got you dead to rights, son," the guard said, unimaginatively. "You and your crew. It's just a matter of time before we round them all up."

That brought Zammi back to the moment and he suppressed a grin. They hadn't caught the others! He didn't really know how any of this worked, but surely the longer they had to get away, the less likely they'd be to get caught. If he had to take the fall for everyone, that was fine. It would be cheap at twice the price.

"Nothing to say for yourself, eh?" the guard asked, and Zammi didn't even shake his head. He did glance over at Ivan, who could not possibly have looked prouder. Apparently, nothing brought a family together quite like a stint in an interrogation room.

The guard's attention was caught by a notification on her holo and she turned to the door. "That will be Ljunggren. And not a moment too soon, either. This was starting to get a little tedious." She walked out the door and locked it behind herself.

"You're doing great," Ivan half-whispered to Zammi. "I'm sure we'll find a way to get you out of this."

"It's OK if we don't," Zammi said and laid a hand on Ivan's arm, but the moment was interrupted by the door opening again. Zammi could see out into the hallway, where a short, stocky, white man of young middle age was commanding the attention of the local staff. Ljunggren, presumably. He was gesturing firmly to a series of enthusiastically positive responses, and at one point he singled out the guard who'd been with Zammi and Ivan, as if for accolades. The look on her face certainly implied that Ljunggren had just gifted her with a solid, "Well done."

The knot of officers began to unravel and Zammi's stomach lurched. Oh no, how was this even possible? There, in between two grinning Helion security officers and looking rather the worse for wear, stood Val.

•••

"This is Zambrotta and Ivan?" Ljunggren said upon approaching but not entering the dinky little room that had been utilized for the purported interrogation.

"Yeah," the local guard said. "That's them."

"Hmm." Ljunggren looked over his shoulder and Zammi followed the little man's gaze toward the tight knot of people outside. Val.

Zammi stood to try and catch a glimpse of her, to see how badly she'd been roughed up, when the guard yelled, "Sit down!" It came out as a single word, and Zammi complied without thinking.

"Hold up, Claudette," Ljunggren said, and the guard stepped back.

"Yessir."

Ljunggren faced his subordinate, and smiled disarmingly. "Come, now, we're all on the same team. Call me Max."

"Yessir. Er, Max, sir."

Zammi cleared his throat loudly and all eyes turned toward him. He didn't know where that came from. Channeling what he'd imagine Marius might do, maybe. It felt good, though. He didn't have any real control over this situation, but getting some attention served as a surprisingly decent substitute.

"Right," Ljunggren said. "The situation is rather a bit more fluid than everyone has been aware, so I apologize if there's been any..." He looked at Ivan and Zammi, as if assessing how physical the detention process had been. "Any untoward experiences."

"This whole thing is untoward," Ivan said, cranky. "But we've not been harmed," he added in a surly tone.

"Good." Ljunggren stepped back out the door, an invitation for them to follow. "Come with me."

Zammi stood again and turned to Ivan, who made a "don't ask me" face, and they stepped out of the little room and into the main office space.

A figure flew at Zammi, and he was wrapped in Val's arms before he could even brace himself for impact.

"It's good to see you, Zambo," she said into his chest. "I didn't know what was going on for a while there."

"It's good to see you too, Val," Zammi said, then thought about it. "Even if I kind of wish I didn't."

Val pulled back and looked up at Zammi, confused. Then she laughed.

"Oh, you think we're all still detained," she said, after an awkwardly long time laughing. "Yeah, no. Sit down, there's a lot to explain."

"So, then it turned out that the dude I'd been talking to was the security chief of the site, and when I told him what you and Dad were doing at Factorum, and that it would probably end up with Helion catching up with you, and he was all, 'I know a guy at the Deimos branch, as soon as we get underway, I'll get him on the horn.' Then we hoisted the Oryx into the cargo bay of the heavy flyer, piled in as fast as we could and took off. Man, those things can really move." Val whistled at the memory of it.

Zammi and Ivan – and probably a good portion of the Helion branch office staff – sat with mouths agape, trying to follow the tale. Val had arrived at the Helion site not long before the nearly live images they'd seen at Factorum, and had hurriedly explained the situation to the people on the ground. Not knowing whether or not the comet had been diverted, they had to move – and move quickly. Val had used up the last of the Oryx's power reserve getting there, but she was reluctant to leave it in the path of destruction, so the Helion team came up with a ridiculous solution, and off they went.

"OK," Zammi said, working it through in his mind. "I understand how you got here, but what about the rest of this?" He spread his hands.

"Yeah, so, that flyer really booked it, but there was still a lot of time to kill. Those things only have two seats, so most of us were slumming it in the hold. That's where these beauties came from." She held up her bruised arms. "And that's also where this came from!" She flicked open a holo to show a document bearing that day's date and the words "Official Writ of Incorporation for Security Union – Helion Branch."

"You did all this and then convinced the guards to unionize?" Zammi asked, incredulous.

Val shook her head, but she was smug and self-satisfied. "They simply heard what I had to offer and agreed that it was in their best interests."

"That's fantastic, Val," Ivan said, the pride now aimed in his daughter's direction. "I'm not entirely certain how that helps us, though."

"We did more than sign some paperwork," a new voice replied. "I called my old roommate, Max here, and he ran it up to Helion HQ. When you break it all down, the three of you have helped us all a lot more than you've hurt us."

"There were more than three of us," Zammi said, then winced as both Val and Ivan smacked him.

"Yes," Max Ljunggren agreed, ignoring the family squabbling, "and I proposed the same treatment for everyone involved. This is an internal Helion matter and, upon my recommendation, HQ decided that there was no need to refer it to the Martian Criminal Board. Indeed, there was no need to do anything further. We're letting it go."

Zammi understood the words perfectly, and yet it didn't make any sense. "That's it? It's over?"

Ljunggren smiled and Val grinned. Ivan said, "We're going to need that in writing. And what about my job?"

The security chief winced. "There had to be some kind of consequence, I'm sure you understand."

"So, I'm still fired."

"Still fired, yes."

Zammi turned to Ivan and tried to read the older man's face. Being fired from Helion was the absolute worst fate he could have imagined for his father. But now, there was a peace in his face that Zammi had never seen before. That was the old Ivan, who lived for his work because everything else he had to live for was so far out of his control that he couldn't allow himself to get hurt again. This new Ivan seemed OK with it.

"Well, all right then," Ivan said, standing. "Kids, why don't we go home?"

CHAPTER THIRTY-TWO

Zammi leaned back in his chair, feet up on the desk, engrossed in the book he'd been reading on his holo. It was the third title in the Cherry Lazereyes series, and he still had nine more to go on his bookshelf. He left her current adventure in the wilds of a jungle-dome on Ceres and gazed at the live feed in the viewport. The foreground was unidentifiable green scrub, with typical Martian dun-colored rock at the edges of the view. But at the center of the image was something both unfamiliar and beautiful. An uneven horizontal line bisecting the vista, green and brown nearest the camera, and into the distance, as far as the image could be seen – blue. An otherworldly ocean of blue.

There was still some debate about what the body of water would be called. He'd secretly hoped for Lake Kaspar, but the Terraforming Committee was officially designating it an ocean and there were nomenclature rules. Someone at Interplanetary Cinematics was trying to drum up support for a naming contest, and Zammi knew that wouldn't end well.

It didn't matter what it was called, whether it was technically a lake or an ocean or even a slough. It was the future, it was life.

A notification flash pulled Zammi away from the screen and he turned to the door.

"Morning, professor." Fern didn't wait for an invitation and settled herself into Zammi's guest chair. "I see you've acclimated back to the dull life of academia."

Zammi grinned. "I don't miss being on the run from security," he admitted. "Honestly, a life of crime just isn't all it's cracked up to be."

Fern shook her head. "You can't fool me. You took to it like a duck to water."

"Now, there's a phrase that's finally going to start making sense to people again," he said.

"Someone's introducing ducks?"

Zammi shrugged. "It's just a matter of time. Soon there will be everything here: birds, fish, predators. Heck, maybe even penguins someday."

"Yeah, why not?" Fern said, serious. "The temperature is right and there is plenty of ice – I should know. Anyway, I finally heard from my cousin Toni. He says that there's been a big shakeup at Factorum. One of the directors is out."

"Oh yeah? I bet it was da Silva."

"It was. How did you know?"

Zammi remembered the meeting they'd had and the acrimonious way it had ended. "It's hard to be the lone voice for cutthroat ruthlessness."

"I guess. Anyway, Toni says things are getting back to normal, finally, and he wanted me to pass on his thanks."

Fern's face was puzzled. "I double checked that's what he meant, and he said yeah. But I don't get it, he's the one who did you the favor."

"And I appreciate it," Zammi said. "I think I know what he means, but tell him it was our pleasure. We're all just happy that everything turned out all right in the end."

"About that," Fern said, grinning slyly, "how are you coping? A brand new tenured professor, plus this new side job of yours? How are you managing?"

Zammi laughed. "Oh, don't you worry. I'm managing just fine. To be honest, Dad and Marius are doing all the heavy lifting. Sometimes I think Val and I are only there for the celebrity name value."

A raucous sound in the corridor preceded the face appearing at Zammi's door.

"Speak of the devil."

Val strode into Zammi's office, chatting gregariously with a spark plug of a man. He nearly filled the width of the doorway, and it was clear even under his bulky Helion security uniform that he was all muscle. Zammi vaguely remembered seeing him at the Helion branch office in Deimos, but it hadn't been the kind of occasion which had led to introductions. Val turned to her companion and said something that made him laugh, then shooed him out the door. Obediently, and maybe little awestruck, he left.

"Who was that?" Zammi asked. "The new shop steward of Hired Goons Local 257?"

"Ha!" Val smacked Zammi on the arm. "Nah, Ljunggren's the shop steward. And of course, they aren't contractors. They're salaried employees."

Fern glanced between Val and Zammi, enjoying if not understanding their easy banter.

"All right, you two, I can tell when I'm surplus to requirements." Fern stood, and both Zammi and Val tried to convince her to stay, but she waved them off. "Nope, you're not dragging me into this business of yours. I'm sticking with ice asteroid science from now on."

Zammi groaned and Val shared a smirk with Fern as they passed each other on Fern's way out.

"So, who's your new buddy?" Zammi asked with raised eyebrows as Val sank into the recently vacated chair.

"Huh?" Val looked at Zammi, then seemed to understand what he was getting at and laughed. "Oh, that's Mike. Anyway, he did a big refurbishment job on one of those old ground transports, turned it into a campervan, can you believe it? I wanted to know how he handled the fuel line issues. They were notorious for cracking but he said you can swap out the factory parts for–"

Zammi raised his hands. "Never mind, forget I asked."

Val shrugged. "Sorry. I can get a little carried away. Still, it's…" She stared at a spot on the viewscreen. "It's nice to talk like this. Like siblings."

"Yeah." And she was right. It was nice.

"Hey, Zambo," Val said after a moment, eyes still locked on the image of the new Martian sea. "Remember that fight in the arboretum?"

Did he remember? How could he forget?

"Yeah. Look, I know I said some things…"

Val shook her head and made herself meet his gaze. "No, that's not it. You were talking about when I left, when you were sixteen. And I realize that you never knew why I did it."

Zammi frowned. He was pretty sure he knew why she left. She was twenty-two years old. She had to start her own life.

"Man, I was just a kid, you know? But I thought I knew everything back then," Val began. "I'd already been recruited by the Mining Guild to take on entry-level jobs at small operations and, you know, agitate. I was working with the other staff at that cargo hauler outfit I was temping for – you remember them? Anyway, their parent company didn't like the idea of their staff getting organized, and they decided to play hardball. A couple of their security team leaned on me – cornered me in a warehouse after hours. What a rookie mistake, being in there on my own. They didn't rough me up or anything, but I sure thought they were going to. They told me to drop it or they'd go after Dad and… you. I was so scared, Zambo, I really believed everything they said. But I wasn't willing to give up my work with the Guild. When they took me on it felt like the only connection I had left with Mom and Papi. I didn't know what to do – I didn't want to lose that but I didn't want to put you in danger, either. So I did the only thing I could think of to have it both ways. I took off. I was convinced that if I could isolate myself from you, I could protect you."

She took a deep breath and let it out in a slow stream. "I didn't want to go. I never wanted to leave you, but I really thought it was what I had to do. And later, when there were no reprisals, I was convinced that I must have been right, so I stayed away some more. The next thing I knew, years had gone by. We had messages and calls every few months and the odd visit, and that seemed like enough. I never even really thought about it. But then one day I did and I realized what a fool I'd been, but by then it had been so long..." She stopped being able to speak then and they both just sat there for a moment.

Zammi couldn't imagine what that must have been like for her. But, of course, she would have known exactly how much it hurt him. Hell, he'd made it pretty clear in that passive-aggressive way he had whenever they'd talked. Everything that had happened since she left took on a new light for him, and Zammi could see now that the past few weeks hadn't been the anomaly. This was the way it should have been all along.

There was nothing he could say, and for once that didn't matter. He stood and came around from behind his desk, pulled Val up, leaned down and put his arms around his big sister.

"Hey, Marius, you ready?" Zammi stood in the doorway of the department chair, Val leaning against the far wall of the corridor with an air of exaggerated casual cool. Marius was his usual dapper self, moustache shiny and bristling, and he tossed an actual tweed jacket with elbow patches over his shoulder. Ancient fashion was becoming a hot trend, apparently, and Marius was always on the leading edge.

"Wouldn't miss it," he said as he joined the siblings in the corridor. "Is Ivan going to be there?"

"Virtually," Zammi said. "He's still busy onsite at UNMI headquarters, but he'll be on holo."

They walked down the corridor to the exit to the main quad. Zammi noticed Marius observing the ease between him and Val, and recognized the flush of happiness in his mentor's face. Soon the trio arrived at the Grand Ballroom, an oddly named hall that was used for everything from conferences to convocation ceremonies to fundraising dinners. This time, it was to be host to the official unveiling of the Standard Protocol Input Read/Write, commonly known as SPIRIT.

Already the large room was teeming with dignitaries, ICN reporters, politicians, half the university faculty and any student who was lucky enough to get an invitation. The event was richly catered, after all.

"I can't believe all these people came out for this," Val said. "It's a data-sharing protocol. Is there anything duller in the entire solar system?"

"Not much," Marius agreed, "but they aren't here because of what it is. They're here because of what it represents."

A uniformed waiter stopped by with drinks on a tray, and they each selected something before the waiter moved on.

"Fancy," Val said, eyeing the sparkling beverage in her hand.

"Shh…" Marius said as a series of well-dressed people trooped up to the stage.

"Welcome, everyone." The speaker's melodious voice hushed the crowd as everyone recognized her. It was Jacqueline "Call-Me-Jack" Running-Bear, the current Chair of the Terraforming Committee. "Thank you for joining us here at Mars University, a beacon of cooperation and research for a unified Mars." There was polite applause and a few grumbles at the overtly political tone at what was meant to be a non-partisan event. Jack Running-Bear either didn't notice or ignored it, and continued her speech.

"For too long, the people of Mars have been fragmented, each living and working in their individual teams and groups.

And there are those who believe that this was a strength, that the competition to prove our ingenuity was the forge in which a strong Mars for all of humanity would be cast. Perhaps they were right, but now it is the time for something more. For us to reap what we've sown, to enjoy the fruits of our harvest."

"How many irrelevant Bronze Age Earth metaphors do you think she's going to use?" Zammi whispered to Val, who snickered loudly enough to be shushed by three different people.

Running-Bear went on. "I'd like now to introduce to you Ivan Michelson, the engineer who has led the creation of SPIRIT, the new, interoperable data protocol that will allow all of Mars seamless and error-free communication."

An absolutely enormous holo lit up over Running-Bear, and Ivan's face filled the screen. He'd have been mortified if he'd known, and Zammi had to stop Val from sending him a live image.

"Uh, hi, everyone." Ivan's voice boomed out of speakers set around the room. "Thanks for all this, but really there were a lot of people who worked hard to implement this protocol. And we couldn't have done it without the cooperation of all the corporations and organizations who have jumped on board. A special shout-out to Factorum and Helion for…" Ivan paused for a brief moment, and Val elbowed Zammi in the ribs.

"He's not going there, is he?" Zammi whispered, but Ivan seemed to reconsider when he spoke again.

"…for their early support. Most of all, though, I have to thank my kids, Valentina and Zambrotta. Without them, none of this would ever have happened."

A bright light came out of nowhere, blinding Zammi, and he realized that this must have been planned. Damn it, Dad! He lifted a hand in shy acknowledgment, while Val raised both arms in self-congratulatory glee. Well, between the two of them they made for one appropriate person, Zammi thought. The spotlight faded away, and Zammi blinked back the temporary blindness.

"Here's to a new era of cooperation," Ivan finished with a triumphant tone, and the room exploded into applause. As Zammi's vision came back he could see Ivan's face on the jumbo holo and realized that while everyone else in the room – on Mars – thought he was talking about the data protocol, Zammi knew it was more than that. He was speaking to him and to Val. To their own new era.

The party went on for hours and at some point or another Zammi had probably spoken to everyone he knew and several people he didn't. Val had flirted with about a dozen people and Marius had pulled together at least that many potential recruits for the Citizens' Oversight Committee, but the two of them ended up together at a small table. Eventually, Zammi found a slightly quieter corner and was taking a well-earned breath, when there was a tap on his shoulder. He turned to see Fern, a plateful of excellent catering in her hand.

"How are things?" she asked, gently.

Zammi smiled. "Things are looking up. I've heard that using SPIRIT is going to become mandatory for terraforming activities. It's going to be a big help, even if the corporations did fight to keep their own systems for internal business. Krissy Huang told Val that Factorum is on track to beat their targets for decontaminating their first lake, so we may end up with more usable water on Mars sooner than we'd thought."

"That's good news, but I meant how are *you* holding up?" she asked, gently. "You know…" She gestured to the boisterous event. Zammi cocked his head and thought about it.

"Actually, I'm having a good time," he said, surprised that it was true. "I guess a lot more has changed than I realized."

Fern grinned. "Glad to hear it! So, what do you think? About time to call it a night?"

Zammi looked around the room, the celebration still in full swing. He turned to Fern, the plate of food in her hand containing a sample of many of the cuisines on Mars. He pointed to something on the edge of her plate.

"Not quite yet. Say, where do you think they're hiding the rest of those little pies?"

EPILOGUE

It took a lot longer than any of them intended, but eventually they made it work. Between Ivan's work coordinating the launch of the SPIRIT protocol, and Zammi and Val's day jobs, finding time when they could all get away was tough. They had their new regular weekly calls which spanned the gap, though, and Val and Zammi saw each other most weeks. It had been surprising how easy it had become to be in each other's lives again.

When the three of them had finally found a time, Val and Zammi drove down to Noctis where Ivan had been based since he'd picked up the new job. He was waiting for them at the northern airlock, and when he saw them pull up in the Oryx, his eyes filled with tears.

"It's exactly the same as I remember it," he said, nearly whispering. "I can almost see them sitting there – Hadley at the console, Julián fiddling with the comfort controls. Some kind of terrible music playing…" That was all he could get out before the tears came and it was a good while of reminiscences before they were all ready to pile into the rover and eat up the Martian dust.

They only had a few days, but they took the scenic route anyway. Irrigation had resumed, transforming the landscape. Past the now lush fields of green grasses to the south of Noctis City, they drove over the desert of Sinai Planum, its eerily flat surface still pocked with craters formed millennia ago. They passed several points that were marked by one corporation or another for planned development. Zammi wondered how long it would be before there was anywhere left on Mars that was undeveloped.

Soon the trappings of humanity became evident more thickly as they approached the Arcadian Communities, and Val eventually brought the Oryx down and drove into the small dome with a hand-lettered sign reading "Welcome to Opportunity." They parked the Oryx next to a couple of rovers of a similar vintage and walked to the town hall.

"Howdy." The voice came from the side of the hall.

Zammi introduced himself, then the person said, "Ah, yes. I talked to you the other day. I'm Ethan Tipton, what passes for the mayor here."

"And you're Ethelbert and Edith's brother." Val stuck out her hand. "I'm sorry for your loss."

Ethan nodded curtly, but shook her hand warmly. "I didn't know what they were planning to do, and I'm sure that's because they knew I would have tried to stop them. I understand why they did it, though. Things were getting real bad here."

"I'm sorry we weren't able to bring you better news," Zammi said, but Ethan waved his words away.

"They made their choice and that crash wasn't their

fault. I'm just grateful for the work you and the Oversight Committee did. We might never have known what happened to them otherwise."

"I'm glad my kids could provide a little comfort for you," Ivan said. "Even if we couldn't do more."

Tipton provided a small cabin where they could stay overnight, and that evening they met some of the other citizens of Opportunity. Everyone in the small town had known Ethelbert, Edith, and Edith's friends Joe and Cier who had died on the *Lupa Capitolina* trying to bring back water for the community. Everyone had a story to tell, and there were both laughter and tears, sometimes at the same time. It was a heartbreaking evening, but it was also one filled with both memories and hope.

The next morning the trio were up early, eager to get to their destination. Val asked Ivan if he wanted to drive, but he just laughed and said that it was always Hadley's job, and he wouldn't take it now. Zammi waved off the offer too, and Val happily slid into the pilot's seat. They cruised northeast for about a hundred kilometers before it began to appear before them.

It was both exactly the same and nothing like the images that Zammi had been watching on his viewscreen. He was no horticulturist, but as they approached the greenery, even Zammi could see that there were several different plants reaching up toward the reflected sunlight. Even the ground was different. The normal pale ochre dust was darker, heavier, as the daily evaporation and condensation spread the lake's bounty beyond its borders.

And the lake itself – it was breathtaking. They rolled to a stop a good distance from its edges and all three of them sat silently for a moment, just drinking in the sight of it. Ivan was the first to make a move, which made Zammi get out and then Val followed. They walked toward it, the very immensity of the body of water overwhelming.

"I've never seen anything like this," Ivan whispered.

"No Martian has," Zammi said. "This is the largest body of surface liquid water other than Earth. And we helped to make it happen."

"Not too bad for a history nerd, an old rocket scientist and…" Val trailed off, as if trying to figure out how to describe herself.

"An agent provocateur?" Zammi suggested and they all laughed.

"Yeah," Ivan took a step forward to put one arm around each of his kids. "Not too bad at all."

The three of them stood there on the frontier between land and sea, looking into the gentle rippling of the Sea of Accord, and seeing the future of humanity on Mars.

ACKNOWLEDGMENTS

Thanks to my editor, Gwendolyn Nix, for her excellent guidance and superb company along the road. Thanks also to my agent, Chelsea Hensley, for always being my champion.

I need to thank my fellow Darklies – Josh Eure, Craig Lincoln, Ben Murphy, and Cadwell Turnbull – for giving me the space and time to work on this project and for reminding me that making stuff up is the best kind of fun.

I'm indebted to David Mack for all the excellent advice and commiseration, and to James Swallow for a great chat about writing in other worlds.

Thanks to the many players of games in my life over the years, particularly Humberto and Kate for reintroducing me to board games back in the day.

Finally, thanks to Steven for everything, always.

ABOUT THE AUTHOR

M DARUSHA WEHM is the Nebula Award-nominated and Sir Julius Vogel Award-winning author of the interactive fiction game *The Martian Job*, as well as over a dozen novels including the *Andersson Dexter* cyberpunk detective series and the humorous coming-of-age novel *The Home for Wayward Parrots*. Darusha is a member of the Many Worlds writing collective and their short fiction and poetry have appeared in many venues, including *Strange Horizons*, *Terraform* and *Nature*. Their poetry has been a finalist for the Rhysling Award. For Aconyte, they are the author of *The Qubit Zirconium: A KeyForge Novel*.

Originally from Canada, Darusha lives in Te Whanganui-a-Tara Wellington, Aotearoa New Zealand after several years sailing the Pacific.

darusha.ca
twitter.com/darusha
facebook.com/M.DarushaWehm